THE WOMAN WHO KNEW TOO MUCH

At first she thought it was a dream. It was raining and she could hear the steady metronomic beat of breathing. She kicked at the comforter trying to free a leg. It was her own breathing, obviously. Panting. More like panting. She held her breath.

The panting went on, harder if anything.

Then she felt a large wet drop of water land on her forehead.

She came awake, eyes wide, and saw the hulk above her. It was dripping on her.

She spun across the bed, tangling herself more thoroughly in the sheets and comforter. She tried to scream but there wasn't much result. She fell out of bed, grabbed at the lamp on the bedside table, knocking it off and turning it on simultaneously.

The light from the floor wasn't all that flattering but no amount of light could have improved what was standing on the other side of the bed.

It was soaking wet.

It wore a beard and the face and hair were covered, matted with blood looking pink because it was diluted by rain.

It was holding a butcher knife high in the air.

It looked at her and said, "Relax."

Which was when she realized she was naked. . . .

The
Woman Who
Knew Too Much

Dana Clarins

BANTAM BOOKS

TORONTO · NEW YORK · LONDON · SYDNEY · AUCKLAND

THE WOMAN WHO KNEW TOO MUCH
A Bantam Book / November 1986

ISBN 0-553-26100-2

Published simultaneously in the United States and Canada

Bantam Books are published by Bantam Books, Inc. Its trademark, consisting of the words "Bantam Books" and the por-
trayal of a rooster, is Registered in U.S. Patent and Trademark
Office and in other countries. Marca Registrada. Bantam Books,
Inc., 666 Fifth Avenue, New York, New York 10103.

PRINTED IN THE UNITED STATES OF AMERICA
O   0 9 8 7 6 5 4 3 2 1

for Tom

BEFORE

❧

The Director wheezed softly. He was enjoying his lunch.

As usual he lunched alone, in his office, listening to opera. He lunched alone because he looked upon eating as a bodily function, most enjoyable when partaken of in privacy. Opera because he had always listened to opera, grown up on opera. His father had been a well-known tenor in his day, at least in provincial circles. Today, feeling rather passionate, if not actually lustful—he never felt lustful, not since his misfortune—he was absorbing the sounds of the great recording of *Carmen* with Rise Stevens. He hummed along as he carved at his veal chop, lathered with a sauce of tomatoes, green peppers, oregano, and capers, and occasionally directed the orchestra with his knife and fork.

Halfway through the chop he paused, patted his thick, naturally pursed lips with a sauce-flecked napkin. He was out of breath, like a jogger, though he had certainly never jogged. Eating had come to wind him like sex once had. Since his unfortunate accident he didn't move around as he once had, and far less exertion winded him far more quickly. Of course, he had grown unconscionably plump. Well, fat. Fattish. Three hundred and eleven pounds as of this morning. He'd put on a hundred pounds in two years. Where, he wondered, would it end?

Well, what could you expect, really? A man had to indulge at least one of his senses. Two, counting the opera. Perhaps things weren't so barren after all. And what would he rather have done than followed a morning of extraordinarily absorbing plotting, on an almost mathematical schematic, with a fine lunch? Alone? He couldn't imagine.

3

He listened thoughtfully for several minutes, tiny black eyes prowling ceaselessly deep in the puffy, purple-bagged sockets. His eyes were the only part of him that got much exercise anymore. His eyes and his mouth. A man in his life, he supposed, did play many parts, and for the moment he felt a little like he suspected God must feel. Seeing all, committed only to the propagation of belief in Himself.

His gaze drifted to the broad bullet-and-bomb-proof laminated window, to the vast green lawn stretching away from the bunker like the world's largest putting green. It amused him to know that it was heavily mined in case of trouble. All around him, the thick, civilized forests of New Jersey; across the Hudson, the upper reaches of the city shining in the spring sun.

A brown Chevrolet sedan nosed up the long curve of driveway and disappeared into the parking lot. The cars these people used were so nondescript as to be virtual advertisements. Nobody bought such cars: they were issued. He worked on his veal chop for a few moments longer, sipped his wine, and the two men from the brown car were shown in by his secretary. The Director nodded but did not rise.

Mason and Friborg. They might have been robots for all the charm and wit they exhibited. In a way they were machines, of course, chosen for their lack of charm, wit, or imagination. The profiles indicated they were highly disciplined, obedient, and violent when unleashed. One wore a blue suit, one wore gray, and the Director wondered what the material might be called. They sat down while he slid a final morsel of veal through the puddle of sauce and popped it into his mouth in a quick movement like an old coin bank swallowing a penny.

Chewing carefully, the Director looked at them. He smacked his lips and lit a Pall Mall with a match from a restaurant called Nanni's, where they knew him. He poured coffee from a wicker-jacketed vacuum jar. He didn't offer them coffee because he couldn't stand hearing them say no, thank you, sir, like a couple of dolls. He stirred a packet of Sweet 'n' Low into the steaming coffee.

"Someone is trying to kill me," he said. He stared into his cup while he blew across the surface, then sipped. When he looked up, he seemed surprised to find them still there. "That's all." He shrugged. "Excuse me, I'm a very busy man so . . ."

"Do we know who, sir?"

"If I knew, wouldn't I have you dissuade them, urge them to mend their ways, stick a claymore in their lunch pails?"

"How do you know someone's trying to kill you, sir?"

"Take my word for it."

"Excuse me, sir, but that's not much to go on—"

"Friborg, no one ever said it would be easy."

"I'm Mason, sir—"

"Mason, Friborg, whatever."

"What would you like us to do, sir?" Friborg was always confused by these little discussions with the Director.

"That's your business," the Director said. "I'm just trying to keep you in the picture. It seems the least I could do."

"But, sir—"

"Do as you wish. But as you may know, my premature death would have consequences for us all. . . ." He may have smiled. He wasn't even sure himself.

"We certainly want to avoid that, sir."

"I daresay." The Director nodded, his chins wobbling slightly. "Well, I *am* very busy. Thank you so much for coming."

Mason and Friborg stood up.

The Director picked up a square gray envelope from beside his coffee cup.

"You will undoubtedly be seeing the General shortly. Might I entrust this to you?"

"Of course, sir." Mason took it, looked at it as if he thought it might be lethal. The Director definitely did smile at that thought: Mason could not possibly imagine how lethal.

"What is it, sir?"

"Friborg," the Director said, swiveling to look back out the window at the birds hopping around the feeder, innocent as eggs. "It is a floppy disk."

"Mason," the man in the gray suit said softly, as if his name didn't really matter.

Once he was alone, the Director telephoned his wife. He liked keeping an eye on her these days. All things considered, it seemed a good idea.

While he listened to the ringing telephone, he reflected smugly on the General. They were rivals of a kind, competitors. The dear old General believed that Mason and Friborg worked for him. In fact, one of them worked for the Director. And the Director knew damn well which was which.

The telephone was still ringing. Where the devil was she, anyway?

Charlie Cunningham lay in the sex-soiled sheets by Bill Blass and peered wearily around the entirety of his studio apartment. A Boston fern had turned brown and brittle from inattention. A wandering Jew was at death's door. Clothing hung from doorknobs and chairbacks, and there were stacks of books on the table and the floor as well as on the crowded, overflowing bookcases. He had to get rid of the books he didn't need or had read. *Had* to. A trip to the Strand was in order. He made a resolution and then caught sight of the open bathroom door, of the incredible mess she'd made within. He clamped his eyes shut. He smelled her perfume and sweat and sex on the pillow and realized that, yes, she had her points, he hadn't tired of *that*. What was driving him nuts was the rest of her. *Really* nuts.

Almost two years it had been. He'd gotten excited just looking at her, surrounded by idiot literary types celebrating the publication of some ex-Mafia moll's memoirs. The raven hair with the widow's peak, the almost translucent paleness of her skin, the heavy breasts that bounced and swung like fruit on the vine when she walked across the Algonquin suite and introduced herself.

"You're tall and fair and kind of messy looking," she said, smiled appraisingly. "Intellectual looking, like you should be thinking about the philosophies of Descartes and Malthus. But you're not, though, are you?" He shook his head. She smiled at the party, surveying it, smiled and waved to the guest of honor who'd told all and was now said to fear for her life— the odd auto accident on the FDR, the gas explosion, the stray intruder. As she smiled, not looking at him, she said: "You actually have a shockingly dirty mind. Or would have if I were shockable. But since I'm not, let me tell you what you're thinking about. My breasts, for two things. And my ass for another. You're sort of innocent, you can't help it. You're thinking about some very nasty things you'd like to do to me." She turned the full wattage of the smile on his flabbergasted face. "Have I got that about right?" He nodded, feeling the blush spread. "Okay," she said. "Deal. No time like the present. Let's get out of here." He followed her round, swaying hips like a man on the road to salvation.

That's how it had started, like nothing he'd ever heard of before. Even now, sick as he was of her ego and her roughriding personality and ambition and impatience and greed and irritation and contempt,

tired as he was of having her leave all the endless
notes and instructions for him, all the orders and
countermanding orders . . . sick and tired as he
was of all that, he had to admit that watching her
slowly pull her panties down and come to him in a
cloud of heat was better than anything else. Anything. But he was going to have to get used to getting
along without it. Wasn't he? It was a perfect example
of a folie à deux, a mutual sexual obsession that
seemed to feed her while it consumed him. . . .

He crawled out of bed, knocked over a stack of
books and yanked them back up, stuck them by the
door for delivery to the Strand, checked for any
instructions she might have left, and tottered into the
shower. He shaved, ate cornflakes dry since he no
longer remembered to perform such simple tasks as
buying milk, drank a cup of instant coffee made with
hot tap water, and put on his blue blazer, fresh
chinos, and blue button-down shirt. He grabbed the
stack of books, dropped them into a Strand sack, left
the building and began walking. He stopped to make
the quick sale at the bookstore, then headed up
toward midtown. It was a little past noon.

She'd begun their affair with a plan that she hadn't
revealed to him until they'd been lovers for a month,
by which time he was addicted to her eagerness to
perform even his most outrageous fantasies. The
plan had a certain appeal. She was a novelist with
access to some highly secret information. He wrote
non-fiction. She'd read a couple of his books. Not
many people had. He was flattered. He'd have
jumped off the Chrysler Building for her. In the end
what he'd had to do made the Chrysler Building
brain dive look like a day at the beach. Working
together, they had written a book. Which had turned
life into a new kind of horror show.

He caught sight of his reflection in the window of
Saks on Fifth Avenue. He was surprised that none of

his problems really showed in the outer man. It was his apartment that reflected what was going on inside, his version of the Dorian Gray thing. Christ . . .

He waited for the light among the crowd of people gawking at St. Pat's and Atlas at Rockefeller Center. Scanning their faces, he supposed not one of them would have believed his story.

He'd been a boring, timid member of the literary fringe . . . and now was a terrified avenging angel, righter of wrongs, kinked-out sex maniac, pussy-whipped punching bag, and would-be murderer. It had been a fairly lurid two years. His mother thought he was writing a book about Yogi Berra. He sighed and crossed Fifth Avenue.

He checked his watch again. He walked past the huge planters full of spring blooms and stood looking down at the yellow awnings in the outdoor cafe beneath the sculpture of Mercury. Was it Mercury? Who the hell cared. He lit a Camel and coughed. Shit. I'm an insult to spring, he mused. He felt the pack of cigarettes for the outline of the small piece of pasteboard inside the cellophane.

Within a few minutes he was going to do something that would save his life, if everything worked out the way it was supposed to, which of course it wouldn't since nothing ever did. But you had to try to cover yourself. Come up with your own horror show and then make it work for you. Oh, boy.

If *she* knew, she'd kill him.

At thirty-four, Jesse Lefferts wanted two things. He wanted to get married and he wanted to be made a senior editor at Pegasus House. Since he'd been afraid to go on a date since his Big Herpes Scare of '84, it looked like his career was the way to go. He sat

beneath the fluttering fringe of the yellow umbrella,
drinking a tall glass of something that wore a paper
hat. The waitress was dark and silky and her inseam
must have gone 36. He idly wondered if she might be
a carrier. You couldn't be too careful, which was a
problem, period.

This lunch represented his best hope for the senior
editorship. Even in the messy wake of the not-so-
funny-after-all first novel about the snake—which
had not only not sold, but subsequently been proven
to be plagiarized—he figured he still had one more
chance. Acquisitions, that was the name of the game
under the new management at Pegasus. Bring in a
hot book with lots of PR and TV news angles and you
were golden. Well, this was his chance, and he liked
the feel of the deal. All cloak-and-daggerish. Make a
hell of a *Publishers Weekly* piece once it hit the lists.
Sort of Deep Throatish. All he had to do was get his
hands on the goddamn manuscript.

Boy, who'd have thought Charlie Cunningham
would be the guy? That bothered Lefferts because
he'd never thought of Charlie as absolutely the most
serious guy around, but then, he'd known Charlie for
years, back to the days when Charlie was always
trying to scrounge review copies out of him at
Scribners. Now Charlie had come to him with his
plum out of loyalty, in remembrance of those days
when they'd cruised chicks on the Upper East Side
and always gone home alone. The good old days.
You'd think the kind of guy who'd come along with a
property like this would be dynamite with the
ladies. He wondered if Charlie ever got laid . . .
which got him to thinking about the faded mossy
ruins of his own sex life, which prompted him to
order another drink with a hat. Ah, there was Charlie
now.

Charlie didn't mess around with well-dressed
drinks. A martini straight up, no twists, no hat,

nothing. He looked awfully tired, like the pressure was getting to him. Gray around the eyes. They drank, and then they ate huge sandwiches and talked about those Yankees, those Mets, and when Lefferts switched to women, Charlie hadn't seemed all that interested. Had he lost the will to live?

"You know why we're outside?"

"Nice day?" Lefferts ventured.

"It's harder for them to bug us out here. Too much noise, traffic, everybody babbling. These people are very bad people, Jess. Bugging is the single nicest thing they do to people. Get it, Jess? This is serious."

"Works for me," Jess said bravely.

"Yeah, well, good for you. Scares the shit out of me. Now, I'm gonna give you a Camel—"

"No, really, if it's all the same to you. I've been off the hard stuff six weeks, Charlie, don't tempt me—"

"You're gonna take the pack, get a cigarette out, and you're gonna slip a claim check out from inside the wrapper. Try not to make a big deal out of it."

The exchange was accomplished.

"Now light up, Jess."

"Aw, please, Charlie—"

"Light the fuck up." He stuck a lighter into Lefferts's face.

Lefferts lit up, inhaled. A broad smile spread across his boyish face. "Oh, it's wonderful, just wonderful."

"Go back to your office. About four o'clock send one of your messengers to the Port Authority luggage claim. Have him claim a briefcase with the check. Inside that briefcase is the manuscript. You will discover that the briefcase is locked. Leave it locked. Scout's honor."

"Come on!"

"Scout's fucking honor, Jess!"

"Okay, okay—"

"Say it."

"Scout's honor."

"Keep the briefcase in your office. Don't make a big thing out of it. Ignore it. The key will arrive later."

"I don't like this—"

Charlie Cunningham said: "I don't care." He stood up. "Thanks for lunch, Jess. Let's hope we live to do it again sometime." He left, wending his way among the white tables with the yellow umbrellas.

Although he didn't like the way things were going all of a sudden, Lefferts decided to have coffee and smoke, smoke, smoke that cigarette.

DURING

Chapter One

❧

Celia Blandings stood in the musty smelling wings and waited for Billy Blumenthal to finish chatting with the author of *Misconceptions*, a new thriller about a woman who was supposed to be pregnant but wasn't. She had read the Xeroxed script over the weekend and knew it needed work. But with work, there just might be a commercial hit about to emerge. Billy had personally called her, as well as her agent, asking her to come in and read with Deborah Macadam, the movie star who was playing the pregnant lady who wasn't. Celia would play Macadam's sister, a perky, funny, sexy lady who gets knocked off in the middle of the first act but returns mysteriously halfway through the second act. If she got the part.

She had known Debbie Macadam off and on for nearly twenty years, from University of Minnesota days where they'd worked under Doc Whiting on the Showboat. They had even roomed together for six months in a stucco earthquake trap in the hills above the Château Marmont and Sunset Boulevard, back before Debbie had gotten her big break in the Michael Caine picture. Now Debbie caught sight of her and came running over to give her a hug. She was wearing white housepainters' overalls and a tee shirt under the bib top. Debbie was a nice girl, and God knew she was built for the part. Her breasts looked bigger than ever, like someone about to start nursing triplets. "The dairy," Debbie had always referred to them, as if they were the family business. In a way, Celia guessed, they were.

"My God," Debbie sighed, "I hope you get this. I'd get to kill you!"

"But I'd get to come back from the dead and scare your pants off—"

"Happens all the time," she laughed.

"But what brings you to work in this dump?" The off-off Broadway theatre was tucked away, three flights up in a rundown Chelsea office building. The dust in the wings had dust of its own.

"Shows everyone how committed I am to my art." She bit a thumbnail, chipping the last of the polish onto her lower lip. "And, you know, the producing thing . . ."

"The producing thing?"

"Universal's producing. They own the screen rights. If it works, I get the pitcha. It's worth it, believe me, for a marginal movie star with big tits and iffy legs." She batted the long lashes that lay like grillwork over enormous brown eyes.

"Who is also not getting any younger," Celia added.

"Aha! That's where you're wrong. Three years ago I was thirty-four and you were thirty-four. How old are you now?"

"Thirty-gulp-seven."

"Right. But I am thirty-one! Read it in Liz Smith's column yesterday in the *News*. That's what happens when you have William Morris in your corner. You've signed a pact with the Devil, but suddenly you're getting younger. Soon I'll be a college girl again, then going to the orthodontist in knee socks, then diapers—I recommend it, dear."

The stage manager brought them hot coffee, and they were suddenly chatting easily about the old Hollywood days, the marriage that each had buried in the past, the way things were going now. Celia said: "Sometimes I think about this acting thing and I really do have doubts."

"Oh, it's not much," Debbie said. "But it's what we do, my darling. It's too late for me, I'm in it. Not complaining, mind you, but it ain't gonna last forever. You could still get out, though. You could do something else."

"I can?"

"Linda Thurston," Debbie whispered enigmatically.

"Good Lord! You remember that?"

"Are you kidding? If I had a Linda Thurston, I'd be gone. Eat all the pasta I wanted, the hell with it. It'd be me and Linda all the way—"

"I doubt that—"

"Take my word for it."

Then Billy Blumenthal was crying her name, kissing her cheek. "Celia, Celia, last time I saw you, you were engulfed—I mean positively dwarfed—in a fur parka in the snow at the Anchorage airport! And here you are, springy and wearing—da-dum—a skirt! Have I ever seen you in a skirt? Indeed, have I ever set my peepers on those toothsome stems?" She hadn't set her own peepers on Billy since the Alaska Rep three years ago, and he hadn't changed.

"Peepers? Toothsome stems? Ick." Debbie Macadam made a face.

"Your chest, darling, and Celia's legs, the makings of a master race! Come, come, Celia, meet our author, Mr. Levy. Have you had time to glance through this, dear girl? Good, wonderful. Morris, I want you to meet Celia Blandings who's ready and willing to expire in act one. . . ."

So they all gathered around a card table under a single dangling light bulb and began reading Celia's sides. The laughs were there, not quite actor-proof maybe, but close. Levy read some stage directions and Billy cocked a head, eyes closed, listening to rhythms and speech patterns. He'd want just the right contrasts. The physical ones were all in place: dark, active, lean Celia would play just fine off busty, swaggering, fair Debbie. And they read and read and read. The problems were with structure rather than dialogue, which made Levy's problems sizable but not impossible. There was something worth fixing.

Celia's mind wandered off, the lines already sticking in her head. Incredible—Debbie was thirty-one now instead of thirty-seven. What did it all mean? Maybe it wasn't much of a life, maybe Debbie really had given it some thought. But remembering Linda Thurston! How had she managed that? Debbie had never seemed to be paying any attention, and suddenly a decade later, in a dreary dusty theatre, she trots out Linda Thurston. Clearly, miracles would never cease.

Celia's agent, Joel Goldman, was waiting for her, consulting his blade-thin gold watch, when she arrived at the Gotham Bar and Grill on East Twelfth. It was a huge, lofty, understated room, grays and beiges and mauves, with tapestry banquettes and flowers. It was across the street from Fairchild Publications, just down the street from Malcolm Forbes's magazine empire, at eye level with the opera hangout Asti's. Wholesale antique dealers nestled like clubs nearby, and the movie theatre in the middle of the block showed classics. It was pure New York. And it was only a five-minute walk from her apartment at the top end of Greenwich Village.

Joel had already ordered a gin gimlet on ice for her, and she took a greedy drink. "How did it go?" he asked.

"Okay. Fine, I guess. I don't know. It always goes fine, you just don't get the job. I'm gonna need another one of these."

Joel beckoned a waiter and pointed to her glass. "Well, Billy was certainly determined to have you in. I think it looks very good, frankly." He ordered a bowl of mussels for them to share.

She felt like complaining, and carried it on through the mussels, interrupting herself only once, long enough to order a Jerry's Enormous, medium well.

"The point is, Joel, I'm thirty-seven and she's only thirty-one, and three years ago we were both thirty-four. The point is, it's just not working, Joel. . . ."

Joel sipped his Perrier and shook his head. He looked like a grown-up New Yorker in his blue pinstripe suit, Turnbull & Asser shirt, and fresh, trim haircut. He had a better manicurist than she did. He lived on West End with a belt designer called Bruno in what he insisted was an asexual relationship. He was neat and conscientious, and in a general kind of way, the perfect example of a man who had his shit together. He was probably her age, but in his company she always felt like an unappreciative, petulant, jam-spotted child.

"The point, Celia, let me remind you, is that it does work. You work. Right now there's a Masha you could pick off just like that—"

"Where?"

"Pittsburgh."

"Ha!"

"There's a Medea in Seattle," he said patiently.

"One Medea in this lifetime was enough, thank you."

"You're in a mood, Celia. I can't talk to you." He prized one last mussel open and did away with it. "Look, you're an actress of power, presence, style, even wit when properly motivated. There's a *Design for Living* in Denver you could do wonders with— just don't pout. Bruno arose this morning in what looks like a long-term pout, all because of some

buckles that cut through the leather or something. I
am a man with a load of troubles, Celia, try not to
add to them."

"Well, I do love you when you do your Clifton
Webb impression."

He nodded. "My mother was frightened by *Laura*
while she was carrying me. I understand your
frustrations. At least I think I do, but you must
understand that I have gifted clients who *never*
work—"

"I know, I know. I'm a wretch, I don't know when
I'm well off. However, as I slither up on forty, I'm
sick of running around to regional theatres. I'm sick
of wintering at the Guthrie, and I'm tired of summer-
ing at the Alley in Houston and having to change
clothes half a dozen times a day. Sweaty in Houston.
I've done my number in Louisville, Cincinnati, the
Arena, ACT, Alaska . . . I'm done with all the
funny little apartments and the mouse droppings
somebody else didn't clean up—I want droppings
from a mouse of my own. I'm tired of renting cars
from Chrome and Punishment—"

He burst out laughing. "That's very clever, Chrome
and Punishment. I must remember that. Go on, I cut
you off in mid-kvetch."

"I'm sick of being a Gypsy."

"You are also the Kladstrup Koff Kandy fairy, a
very nice job, that. Here, stuff yourself with Jerry's
Enormous."

It was her favorite hamburger. Ten bucks of it filled
the plate, along with little frizzled onions, corn
relish, bits and pieces, all of which Joel could well
afford. He picked at a bit of cold salmon. Looking
with some distress at her preparations, he said:
"Please, have some hamburger with your ketchup."

"I'm really serious, Joel," she said. "I feel like
hibernating for a while—"

"Fine. If you can afford it. Can you?"

"In Manhattan? Get serious. Nobody can actually afford a damn thing. It's all part of the trap."

"Well, you could get married."

"Oh, God—"

"A nice doctor, maybe. An investor, a lawyer, even a producer—just not another actor. Merely hire yourself out as a wife." He reached across the table and patted her hand. "I would be more than willing to volunteer for the position of husband had I not been neutered at an early age by a desperately maladjusted aunt who wanted my mother for herself. Pity."

While she mopped up the last of Jerry's Enormous, she said: "I'm thinking of taking six months off and getting down to my life's work—"

"Oh, no, this isn't what I think it is—"

"Joel, I've wanted to do this all my life. I've done a lot of research. This may be the right time. I should give it a chance."

"Oh, God, not Linda Thurston. . . ." He searched her face. She grinned fetchingly. "It is, it is Linda Thurston. My worst fears realized." He sighed dramatically, plucked the lime from his Perrier, and made a face as he began to suck it.

Chapter Two

❧

Celia strolled along Twelfth Street toward the Strand and its famed eight miles of used books, stopping for a moment to gaze at the monster masks in the windows of the science fiction bookshop, Forbidden Planet. The masks were both realistic and intriguingly repugnant, eyeballs bulging bloodily out of cheeks, a face made entirely of tentacles. She was standing at the corner when Vanessa Redgrave and her son, she supposed, came out of the store. The boy was leafing through comic books, and the movie star looked motherly and a little distracted. Watching her, Celia wondered who the boy's father was. Franco Nero? Well, whoever it was, Ms. Redgrave had survived an admirable career, some unpopular political stances, a great theatrical name . . . and she had a son. If acting really wasn't so great, she still had that son. Which put her way ahead of Celia.

Celia's husband, Paul Landover, was long gone, though he remained a distant friend, and he skittered across her mind—in his doublet, since he always seemed to be doing a costume thing—for the few seconds it took her to cross the street. Just as well there wasn't a little Paul Landover, now that she thought about it.

She'd sat over a second cup of coffee at the Gotham once Joel had departed to conduct bigger and doubtless better business. Once he was gone, of course, she'd thought of plenty of things she should have said while he was blithering on about her wonderful career. She could have recounted all the jobs she'd wanted but hadn't gotten in the last couple of years because she was too old, too young, too pretty, too ordinary, too dark, not exotic enough, too damn exotic, too tall, too short, too thin, not motherly enough, too damn motherly, not housewifey, and too glamorous. A *Vanities*, gone, a *Talley's Folly*, a *Death Trap*, a *The Dark at the Top of the Stairs*, a *Loot*, a *Midsummer Night's Dream*, a *King Lear*—the list went on and on, all productions in or near New York, where she could have maintained a life.

She sat thinking of all the ripostes she might have made, but after all, they were too ordinary, too obvious, the warp and woof of every actor's life. So what, Joel would have said, the bottom line is work—and you have worked. It was true. So why wasn't she just thankful for that? And why didn't she shut up?

Presumably because she wanted some kind of settled existence.

Did that mean she was getting old?

Of course it did.

But not *that* old. Entering her prime, she thought, remembering how she and Debbie Macadam had once played students of Miss Jean Brodie at the U of M.

Maybe she was tired of always interpreting a role, saying someone else's words, inhabiting another creature's body. Unlike some actors, she'd never hidden within a role, had never needed that particular kind of refuge. She'd simply done the work and enjoyed it. But perhaps she was losing something of Celia Blandings in all the transformations she'd accomplished over the years. Maybe that was why so many actors painted and sculpted and jotted down stories and kept diaries and labored over poems. Reminding themselves that they existed once the lights had gone down, the curtain fallen.

There was something about the act of creation that was never fully present for the actor. Or that was how she felt, anyway. You were bound by the character as written, by the author's vision; you were bound by the director's conception. You were controlled by the necessity of tuning your performance to your fellow actors. You were even controlled by the audience, by the need to make them laugh or cry or gasp on cue.

None of that mattered with Linda Thurston.

At the Strand she fell upon the tables of review copies like a Hun on a defenseless hamlet of fair damsels. It was midafternoon and there were only a few browsers picking over the three large tables of new arrivals that sold for half price. She let her eyes roam happily over the brightly colored dust jackets, the relatively virgin pages. That was what Debbie Macadam had called herself when they met as sophomores. *A relative virgin.* And that was how Celia was coming to view the last few years of her life—relatively virginal. Uncomplicated, all work. Which was just the way she'd planned it, except now she didn't think it had gotten her anywhere. Not anywhere she particularly wanted to go, anyway.

After giving the tables a onceover, she settled in, noting each title, each author. She was looking only for mysteries. When she traveled, she carted along more of them than clothing, somehow, and it was mainly a case of fearing she'd run out. It was like chocolate for some people. She couldn't get enough, though she was a discriminating judge. No junk. Not even very much of the stuff that was mainly plot or puzzle oriented. She had, therefore, never become a devotee of Agatha Christie. The characterizations were usually just too thin, too superficial. Her favorites from that classical age were Dorothy

Sayers, Josephine Tey—though she came a bit later—Edmund Crispin, Anthony Boucher, Ngaio Marsh, Michael Innes. . . . They were less writers of a particular era than of essentially-like minds. However ingenious or fanciful their plots, they dealt in character.

Today she was in luck.

Someone must have brought in a load earlier in the day, and she was the first scavenger. She found a Donald Westlake, so funny; a Ross Thomas, so precise and ironic and bemused; a Martha Grimes, the best of the new eighties writers, possessed of a positive genius for doing children, as well as for building her protagonist Richard Jury into a figure of depth and texture; a Robert Parker, whose concentration on Spenser's relationship with Susan Silverman was as good a disquisition on up-to-date love affairs as she knew; a Simon Brett, because he wrote with such insight and wit of the theatre; a Michael Gilbert, because he was a true master who'd stood the test of time; a Tony Hillerman, because you learned so much about the Navajo culture, and by reflection, your own; a James McClure for the same reason, though South Africa was his turf; and several other books by writers she knew she should try but never had—Rick Demos and Sandra Elliott and Miles Warriner, among others.

Her shopping bag was full, thirteen volumes. She staggered away and went downstairs, where among the dust and the maze of aisles and the countless tens of thousands of books, much of the staff conducted their strange subterranean existence. There were more eccentrics per square foot in the basement of the Strand than anywhere else in New York. The first thing she saw was a black gentleman seated at a run-down, cluttered desk, carefully inserting pins in a tiny cloth doll while he munched a jelly-filled doughnut.

"Is Claude around today?" she asked, inquiring after a friend who had once acted with her at the Guthrie before coming to his senses and joining real life full time.

Slowly a needle penetrated the puffy chest of the doll, then nosed through the back. The doll didn't really have a head, just a tied-off topknot. Funny little arms. "Just a minute, lady," the man said. He slid another needle. Into the crotch. The dark purple black face looked up, grinned. The teeth were filed to points. "Claude?"

"Look," Celia said, "who is that doll supposed to be? Young Duvalier or somebody?"

The face scowled. The man wore a blue sweatshirt with the Miranda warning printed on it in white lettering. "The man," he said. "The man who owns this place. We of the netherworld, of the underground, we seek release from our captivity. Death to the man. He's not here."

"What?"

"Claude. He left at noon. Said he was going bowling." He shrugged. "Different strokes. Now me, if I could get outa this place today, I'd go buy myself a nice chicken. Y'know, feathers, alive, squawking. Then I'd have me a nice little sacrificial rite. I give the gods a goddamn chicken, maybe they'll deliver unto me the asshole that owns this place."

"Right. Whatever you say."

She went down one of the aisles, looking to see what might have been squirreled away before landing on the upstairs tables. Two employees were loading shelves, chatting.

"You say this guy is famous?"

"Really famous, yeah."

"You know this guy?"

"See, he's got this collection. Food. He collects real food. But it's like old."

"Old food?"

"That's what I'm tellin' ya, man. A cheeseburger seven years old—"

"Gross. Can he prove it?"

"Ya look at it, you believe. Gross but neat. The thing is," lowering his voice to a whisper, "I'm startin' my own collection."

"Of what?"

"Food. What else we talkin' about, man? I mean, if it made this guy famous, got him on Letterman, why not me? I got a piece of Ray's pepperoni pizza a week old already, you might call it the keystone of my collection, it's where I'm startin' from, buildin' my collection from this simple piece of pizza—"

"You actually know this famous guy, then?"

"Well, I know a guy knows his roommate. We're gonna go over to see his whole collection sometime. Got a nine-year-old piece of wedding cake."

"Really? Nine years old?"

"Yeah, he says it's already lasted five years longer than the marriage. . . ."

Celia went back to the main floor, where she set down the thirteen books on the counter.

"Wow, you want all these?"

"Here's my Visa."

The guy behind the counter brushed long black hair out of his eyes with his fingertips. Celia had once had a typing teacher who made exactly the same gesture.

"You must be a real mystery buff."

She watched the total rise as he flipped through the books, punching out half the list price.

"Yes, I guess that's what I am."

"Me too. Always thought I'd write one, but I never had the time—"

"Takes more than time," she said.

"Think so?"

"It's hard, writing a mystery." Then, without really thinking about it, she blurted out: "I'm writing one myself."

"Hey, really? That's great. I suppose you're right, I could never concentrate that long, like we've got this nut in the basement here. You're not gonna believe this, he's collecting old food. Like art. Now that doesn't take *any* concentration . . . well, let's see here, you're putting quite a dent in a hundred bucks."

She left the bookstore, stood blinking in the sunlight, waiting to cross. She couldn't believe it, but she kept hearing the words.

I'm writing one myself.

She felt as if she'd slipped out of gear and the motor was racing. She'd never actually said it before, without qualifiers and conditional clauses hanging all over the place. But now, out of the blue, she'd just said it.

She lugged her books in the red-and-white Strand bag over to the drugstore, where she picked up some toothpaste and a new brush. A girl of ten or so with blond hair in two pigtails tied with blue yarn was tugging at her mother's skirt, pointing at Celia. Celia smiled down at her. The big blues were stuck on Celia's face.

"You're the cough-syrup fairy."

"Me?"

"Mommy, the cough-syrup fairy!"

The woman smiled at Celia. "You are—"

Celia shook her head and smiled. Not me, she thought, testing the words in her head, I'm a writer.

The girl gazed up at her, ducking behind her mother's skirt.

"Louanne, she looks like the fairy. But she knows who she is. Don't you?" She winked at Celia.

"I'm not altogether sure," Celia said.

She left the drugstore and walked on the sunny side of the street, feeling determined and fresh and even a little silly.

It was time she sat down with Linda Thurston.

Chapter Three

❧

Celia lived in two rooms, one tiny, one immense, in a building on Tenth Street near Fifth Avenue. It was on the historical registry—the building, not her apartment, which had been created in the late sixties by knocking out a couple of walls, relocating a bathroom, and raising the ceiling, which had inexplicably been dropped in the fifties. No decade had a lock on the inexplicable.

Celia did almost all her living in the big room. And most of the living centered on the ornate pool table which, with its slate bed, had required the services of four men and a crane and had pretty well tied up traffic the day it was installed. The men who came later in the week at the landlord's request had listened to the house with stethoscopes and concluded that there probably wan't any structural damage. Still, she would be well advised to listen for excessive creaking in the walls and under the floorboards. And for the next few months she heard nothing but excessive creaking. In the end she learned to live with it, like San Franciscans and Love Canalites.

A carpenter had built a top that fit on the pool table, making it her desk, her dining table, and with the addition of an air mattress, her guest bedroom. There were a couple of long, deep couches, a fireplace, white brick walls, just under eight miles of books, an enormous pretend-Oriental rug, and a galley kitchen backed into a faraway corner. There

was a long three-bulbed lamp hanging over the table
with three green glass shades and all brass hardware.
Like the table itself, it was very old and had belonged
to her paternal grandfather, who had owned a
poolroom in the Chicago Loop.

When she banged in the door, she awakened Ed-
the-Mean, who came at her in a frantic flurry of
purplish blue like a very scary special effect or a
demon from the void of eternity. She had been
through it all before. She stood her ground.

"Ed, you're not only mean and dumb, you're one
silly ass. Now get out of my way!"

She dropped the bag of books on the table.

She watched Ed, standing quietly now by a book-
case that was spilling its guts onto the floor.

Someday Ed was going to raise hell with the wrong
guy and wind up in the next morning's trash.

She put her tape of *Gilda* into the VCR and got it
going. It wasn't absolutely her favorite movie, but it
was close, up there with *Dead Reckoning* and *The
Blue Dahlia* and *Murder, My Sweet* and *Out of the
Past* and *The Big Sleep* and *Ride the Pink Horse*.
She'd fallen asleep the night before, had clicked the
movie off with the remote control. Now it picked
right up near the end, when Glenn Ford sees the
mysterious louvered window in the nightclub's office closing, and knows that George Macready isn't
dead after all but back from the watery grave, with
Rita Hayworth on his mind. . . .

She watched the end, then rewound it and started
it again. Then she went to the closet in her tiny
bedroom and brought a large cardboard box back to
the couch.

Inside it lived Linda Thurston.

Ed-the-Mean cocked his head and peered down
from the mantelpiece as she emptied the box and

spread Linda all over the Oriental rug. Celia leaned back against the couch and surveyed the file folders, the notebooks, the loose pages, the newspaper clippings, the three-by-five and four-by-six file cards in a rainbow of colors—all of which added up to one Linda Thurston.

Linda Thurston, the heroine of the unwritten mystery novels she'd contemplated for so long. The heroine of so many incarnations across the years. Celia hadn't told more than a half-dozen people about Linda. Hilary Sampson, Debbie Macadam, Paul Landover in the flush of newly married ultimate-secret telling, Joel Goldman, maybe a couple of others . . .

She poured a glass of Chablis, checked *Gilda* to make sure the story hadn't changed, glared at Ed-the-Mean with eyes that said if-you-dare-even-think-of-shitting-on-the-floor-you-die, and turned back to Linda.

Celia had imagined her in a variety of guises as the years and manners and mores had marched onward. She'd been a tough, perky, driven Civil Rights marcher and anti–Vietnam War protestor in the sixties; a tough, perky, driven reporter like Jane Fonda in *The China Syndrome* in the seventies; a tough etcetera muckraking newspaper woman; a tough blah-blah lawyer defending wronged underdogs; a ditto actress. . . .

All those Lindas had taken their places in the cardboard box, and finally one day the real Linda had appeared, as if she'd been waiting all along for the right moment, like a Botticelli Venus rising from the note cards. She emerged from Celia's own life and imagination, but was not Celia herself from the world of theatre, not an actress.

Linda had begun as a newspaper feature writer, then become a drama critic because of both her education and inclination. From there she'd hopped into a spot as a TV drama critic, largely due to her personal style. Subsequently, because of her love of the sweaty, gritty, greasepainty world of theatre itself, she went to work for one of the great regional theatres in administration—first in PR, then as assistant to the company manager, then as a fund-raiser, then even getting her feet wet directing a summer touring show; one job after another.

And with each new job a new mystery would present itself, sometimes a murder, but sometimes something more subtle—financial skullduggery on the board of directors, the undermining of the theatre's eccentric founder, a poison-pen letter writer driving a well-known guest star to a nervous breakdown. Celia had seen just about everything but murder in the companies where she'd done time, and this most recent version of Linda Thurston had seemed so right.

Celia had outlined the first Linda novel a couple of years before, but had then spent nearly all of the next two years working hard at her acting, with not enough energy left to spend on writing. But now, now she might just make the time while the Kladstrup Koff Kandy fairy paid the bills. She had a plot and a title, *Murder in the Round*. It was the story of a woman who'd founded a theatre and was renowned for bringing the men in her life—actors, directors, authors, critics, moneymen—to heel in the most peculiar ways. Celia had watched the woman in action, more or less, and knew her inside out. It seemed like a promising beginning.

She worked at the covered pool table, perched on a stool, hunched over a pad of graph paper, sketching in the outlines of her novel, jotting down the events of the first few chapters, the aspects of character and setting to be revealed therein, the point each action was to make. It was satisfying but exhausting work, and after three hours of it she looked up, feeling red-eyed and stiff, her facial muscles aching from grim determination. She leaned back, stretched, and got up to take the long concluded *Gilda* out of the VCR.

She went to the kitchen counter and ground coffee beans, brewed a fresh pot, and while waiting for it, talked to Ed-the-Mean.

He was an Anodorhynchus Hyacinthinus, more commonly known as a Hyacinth Macaw, at about three-and-a-half feet from stem to stern the biggest goddamn parrot in the known universe. Ed happened not only to be slothful but truculent, particularly in the presence of the unknown or unwary. He was also such a beautiful creature that Celia sometimes came near to crying just looking at him—when she wasn't mad at him.

He was, for the most part, a deep, unique blend of purple and blue, with a periophthalmic ring of golden yellow and a small naked yellow streak along the base of the lower mandible. Ed was a native of western Bolivia. The bird books described his kind as "not shy," which in Ed's case was so far from understatement it bordered on criminal. Normally the hyacinth macaw is thought to be unusually gentle, intelligent, and affectionate, but the standard reference work also observes tht he is "fierce toward strangers." Ha! Enter Ed-the-Mean.

The grayish-black beak is not merely large. With three hundred pounds of biting pressure per square inch, a human finger, for example, is child's play. A snack. Ed, for exercise Celia assumed, frequently amused himself by turning pool cues into neat little bits of kindling. He was also a roguish free spirit. His cage, an enormous affair made of welded and bolted steel which had cost seven hundred dollars—still making it only a fraction of what Ed himself had cost—was only a toy. He regularly let himself out in the morning, and when the mood was upon him, locked himself back in at night. As a companion on lonely evenings he was almost ideal: he didn't say much, but was a good listener. And while she waited for the coffee, he came and pushed against her hand, a cat wanting to be stroked.

Celia cooed to him: "You are a big bad birdie, a disgrace to your gentle, intelligent, affectionate race. Naturally, I love you. On the other hand, I rather resent the fact that you will outlive me." He clucked happily. "I love you, unless, that is, you do naughty on my kitchen counter. In which case, I will kill you." Ed clucked derisively, knowing she didn't have the nerve, wouldn't have a chance if it came to hand-to-hand combat. She was only a woman, and he seemed to know perfectly well that she'd have trouble biting through a swizzle stick.

She sat with her steaming mug of coffee and emptied the bag of books onto the floor around her. She'd put a *Rockford Files* tape on the VCR, which meant seven or eight episodes could run without interruption. She loved *The Rockford Files*. She'd actually been featured in a couple of them, once as a girl good old Jimbo got mildly stuck on. Jill Clayburgh was starring in this one, and some village thugs were giving Jimbo the usual rough time.

Eventually she began looking at the books, reading the first page or two of each, getting a feel for the story and the approach. She was just enjoying herself in an uncomplicated way when she picked up Miles Warriner's *Littlechild Takes Aim*. She'd never read any of Inspector Littlechild's adventures, and friends assured her it was time. She flipped the front cover back and watched a sheet of white paper slide out, flutter to the floor between her outstretched legs.

It was probably another press release that accom-

panied review copies. She'd already come across
several in this single batch of books. She picked it
up, glanced at it in passing.

It wasn't a press release.

It was a letter. Sort of.

She read it. She put it down and shivered. She
picked it up and read it again. It didn't take long. It
was short.

She looked at Ed, who seemed about to fall asleep
on the mantelpiece.

"Holy shit," she said. Her voice was shaking.

Ed blinked sleepily.

She went to refill her coffee cup, came back and
read the damn thing again, trying to believe it was a
joke. She tried to put as many interpretations on it as
possible, but there wasn't much leeway.

> MM
> In re the murder of the Director.
>   1. Door unlocked.
>   2. Working west wing.
>   3. D in study. Dan Rather.
>   4. Prowler shoots.
>   5. Trunk.
>   6. Rolls.
>   7. Clean getaway.
>   8. Try not to be STUPID!
>   9. 21. 7. Don't forget.
>   Z.

She felt as if Linda Thurston had just taken shape
and was reading over her shoulder. It was eerie, and
of course absurd, but she took a minute to rid herself
of the feeling. Sure, she was alone. But Linda was
like a genie: Once she got out of her box it was going
to be trouble getting her back in.

What would Linda Thurston do if she found such
a letter of intended murder?

To begin with, she'd make her hands stop trembling.

Then she'd try to figure out exactly what it meant.

Who was M.M.?

Who was the Director?

What did Dan Rather have to do with it?

What Prowler?

What trunk?

Who needed Rolls? This didn't sound like a coffee break. . . .

What was 21? 7?

Who was Z?

And who the hell was that knocking at the door?

Chapter Four

❧

Hilary Sampson, a lanky redhead with hair cut the length of your thumb and eyes of pearl gray separated by a freckled nose, was standing at the door in her dark blue Auxiliary Police uniform, billed cap pulled low on her forehead. She was holding a yellow plastic bag from Hunan Royal on Sixth Avenue. Dinner.

She'd finished her evening's patrol and as usual made her final stop at Celia's, though in her excitement at thinking about Linda Thurston, Celia had let the custom slip her mind. Hilary always used the key Celia had given her in case of emergencies.

Hilary was at her best in emergencies, whether you were in need of a nightstick, the paramedics, or the Heimlich Maneuver. She'd once given mouth to mouth recusitation to a drunk fallen in a stupor outside Steve's Ice Cream at Tenth and Sixth, saved his life, and managed not to throw up afterward. She'd once given Ed a swat with her nightstick, following which his greetings became markedly less effusive. A friend had once given her a framed sampler with daffodils and bunny rabbits embroidered around the words DON'T FUCK WITH ME. Hilary hung it on the closet door in her tiny front hall.

"Cold sesame noodle, chicken in garlic sauce, orange beef," she said, proceeding to the pool table. "Evening, Ed, how they hanging?"

While Celia brought in the bottle of Chablis from

the fridge and another glass, Hilary looked at the mess on the floor and shook her head. "Do my eyes deceive me or have you decided to be a writer again?"

Celia went back to the kitchen for chopsticks. Hilary opened the little white pasteboard containers. Celia went back to the kitchen yet again, her mind racing with other things, and returned with plates and paper napkins.

"More like a detective," Celia said.

Hilary rolled the pearls heavenward. "Oh, Ed, what has she done now?"

"You eat," Celia said. "I'll talk. The craziest thing has happened."

She told her the story of the day, how Debbie Macadam had gotten her thinking about being trapped and wanting escape routes, about Linda Thurston. She told her about how Joel had tried to convince her that the career was going strong, and making perfect sense, and she really ought to do this or that in some faraway place, on and on through an infinity of mirrors. She told her how she'd gone down the street and seen Vanessa Redgrave, then gone to the Strand and quite unexpectedly announced to a total stranger that she was writing a mystery. And she had practically lied to a little girl who'd identified her as the cough syrup fairy.

Hilary listened intently while bravely fighting it out, chopsticks versus sesame noodles, casually using a finger when it was required. Ed watched the finger while pretending to groom a wing, seeming to calculate his chances, knowing perfectly well he was overmatched against that damn log she'd once hit him with.

Having calmed herself about everything else, Celia finally came to the murder letter. She handed it to Hilary. "You read, now I'll eat."

Hilary read. Her eyebrows slowly rose. She took a

long drink of wine. Eventually she picked up War-riner's *Littlechild Takes Aim*, shook it by the covers to see if more goodies might emerge. None did. She leafed through the pages, stopped at the title page for an extra moment, then closed the book.

"Looks like a case for Ms. Thurston," she said.

"Mmm," Celia said, shoveling in a mouthful of chicken in garlic sauce.

"Unless it's just a plot from the perverse mind of some other would-be mystery writer—"

"In the form of a letter to M.M.? Read it again. Those are directions to M.M. from Z. Not notes for a novel. I've made notes in every imaginable form, but nothing like that."

"So someone's going to kill the Director," Hilary mused.

"Well, I'd say M.M. and Z are going to kill the Director—"

"Two out of work actors plotting to kill—let's see, a director so important he gets a big D—Mike Nichols maybe?"

"Actors only *talk* about killing the director. They hardly ever do it. And then only in fits of pique. Extreme, aggravated pique. Never, ever in the study with Dan Rather."

"That shows how much you know," Hilary said. "If Colonel Mustard can do it in the library with a candlestick, then an actor could do it in Mike Nichols's study with Dan Rather doing a live remote—"

"Come on! That's ridiculous and this is no joke—"

"Ed's ridiculous but there he is. Definitely no joke."

"Okay, okay, let's get serious. First, we don't know who M.M. is and we're not going to find out tonight. And there's no way yet to figure out who the Director is either—all we know about him is he's the victim.

Now, what about leaving the door unlocked? Maybe the Director always leaves the door unlocked."

"Or maybe Z is going to leave it unlocked for M.M. Look, we're just treading water here, Celia."

"Let's just stick with it. Someone is working in the west wing. While the door is unlocked. The Director? West wing. Sounds awfully grand—"

"No, the Director—that is D, if that's the Director— is in the study with Dan Rather. Could there be some other Dan Rather?"

"Somehow one doubts it, wouldn't you agree?"

"I suppose," Hilary conceded, tangling with the chicken now.

"Now there's the Prowler—is that a third murderer or what?"

"I wonder. Could be M.M., I suppose. I mean, Z wouldn't be reminding M.M. if Z is the Prowler. Would he? Well, I don't think we can tell, really."

"Trunk makes no sense. Maybe there's something in the trunk they want. Treasure of some kind. Rolls? Wouldn't need arsenic in the rolls if you've got a gun. Trunk and rolls. Maybe they're planning to work up an appetite. It's gibberish. At least Clean getaway is self-explanatory."

"The next one makes you think Z doesn't find M.M. the brightest guy around—"

"Agreed."

"But 21 and 7 baffle me—"

"Could be the date written in the English manner," Hilary said. "Twenty-first day of the seventh month. That'd be July—"

"But this is only May nineteenth. Why the big note to M.M., all this checking up on details? Sounds like it's urgent last minute stuff—"

"Dan Rather," Hilary reflected, wiping orange beef from the corner of her mouth. "God, I wish you'd let me use a fork!"

"Dan Rather what?"

"The evening news comes on at seven here. That's Dan Rather. He's not in the study with the Director. The Director's in the study at seven o'clock *watching* Dan Rather. And he's always there at seven because the Director is a creature of habit. The more habitual your routine, the easier you are to kill. So . . ."

"You're saying—look, that means the murder takes place on the twenty-first of this month at seven o'clock!"

"And today's the nineteenth. . . ."

For the second time that evening Celia said: "Holy shit."

"We know something else," Hilary said once the plates had been rinsed and stacked in the sink. The wine was running low. "You didn't look at the title page."

"What do you mean? I was so amazed at the letter—"

"Well, there's another connection. The title page is signed by the author." She reached for the book and handed it to Celia.

Celia looked. Written in ballpoint pen, slanted across the page above and below the title itself, were the words: *For MM with love and other things,* "Miles."

"So M.M. knows Z *and* Miles Warriner," Celia said. "Would one man write 'with love and other things' to another man?"

"Probably. In the Village, anyway."

"Mmm. I suppose. I wonder why someone would sell an autographed copy at the Strand?"

"Well, that's obviously a mistake," Celia said. "M.M. didn't mean to sell that book. Not autographed. Not with a plan to commit a murder included. All this is a big mistake."

Hilary pointed a finger at Celia, cutting her off.

"Now we have a name! Miles Warriner must know who M.M. is! So all we have to do is find Miles Warriner and ask him—"

Celia was shaking her head. "That might not be so easy. Look at the quotation marks Warriner put around his first name—what does that mean to you?"

Hilary shrugged. "A nickname?"

"A pen name," Celia said. "I'll bet Miles Warriner is a pseudonym." She flipped to the back cover, which was taken up by newspaper quotations about the Littlechild series. The inside dust-jacket flap contained no author photograph but merely the listing of the Littlechild titles, seven of them, and the enigmatic sentence: *Miles Warriner lives in New York City but is intimately acquainted with the villages of England about which Inspector Littlechild seems to know everything.*

Hilary read it and looked piqued. "Cute. Smarmy bastard. So if it's a pseudonym, where does that leave us?"

"Depends on how seriously the secret is kept. Sometimes it's common knowledge, maybe the leisure writing of a heavier weight literary type. Could be a professor somewhere who fills his holidays with mystery writing. Or it could be a dark secret for a million reasons. But the thing is, whoever it is, he knows M.M. I wonder if Miles Warriner knows Z?"

"How can we get the real name?"

"Just ask," Celia said. "The publisher, the Mystery Writers of America . . . maybe Otto would know—"

"Otto?"

"Otto Penzler up at the Mysterious Bookshop. He knows funny things sometimes. Like where the bodies are buried, so to speak."

Celia had turned the lights low and lit a couple of

candles. Rockford's gold Firebird spun wildly
around a mountain road, the bad guys in hot pursuit
through the clouds of dust. Hilary sat at the other
end of the couch. The magnitude of the letter was
just beginning to sink in. A man was going to be
murdered, and the sheerest of accidents had let them
in on the secret. Now there was a moral question
involved. It was none of Celia's business. She was
the perfect Hitchcockian innocent bystander—the
Jimmy Stewart character, stumbling over a body. The
woman who knew too much. . . . But could she
ignore the fact that she knew? Wasn't there an
obligation to do something? To try and save the
man's life?

Celia's first reaction had been to take the letter and
their story to the police. Hilary, who was fascinated
by police procedures and had been an auxiliary
volunteer patroling the Village and hanging around
with cops for five years, just laughed.

"They'd think we were totally crazy," she said,
"and nothing would happen. There's nothing for
them to go on. It's too off the wall. No crime has been
committed, there aren't names and addresses, nothing. If the murder had already been done, then the
letter would be evidence, which we've screwed up
by playing with it. . . . Nope, not a chance." Her
arguments were persuasive.

Now Hilary was sighing. "I'm going to regret this
next part, let me make this absolutely clear right at
the outset. What, I wonder, would Linda Thurston
do? I ask only because I once had a therapist who
was always suggesting that we put ourselves into a
third-party point of view—she kept telling me I
should use a role model, try to think what the role
model would do. She said fictional role models were
as good as real ones, better actually, because their
personalities were often clearer. Anyway, you're
supposed to think like Linda Thurston—"

"I feel foolish."

"Linda wouldn't. So you mustn't. Okay, look at it this way. If you were writing a Linda Thurston story, what would come next? She finds the letter and . . . what?" Hilary lit a True and took a deep drag, which she'd convinced herself couldn't harm a fly.

"Well, that's different because Linda—in the first one I want to write—is having an affair with an actor in the company who's playing Sherlock Holmes, who's made a career of playing detectives on TV and in the movies. She takes the problem to him and they sort it out very romantically, you know, like in a movie. But I don't have a boyfriend, and if I did he *wouldn't* be an—"

"But," Hilary interrupted, turning to grin maniacally, "I had a boyfriend who was a cop. He still is a detective—wait, no, he isn't actually. But he counts as a detective even though he's retired—"

"He's old?"

"No. But he's . . . disabled. Only has one eye."

"Wonderful."

"Smart guy, though. I'd say he's your best bet."

"Does he have a name?"

"Greco. Peter Greco. I'll call him right now."

But he was out so she left a message on his machine that practically assured she'd get a call back.

Once Hilary had gone, Celia lay in bed, listening to the faint, steady hum of the city. She heard Ed banging around in the other room, climbing back into his cage and locking up for the night.

Alone in the darkness she wondered what in the world she was getting into. It had seemed like a titillating game at first, but as the somber facts of a murder plot grew clearer, its appeal was fading.

Murder was desperate, serious, brutal, not the stuff of games.

Yet she was dabbling in it. As if she were only Linda Thurston, safe in the pages of a book, with a benevolent creator looking out for her.

Who would be looking out for Celia Blandings, who had always taken a certain pride in admitting her physical cowardice? Where was the fun in doing something that could wind up with you dead?

And what did she think she'd do about the murder plan anyway? Did she think she was going to keep the murder from happening? She had a couple days, and she didn't really know anything about the impending murder. Maybe the time. Probably the means. But surely that wasn't enough. . . .

Still, there was one big unknown that hadn't been in the letter.

Peter Greco.

Chapter Five

❧

The game had gotten out of hand along about ten-thirty, when the one-eyed guy had blown an easy shot and narrowly missed a three-rail nine ball that would have left him in a position to run the table and climb back to within a couple hundred bucks of even. Instead he'd gone four bills down, then five, and with the growing deficit, he seemed increasingly determined to wipe himself out. Some guys are like that, pushing a losing streak as far as it will go, hoping it will turn around, maybe hoping it will teach them a lesson.

A tall black guy called Slick was calmly, deliberately taking him to the cleaners, smiling all the time, keeping everything nice and friendly. Slick was bankrolled by a couple of greaseballs in Italian suits that might have fit them fifteen, twenty pounds ago. Slick was their boy, and while the score was being clicked up and the balls racked, they chatted together—Slick, his backers, and the guy who held all the money. The thickset, one-eyed guy didn't seem to mind losing. He had all the confidence of a man who thought he was a whole hell of a lot better than he was. A born mark.

He was five-nine maybe, and his thick, curly black hair was receding on a rounded forehead that wore a couple of scarred dents. Where his hair wasn't receding it was speckled with gray. His shoulders sloped confidently beneath his gray sweatshirt. The sleeves were pushed up almost to the elbow. There was a lot of wiry black hair growing out of the muscles. He'd pumped a little iron in his time.

He shot pool erratically, brilliant and creative one moment, blowing an ordinary shot the next. A born mark. And on top of all that misplaced confidence and the inconsistency, he was actually blind in one eye, wore a black patch with a black elastic band sunk into a groove across his forehead and on into his hair. Slick got a kick out of the mark's sweatshirt: IN THE LAND OF THE BLIND, THE ONE-EYED MAN IS KING. Slick thought that was pretty good, and said so.

The mark said: "Can't afford to lose your sense of humor, man. Never take anything too seriously. Particularly your own misfortune."

"Right on," Slick said, his thick pink tongue sliding along his lower lip. Slick wore a purple suit, a black shirt, and a lemon-colored tie. The one-eyed guy thought Slick was pretty funny, and the four of them were getting along just fine as Slick kept rolling up the score.

It was a second-floor poolroom on the Lower East Side. It reeked of smoke and chalk and flop sweat. It had been there a long time, and it didn't look like much, but it was the kind of dreary, dark place where a lot of money changes owners. Half of the tables were in use, and there were some of the usual creeps and rummies hanging around watching the action, ready to bet the rent on guys like Slick, guys on hot streaks.

The one-eyed guy came back from taking a leak and said, "Shit, I got five bills left. Might as well lose it all and go home to bed. Honest and poor." He handed the money to the old crock with the dead cigar stuck in the corner of his rubbery mouth. Christ, the one-eyed man thought, it's a low budget, off-the-books version of *The Hustler*. Now I'd better turn into Fat Jack Gleason. "Let's shoot some pool,

Slick," was what he said. Slick handed five hundred to the holder.

Slick ran four balls, then missed a tough shot he'd been making all night, smiled like a piano keyboard, and gave the table to the mark.

He didn't have much to work with, but sneaked the seven ball into a corner pocket. Then he ran the table without having anything tougher than your grandmother could handle. That was about eleven-thirty.

Funny thing, but he didn't have a tough shot for the next hour and a half. In that time he missed only three shots, three of the very easiest. Whenever old Slick missed one, the one-eyed guy ran the table. Always easy shots. It was like watching Bernard King turn Madison Square Garden into a basketball clinic. "My lucky night," he said, as if he couldn't believe his good fortune.

It was all very quick. Click, click, click, plop, plop, plop. Slick was looking very tired by one o'clock, which was funny because he hadn't been doing much for quite a while but standing around chalking his cue, watching.

At one-thirty the one-eyed guy was $3600 ahead and the guys in the bad suits were dry. They were going to have to borrow carfare home. The game was over. The guy with the one bad lamp had all the money.

Slick was sitting in a heavy, smooth chair, looking at the table, realizing what had happened. The two suits were whispering at each other, nobody listening. The mark put on a beat-up old Yankee warm-up jacket over his sweatshirt. He peeled off a hundred and gave it to the holder.

"Thanks for the game, Mr. Slick," he said, then nodded to the two fashion plates. "Just one of those nights, gentlemen. I was due."

They frowned, muttered. He went down the creak-

ing stairway to the street, looked at the night, saw
that it was good, took a deep breath and told himself
he'd been a very bad boy. The thought rather pleased
him. He grinned. With the thick, slope-shouldered
body, the neck like a fire hydrant and the rounded
dome, he looked like a mortar shell out for a walk.

They came at him with a minimum of subtlety, as
he knew they would. They weren't up to much more.
He heard them panting along behind him. Amateurs.
Punks who leaned on you for the love of leaning on
you, anybody. He stopped beside a junky free-lance
parking lot. The bums who lived there might enjoy
this. He turned around and watched them come.

Slick was doubtless still contemplating the playing field of his defeat. The suits had traded him in on
a hulking pile of muscle who trotted heavily beside
them.

"Look," the one-eyed man said, taking his hands
out of the pockets of his Yankee jacket, "you're not
going to get your money back. You lost it fair and
square. That's a fact. Your friend in the purple suit
choked and you got stuck with the tab. That's life. Go
home, learn from the experience, reflect on your
mistake. It'll be easier that way, believe me." He had
a nice, low voice. Reassuring. Take my advice, it
seemed to say.

One of the suits said: "You gotta gun, man? Better
show it if you do."

The man shook his head sadly. "Don't need a gun,
to tell you the truth. I'm that tough."

The other suit laughed. "Yeah, you gonna wish
you had a piece, man."

He pulled a switchblade. It made the faint clicking
sound the one-eyed man had been hearing for years.

"Last chance to get home in one piece, guys," he
said.

"Fuck you, blind man."

They were a sorry lot. He almost felt badly about what was coming next. Almost but not quite.

The one with the knife nodded to the hulk, who came wading in like a side of beef looking to be lots of steaks.

The one-eyed man took the hulk's arm and broke it with a swift blow that nobody quite remembered afterward. Then he spun him all the way around and rammed him into the guy with the knife. The knife tore through the fabric of his clothing with a faint ripping sound, and the big man sagged to his knees, then lay down in a puddle of stagnant, gravelly water.

The guy with the knife left it sticking in the big man, and while he stared down at his empty hand, the one-eyed man broke his jaw with a forearm like a crowbar. The other suit grabbed a brick from the rubble by the parking-lot fence.

"Why not just call an ambulance for your pals?"

The guy with the brick took a swipe at him. The one-eyed man drove a fist into the man's chest and felt a rib break. He took the brick from the weakening fingers. The man tried to kick him, missed, and sat down. The one-eyed man dropped into a squat like a catcher and broke the nearest kneecap with the brick. The night was full of howling and gurgling and faraway sirens.

He bent over the hulk, who lay still in the water. "Are you dead or anything?"

"I don't think so. But I'm gettin' there."

"I'll get somebody here. You got a quarter? I haven't got a piece of change."

"Pants pocket," the big man groaned.

He felt in the pocket, came out with a quarter, showed it to the big man.

"Hey, it's okay. Hurry." The big man groaned some **more**.

The one-eyed man went to the corner, where he found one of the few public telephones in the city that actually worked. He walked across the street and waited in a dark doorway until the paramedics arrived and began sorting out the wounded. A cop car arrived, siren dying as it slowed to a halt.

The one-eyed man waited until the street was empty again. Then he walked toward an all night coffee shop at the edge of the Village, had a cheeseburger and a cup of coffee and made small talk with the waitress until it was time to go home.

Chapter Six

❧

The General didn't know what the hell to make of it.

But, then, everything had been horseshit all day. Admiral Malfaison had caught him kicking his Titleist out of the rough on eleven and neither of them had known what to say. Sticky. Then he'd discovered that his wife had lumbered them with a dinner party at an outgoing under secretary's godforsaken farm. Farm! Pretentious little bastard. The whole evening was incredible because the courier from New York had brought the goddamned floppy disk with the urgent request from the Director at the Palisades Center to attend to it as quickly as possible.

The courier, chap named Friborg, had said of the Director, "He's up to something, General. He's playing some weird angle. Says somebody's trying to kill him, won't elaborate, just whispers oblique threats." The General had not found Friborg's observations particularly enlightening.

The dinner party had been even worse than he'd expected, and with absolute predictability his driver had gotten lost in the dark coming home. Farm! The under secretary had once served time in New Delhi, where he'd acquired an Indian wife whose curry was causing the General a good bit of remarkably audible discomfort now that he was back in his library. It was well past midnight, closer to two o'clock, and he'd turned the last of the hundred-odd pages of type-script the printer had derived from the floppy desk.

He filled his pipe for the third time. And he still didn't know what the hell to make of it.

Friborg was right, Emilio was up to something weird.

The hundred pages was like . . . like what?

An MX missile shoved up your ass—that was as close as he could come to the *mot juste*.

The Palisades Center would become the biggest, nastiest toxic waste dump in the history of the nation's intelligence gathering if any of those pages became public. There would be all the standard, tired old stonewalling and dragging out of the principles of deniability, but nobody believed all that shit anymore. Nixon had seen to that. Post-Nixon, you were guilty until the TV networks declared you innocent. Nixon had ruined it for everyone who came after him. *That* was his crime, the bastard—screwing it up for all the guys who had to do the dirty work.

But there was no point in picking through all that again. It always gave him the runs when he dwelt on Nixon and that bunch. Spoilers. They'd spoiled everything. He felt his intestines twitching ominously, and he shut Nixon out of his mind.

Why in the name of God had Emilio sent the fragment of manuscript to him?

Well, it was a threat, and not a subtle one.

But why? What did Emilio want him to do about it? What were the implications? What responses were possible? What inferences did the Director want him to draw?

And who could have written the damn thing? Who could have such access?

Or had Emilio himself written it?

Whoever wrote it, what could it be but blackmail?

Suddenly the General had to make a run for the bathroom.

* * *

He sat on the toilet smoking his pipe. His thinking was always best while installed upon the commode, as his sainted mother had always called it.

The leakage, the publication of such a manuscript, would blow them all into something his cat could swallow without chewing. All of them. The President, the General, all of the Eye-talians, the spics, and Emilio too. That's what the General couldn't figure out.

What good was a threat if the fella making the threat would face the music too?

Who would benefit?

Nobody but the goddamn do-gooders who didn't know their ass, that was who . . . and the author of the best-seller.

Maybe it was Woodward and Bernstein again, and the goddamn commie *Washington Post.*

Back at his desk he stared at the manuscript.

This wasn't going to be another Pentagon Papers fiasco, no way, José. Not this time. One of those was enough. Something could be done. What exactly would come to him later. Maybe they'd have to turn the Psycho Branch loose again. Okay, so be it.

Damn it to hell. So Emilio said someone was trying to kill him. Now what was that supposed to mean?

The General hated puzzles almost as much as he hated Democrats.

There was a knock on the library door and Friborg appeared, yawning, his tie pulled loose, a bottle of scotch in his hand. "Drink?" he said.

Friborg was a good listener, so the General talked for quite a long time, smoked three more pipes, and together they finished off the scotch. The sun was coming up on a green and dewy Virginia estate, not a goddamn farm, when he stood up and went to the window and surveyed his domain.

"It always amazes me how people think our little outfit knows everything," he said. "When the truth is we seldom know nearly enough. We have to act on crummy little scraps of information that are wrong more often than not, but we act because we have to. We have to do something. Anything. And that's where people always get their heads fucked up. They mix up action with knowledge. Stupid bastards don't think it through. Because we're ruthless, they assume we must *know* something."

He threw the window open after unlocking the security sensor lodged in the wall. The fresh morning breeze rustled the draperies, filled the room with the grassy sweetness.

"In fact," the General said, turning back to Friborg, pointing with the stem of his corncob pipe, "it's exactly the opposite. The more you know, the harder it is to act at all. With ultimate knowledge comes complete paralysis of will. The less you know, the clearer it all seems. The less you know, the more decisive you can be. You can be confident, you can be ruthless. It's the real lesson of our business, Friborg. I kid you not."

Friborg stifled a yawn. "You mean a little knowledge can be a dangerous thing, sir?"

"Hmmm. Well put. You grasp the essence, I see." The General looked at his watch. "My biological clock is all out of whack, young man."

"Mine too," Friborg said. "What do you want me to tell the Director, sir?"

"Not a goddamn thing," the General said. He knocked the dottle out of his pipe, into a large cut-glass ashtray the President had given him for saving the republic or something, a long time ago. It had been Carter, of all people. "Let's surprise the Director, he wants to be so cute. Somebody wants to kill him . . . so fine, we'll let 'em, whoever it is, kill him. Who needs him? Hey? We're better off without him . . . but we've got to find out about this manuscript. It's part of a book, sure. Well, who wrote it?

Where is it going? Somebody gonna publish the damn thing? Well, they can't! I won't let 'em. His wife's the writer in the family. Let's ask her. . . ."

"Can we ask her hard?"

The General shrugged. "I leave matters of degree to you lads, surely. You won't find me poaching on your preserve. I'm merely a policy maker." He stretched. "I'm going to bed. I'll sleep well, knowing he's a dead man. But you, you just make sure nobody gets in the way of whoever's gonna kill the bastard. For once, just once, we have somebody doing our dirty work."

He was chuckling when he left the room.

Friborg sat in a half stupor for a while. He wished he knew what the Palisades Center really was. For that matter he wished he knew who Emilio, the Director, really was.

He yawned, stood up, dropped the empty bottle into the wastebasket. Christ, he wondered what the hell was going on. Any of it. But Psycho Branch didn't have the license to know. Psycho Branch was strictly Operations. Not Policy.

Chapter Seven

❧

Celia had been awakened early by a call from a man who said he was Peter Greco. He sounded sleepy and disinterested but had just gotten a call from Hilary Sampson, who told him it was important that he call Celia. Well, yawn, here he was, and she could buy him breakfast if she wanted because it would definitely take a bribe to get him abroad so early. She was underwhelmed by the offer and said so, and Greco told her that that was certainly all right with him. She could tell he was about to hang up. He couldn't have cared less. The problem was, she did. She couldn't stand this guy already, but the morning wasn't making the letter any easier to take.

So now she was sitting in the window at Homer's, on Tenth where it turned between Sixth and Greenwich. He was already fifteen minutes late, and she was on her second cup of burned coffee, when she saw this guy about her height but built like a ticket booth come in. He was wearing a Yankees warm-up jacket. She should have guessed. It was just perfect: she'd always been a Mets fan.

He was the type who passed a witticism from the corner of his mouth to the girl at the cashier counter, making her laugh. Probably very big with waitresses and meter maids. Cool. He made straight for her, dropped the *Daily News* and his sunglasses on the table, shrugged out of the jacket and sat down. "Hi, toots," he said. "What's new?" He signaled to the swarthy, mustachioed Greek waiter for a cup of what Celia just knew he'd call java.

"How did you know me?" she asked. "Or is there some hope you're just a masher and not the man I've been patiently waiting for for half an hour—"

"Hey, hey, take it easy on a man with only one eye. Hey, Demetrios, is this the fresh pot or the crud you've been giving her?"

"Fresh made, Mr. Greco, just for you."

"Way to go, my man. Write this down, cheese and onion omelette, toasted bagel, and a big smile. How about you, honey?"

"Two poached eggs—"

Greco interrupted with a moan. "And dry whole wheat toast, don't tell me. Diet doesn't make any difference, you know. When your number's up, your number's up—"

"And dry whole wheat toast," she said through gritted teeth.

He shook his head. She found herself staring at the eye patch and the tracery of scars across his forehead and nose. It wasn't disfiguring, just interesting, like seeing a vintage car that had been used hard. He had thick black eyebrows, and the lone eye glittered like a chip of hard shiny coal.

"Some kind of face, right? Been around." He poured sugar into milky coffee.

"Looks a little the worse for wear," she said.

"You should see the guy who was standing next to me. You'd have to dig him up, of course. They buried what they could find in a shoe box. It was the cough candy."

"I beg your pardon?"

"I had this cough last winter so I tried the stuff I saw on TV. The pretty cough-candy fairy. Hilary said it was you. That's how I knew you, the cough-candy fairy."

"Did the stuff work?"

"You gotta be kidding. So, what's the story on this murder thing?" He enjoyed his coffee. She could tell by the amount of noise he was making.

She told him the whole story, and by the time she had finished, his omelette and bagel were gone and Demetrios had refilled his cup three times. Her eggs were cold and untouched. She took a deep breath and broke off a corner of toast, popped it into her mouth, and prodded an egg. "So what do you think?"

"Hilary was right. The cops would say you were wasting their time."

"What do *you* say?"

"I think you're an actress with a flair for dramatizing things. Chances are there's no murder being plotted. Somebody's making notes on a book. For a review maybe. I don't know. Forget it, that's what I say." The eye kept raking her face like a searchlight. He lit a cigarette."

"Please don't."

"Don't what?"

"Smoke. At least wait until I'm through eating."

"Wonderful." He ground out the butt.

"Hilary was wrong."

"About what?"

"You. She said you were smart."

He laughed. "For that, lady, I smoke." He lit another Lucky. "And cut out the sweet talk. You're not my type. Cute little blondes for me—"

"How disgusting!"

"Don't be absurd. Most of them turn out to be perfect ladies. But once in a while, just often enough to keep me interested, I find a disgusting one. Whatsa matter, you don't like Homer's eggs?"

"What I don't like is too involved to go into—"

"Your ears are getting pink. Can you do that whenever you want?"

"No, I need help—"

"Look, your ears are cute. Cutest thing about you so far." He grinned and winked his good eye.

"This is all so funny, why don't you just go away? I don't need this schoolboy aggravation—"

"Okay. But I'm telling you, you've just seen me at my best. You still want me to hold your hand on this murder thing?"

"Not bloody likely—"

"You're gonna have to cut out the begging. I'll do it, I'll do it. You're drooling egg down your chin, honey."

She wiped her chin. "A little of you goes an incredibly long way."

"About as far as Twelfth and Broadway, how's that?" He was amused by her in all the wrong ways. She hated that.

You never knew what you might find at the Strand.

The man standing behind the counter where you brought books to sell looked like he'd been kidnapped from the real world. He wore gold-rimmed glasses, had sandy hair cut short and neat, and wore a tie. He listened while Celia described the books she'd bought, rattling off a few titles and suddenly the man nodded. Peter Greco was browsing nearby, half watching, half listening.

"That must have been Charlie Cunningham, he's a regular around here. Nice fella, Charlie. Been coming in for years." The memory of what a prince Charlie was caused a smile to spread across the buyer's bland face. "Y'know, I think he brought those books you found the same day, just around lunchtime. I put 'em right out on the tables."

"So who is this Cunningham character?" Greco didn't look up from the lavish book about luxury ocean liners of long ago.

The buyer shrugged. "Charlie Cunningham. Just a

guy who gets lots of mysteries in his mail, I guess. I never asked him, he never told me. What can I say? Why do you want him, anyway?"

"It's not all that important," Celia said. "He left some papers in one book and I'd like to return them. You don't know where I could reach him?"

He shook his head. "He'll be in again one of these days, he's a regular. I'd be glad to hold them for him, if you like. Best I can do." He stroked his chin. "Maybe he's in the book. You could try."

"Thanks. We will. You've been very helpful. And strangely normal," she added with a grin.

"I know," he said, not grinning. "I've heard that before."

Peter Greco went to the corner, patted his pockets, and came back to Celia. "You got a quarter? I'm out of change." She gave him the quarter and he called Information, but there was no listing for Charlie Cunningham. "Who the hell does he think he is, anyway?"

"Charlie Cunningham," Celia said as they walked along in the morning sunshine. "C.C. is not M.M. But for some reason C.C. had M.M.'s book. Why?"

Greco shoved his hands into the pockets of his faded jeans. "So M.M. in your view is a murder conspirator. This Miles Warriner—"

"*If* Miles Warriner is his real name."

Greco looked at her in exasperation. "Look, all we know at the moment is the name on the book, so let me call him Miles Warriner without correcting me each time, okay? Jeez, really. This Warriner autographs M.M.'s copy of the book. But somehow this book, this whatchamacallit—"

"Review copy."

"Is sold to the Strand by Cunningham. Now how the hell did Cunningham get M.M.'s autographed copy? Or, other way 'round, why would Warriner sign Cunningham's review copy for M.M.? Doesn't make sense." He scowled at her as if it might be her fault.

"Well, it looks to me like Cunningham probably knows both Warriner and M.M. And Z is still a blank."

"I don't like it," Greco said.

"Don't be petulant. Are you quitting on me?"

"I'll give it until lunch, okay? Lunch which will be on you."

"What a guy."

"This isn't a date, Blandings—"

"You're telling me."

"Are we walking this direction on purpose?"

"I still think we should find Cunningham, the guy who had the book immediately before I did. Technically the letter is his. Maybe we can find him and tell him what's going on—"

"He *knows* what's going on. He must have read the letter."

"Look, I want to find him. You can take a hike. I'm still going to find this man." She threw him her best defiant glare, dredged up from a bad production of *Agnes of God.*

"Sure, sure," he said. "Where are we going?"

The logo looked amazingly like the flying red horse that had once been the symbol of a huge oil company with gasoline stations everywhere. Now the flying horse was white against a black background. It decorated the spines of all the books in the reception foyer. It hung on the wall behind the receptionist's desk. It was woven into the carpet. Peter Greco said: "Get a load of all the horses. Looks like Mr. Ed and his whole family."

The young, very pretty receptionist looked up from her empty desk. "This is Pegasus Books," she said, past a tight imitation smile. "The horse is not Mr. Ed—"

"Yeah, Mr. Ed." Greco looked pleased. "He talked. Had his own TV show. Right, Blandings?"

"This horse is Pegasus, the mythological winged horse. You might try reading rather than watching television." The receptionist's smile never wavered. "How may I help you?"

Celia spoke up quickly, anticipating just what Greco might have to say. "We'd like to see Susan Carling, please. Charlie Cunningham's office sent us."

The receptionist rang through, and a few moments later a short, round black woman with huge glasses perched at the very tip of a pointy nose appeared. She couldn't stop smiling, as if she were on the verge of real hilarity.

"Charlie's office sent you? Come on in, can't keep Charlie's office waiting."

Her office was a kind of Rube Goldberg diagram of confusion. Everywhere, including the seats of the visitors' chairs, there were books, file folders, stacks of author bios and photos, newsletters, press releases, dust jacket mock-ups, empty coffee cups. The window on the thirtieth floor looked up toward Columbus Circle and downtown to Times Square, Chelsea, the World Trade Center, and the Statue of Liberty. The sign on her door, which she closed, said she was Senior Publicist.

"Now come on, you guys," she said, picking a glowing cigarette from the ashtray where she'd left it, "what's this gig all about? Charlie Cunningham has an *office*? Who are you guys anyway?"

"Humane Society," Greco said, getting in ahead of Celia. "We're taking the horse away, lady—"

"No horse jokes allowed," Susan Carling said. "We know all the old ones, and there are no new ones. "Did you really come from Charlie?"

"Not exactly," Celia said. "We're looking for him—"

"And you come to me? *Me?* What do I know from Charlie? Why me?"

"Because Charlie gets Pegasus review copies. Miles Warriner's books, for instance. We thought you might know how we could get in touch with Charlie or Warriner, or both."

"Lotta nuts running around out there," she said with a wave of her hand at the outstretched city. "Are you two of them?"

"My name's Celia Blandings—"

"The cough-candy fairy," Greco said.

"—and I've got something of Charlie's. I'd like to return it to him."

"Warriner is a pseudonym," Susan Carling said, "and I don't know who the writer is. And Charlie? I'm not allowed to give you his address. But I can send whatever it is to him. Is it smaller than a breadbox?"

"Much," Celia said. "But I've got to deliver this by hand."

"Sorry then." She cocked her head and shrugged helplessly. "I'm out of suggestions."

Greco nodded. "Understood. Perfectly sound security. But maybe you could just tell us who Charlie Cunningham is? Why does he get review copies?"

"Oh, that Charlie!" Her laughter was rich and warm and sexy. "Charlie Cunningham is the last of the independents. He's written a couple of books, I guess, but who is he really? Charlie Cunningham is none other than Mr. Mystery himself." She waited for the nods of recognition. "You don't know about Mr. Mystery?"

"In a word," Celia said, "no."

"Last of the independent what?" Greco asked.

"Oh, Charlie's always got an angle, any way he can keep from working—I'm quoting Charlie there, by the way. He came up with the idea for a syndicated column devoted to mysteries—books, TV, movies, any kind of mysteries. He writes about all of it, sells his column to little newspapers, shopping guides, Sunday supplements—they all need filler. He calls himself, the column I mean, Mr. Mystery. I call him the last of the independents."

"Cute," Greco said, "but a guy named Charlie Varrick was the last of the independents, Miss Carling. Don't ever forget it."

Susan Carling looked momentarily alarmed. "Right," she said, giving the word about four syllables.

Waiting for the elevator, standing in the shadow of a life-size statue of Pegasus, Peter Greco grinned wickedly at Celia, then waved to the receptionist as the elevator opened in front of them.

"Walter Matthau played Charlie Varrick. Love that Matthau. Man's a gambler. Life is a risk, Blandings. Matthau knows it, I know it, but do you know it?"

Back on Sixth Avenue Celia led the way to a Sabrett's hot-dog stand. "Be my guest," she said. "Lunch is on me."

"This is a very cheap move," he said.

"Precisely my point."

He was halfway through his second dog when he said: "Well, now we know that Charlie Cunningham is a man who's in the middle of the murder of the Director." He finished the dog in two bites and polished off his orange drink.

"Now that's what I call a three-rail shot. What do you mean?"

"Hey, you play pool?"

"Yeah, I'm pretty fair actually—"

"Sounds like we got a game, then. A one-eyed guy and a . . . a—"

"Woman is the word you're groping for, and what do you mean Charlie Cunningham's in on the murder?"

"Elementary, my dear Blandings. Mr. Mystery. M.M."

Chapter Eight

❧

Charlie Cunningham wasn't feeling so good.

As the day itself approached, she had become increasingly insistent that he reassure her about knowing his instructions, letter perfect. And the more she insisted, the more nervous he became. The mere ringing of the telephone in his tiny apartment caused a chemical change in his body. His mouth would dry, his limbs would weaken, his voice would quaver. The symptoms sounded like love. It wasn't love. It was awful.

But nothing nearly so awful as this last call. She'd wanted to run over all of it again, and as she repeated for the umpteenth time how he must be absolutely sure of himself, his actions, most importantly his nerve, he began looking for the last sheet of boiled-down instructions she had left with him. He knew he'd put it somewhere. He cradled the phone between shoulder and jaw, staring dumbly at the room and its scattered, piled, and flung contents. He'd been so careful, putting it where he couldn't possibly forget it. But where, for God's sake?

He'd had too much on his mind, that was the problem. Double-crossing someone was a complicated business, more so than he'd dreamed possible. The thing was, she was apparently cut out for murder. She seemed to enjoy the plotting, the details, the research, the game aspect. As if you weren't going to have a guy covered in blood when you got done. Well, not for Charlie Cunningham, he thought, no damn way, as he threw underwear and towels and papers and books onto the bed. He found a pair of her sunglasses that had been given up for lost weeks ago and a shriveled piece of pizza in the dust balls under the bed, but not her list of the murder-day arrangements.

He fumbled with the answers to her questions, made a mess of the timetable. Her voice fell to a low, venomous whisper, a hiss, which he'd come to know so well. He'd better pull himself together, she warned; the consequences of his failing to do so made him break out in a cold sweat. The things a man will do, he lamented to himself, for a great piece of ass.

Once he'd gotten off the phone he slumped into a chair and tried to make himself remember. Miraculously it came to him: *Littlechild Takes Aim!* He'd tucked her letter into the pages of the novel for safekeeping. He smiled smugly. Old Charlie hadn't lost the touch yet. And it wasn't easy, keeping her plan clear in his mind while working out a plan of his own simultaneously. Now, to find the book.

It took less than fifteen minutes for a new, infinitely more dreadful panic to assert itself. It was a small apartment. There were only so many places a book could be. And the Miles Warriner novel didn't seem to be in any of them.

Christ, he was dripping wet again. He did all the logical things, then hastened on to the illogical. Like looking behind the refrigerator and under the bathmat. He was looking in the fridge, between a slab of long forgotten pâté that needed a shave and a cellophane bag of carrots that had taken on the consistency of overcooked linguini, when he remembered the stack of books that had fallen over, which he had impatiently righted and grabbed at the last minute, in a spasm of uncharacteristic efficiency, to sell at the Strand. . . .

Oh, Jesus H. fucking Christ! Had it been among them?

It must have.

It wasn't anywhere else.

This was bad. Worse than bad, of course. The merely bad was part of his everyday life. Catastrophic was more like it. *Really* bad. If someone found the plans . . .

Why on earth did she have to bombard him with written instructions and reminders? He took a beer from the fridge door and sucked on it desperately, wondering how much sense her note would make to anyone finding it. What exactly had she written?

He wondered if what he was having might be a nervous breakdown.

What if she found out he'd sold the goddamn thing to the Strand? She might spontaneously combust.

No. She'd have his guts on a plate, is what she'd do.

But no one could possibly trace it back to her. And that left him. Could it be traced back to him?

Murphy's Law, which had always seemed to govern his life, said yes, of course, why not, it's a certainty, you twit! It wasn't important how. It could happen, and if it could, it sure as hell would.

He had to get it back. There was no other way.

Chapter Nine

❧

Celia led the way up Sixth Avenue to Fifty-sixth Street, where she hung a left and kept walking. Somehow it wasn't quite so scary with Peter Greco grousing along about the cheap lunch and acknowledging that he'd stick with it for a few hours longer, since they'd actually made some headway. He'd also gotten an ego boost out of putting Mr. Mystery and M.M. together before she had. And the point was well taken: Z had written the murder instructions to Charlie Cunningham.

Otto Penzler's Mysterious Bookshop was located directly behind Carnegie Hall, just before you came to the Carnegie Tavern. They took a couple of steps down into the first floor, which was lined floor to ceiling with new paperbacks devoted solely to the mystery novel. In the center of the room was a large table devoted to games, stationery, jigsaw puzzles, and a variety of other paraphernalia related to the great mystery writers, like Black copies of *The Maltese Falcon*, baseball caps with Nero Wolfe and Spenser and Nick Charles written on the fronts. Next to the table a tight circular iron staircase led to the second floor, which was also book-lined, but here it was all hardbacks arranged alphabetically by author, primarily hard-to-locate used copies as well as the latest titles. The room had the look of a comfortable study appointed with mystery memorabilia ranging from a stained-glass window depicting Sherlock Holmes to a colorful movie poster featuring Edward

Arnold as Nero Wolfe and Lionel Stander as Archie Goodwin.

Behind the desk sat a compact, gray-haired but youthful man screaming into a telephone. "All right, Gifford, this time you've gone too far! Westlake never treats me like this . . . yes, I know he has seventeen pseudonyms . . . Garfield never treats me like this, no one has ever treated me like this. . . ." He broke into a cackle of delight. "Yes, yes, I know I love abuse . . . but that's our little secret, okay?"

The conversation ended and the proprietor looked up. "Celia, don't tell me you've come to pay your bill, my heart couldn't stand the shock. Or did my threatening letter work?"

"Otto, we need help—"

"That's the trouble with all you bleeding-heart liberals, always coming around looking for handouts, asking favors." He got up and kissed her cheek. "What is this . . . this person you've dragged in? A Yankee fan?" Penzler regarded Greco with vague curiosity. He had once in the long, long ago been a sportswriter.

"Greco's the name, pool's the game." He looked around the elegant room. "You really make a living outa this? Maybe it's a front—"

"Whether or not I make a living is beside the point, my good man. I have both eyes and a good deal more hair than some of us—Celia, is this man bothering you? If so, I'll summon someone and we'll catch him in a crossfire of withering sarcasm—"

"Oddly enough, he's one of the good guys," she said. "Otto, we're looking for someone, two some-ones, actually, and if you don't know where they can be found, I'm going to lie down right here and cry. Greco here is one of New York's finest, by the way—"

"Finest whats?" Penzler said dubiously. "Pool hustlers?"

"Right the first time," Greco remarked, stunned.

"No," Celia said. "Cops."

"My God, they've come to that, have they? Well, I'm not surprised they've finally caught up with you, Celia. It was bound to happen. You've owed me fifty-six dollars since Christmas two years ago—"

"Otto, please, this is serious—"

"You're telling me. Next I send the pay-or-die letter. But enough of that. Who're you looking for?"

"Charles Cunningham and Miles Warriner," she said.

"Charlie? Haven't seen him since the last Edgar party here at the shop. But I know where he lives. Down in your part of town, sort of." He leaned back against a bookshelf and tweezed his lower lip between his thumb and forefinger. "Miles Warriner I've never actually met. Don't know anyone who has. He's on our mailing list, of course . . . but a real mystery man, you should pardon the expression. Pegasus is his publisher, of course, but what the hell? They'd never give you his address. What's this all about?"

Peter Greco said: "It's possible that Cunningham has gotten mixed up in something that could be dangerous, to himself and to others. Miles Warriner may be involved too. We just don't know, but we need to talk to both of them. You understand I can't divulge the particulars."

Penzler turned to Celia. "He's a cop?"

"I'm involved in this," Greco interjected, "only as a friend of Miss Blandings. Nothing official. Yet. She thought you might help us out."

Penzler frowned. "Here's the deal. I'm going downstairs to check on some shipments I'm expecting. If you come across any addresses in my Rolodex here while I'm gone, that's your business. And if Celia didn't owe me money, if I weren't afraid she might skip town if I got snotty, I wouldn't dream of leaving you two in this room alone—get it?"

"You're a dear," Celia said.

"Funny," Penzler said, descending the spiral staircase, "most people have tended to see me as a kind of great stag."

Miles Warriner lived in Sutton Place, which was good to know and certainly very nice for him, but for the moment Charlie Cunningham was more important. He lived on Perry Street in the West Village, not more than a fifteen-minute stroll from Celia's apartment.

Greco got a cab at the corner, and when they got out he took Celia's arm and stopped her.

"Wait, lady. Now what is it you have in mind here?"

"Well, I . . . I guess I don't really know. Go ask Charlie what he's up to, something like that." It occurred to her that she wasn't using her head à la Linda Thurston.

Greco, continuing to hold her arm, walked her across Seventh. "Now look," he said, his voice softening, the pose falling away, turning into what struck her as something like a regular guy, "we've just about reached the point of no return on this thing. There's a chance that what you found may really have something to do with a murder, or at least the planning of one. And now we're not dealing with a name on a piece of paper. This Cunningham, this Mr. Mystery, is a flesh and blood man. And if he's thinking about murdering someone—well, hell, figure it out for yourself. You walk up to him and tell him you know what he's doing, he could get real upset real quick. People planning murders are grouchy. So we've gotta be careful."

"Okay, so what do we do? After we're done scaring me out of my wits?" She was back to thinking about it as she had last night. It wasn't a lark, after all, even if Greco was sticking with her for the moment. And anyway, she didn't even *know* Greco. Linda Thurston was having a love affair with her actor/detective. But then, Greco was a real cop. . . . She wondered what had happened to him, what had taken the eye and scarred the face.

"Well, I'm thinking."

"Time is not on our side—"

"I know, I know. But neither is this our problem. We're strictly volunteers."

"We can save a man's life!"

"Maybe, maybe not. We don't even know who this Director is—we're a helluva long way from saving anybody's life." He looked up at the house numbers. "Let's just do a little surveillance, maybe I'll think of something. You're safe now, we're the only ones who know you are, the only ones who know you know. I'd say the last thing we want is to have Cunningham find out you know anything about him."

The building where Cunningham lived was a small converted brickfront, probably eight units, that had been fancied up in the not too remote past to take advantage of the high Village rents. The street was quiet and sunny. Two men were leaning on the fender of a nondescript brown Chevy halfway down the block. They seemed to be lost in contemplation of a street map.

"We're just going to stand here?"

"And wait," Greco said. "That's what cops do."

"Is this a stakeout?"

"Make you feel better?"

"A little."

"Blandings, you're what they used to call a fighting gamecock in boxing circles."

"Ugh," she said. She could have kicked herself for being pleased with what may have been a compliment. He was just a broken down, one-eyed cop. Big deal.

* * *

Charlie Cunningham came out the front door and down the steps struggling into a tan corduroy jacket, managing to be out of breath before he started. He was acutely rumpled and wore a disconcerted expression, like a man about to chew his mustache off. He struck briskly off, and Celia and Greco fell in behind him. He crossed Seventh against the light, leaping from the path of an ambulance, hurried on across Sixth, then Fifth.

"This guy's in a panic." Greco didn't seem to be hurrying. "Ring any bells?"

Celia was out of breath. "Absolutely." She wasn't going to let him go two up on her after the Mr. Mystery/M.M. blunder. "He's realized he's lost it and he's figured out what might have happened to it. He's going to the Strand."

"Well done," Greco said. "Am I going too fast for you?"

'Never," she said grimly.

He laughed.

They followed him along Twelfth Street and watched him rush into the bookstore before they crossed. "Wait," Greco said. "We can't go in there after him—"

"Why not?"

Greco sighed. "We don't want to run the risk of you two being brought together. They know you in there. . . . Don't you understand? Jeez, you're just not trying! You're very dangerous to this guy, and he's scared out of his wits. Just stay here and try to get a look through the window."

She could just see Cunningham as he disappeared down the aisle beside the counter. He'd given the tables in front a quick once-over, been unable to find *Littlechild Takes Aim*, and gone off to find someone to talk to. Celia realized she was holding her breath. Suddenly he was storming back up the aisle.

Greco pushed her over to the outdoor racks. "Look at the books, head down. Pay no attention to him."

Cunningham came out of the door, so close she could smell his cologne, looked around until he saw the telephone at the corner. He dashed across on a red light, narrowly beating the oncoming traffic, and made a call at the corner booth. It didn't take him long, and at one point they could see him gesturing frustratedly, as if the person at the other end could see him, would be persuaded. Then he slammed the phone back in place, checked his watch, reached for the telephone again, stopped, fished a card out of his wallet, took the phone again, made another call which was considerably calmer, hung up, looked at his watch again, and headed down Twelfth. He stopped at the Gotham Bar and Grill and went inside.

"You want a drink?" Greco said.

"What if he sees us, wise guy?"

"In there it doesn't make any difference. The clerks at the Strand were the problem. Come on, I'm hot and thirsty."

The luncheon crowd had thinned out. They sat at the bar and spotted Cunningham at a banquette below them, across the room. Greco ordered a gin and tonic, Celia an iced tea.

"Most stakeouts take days and days," he said. "You don't know how lucky we are. Cheers." He took a long cold drink and closed his eye, savoring it. Then the eye clicked open. "Our man's about to eat the tablecloth. Who did he call?"

"Is this a test?"

"You bet."

"I'd say he called his accomplice. Mr. Z."

"Maybe. Who else?"

"What?"

"He made two calls. He used his credit card for one. Who was that?"

She shrugged. "I'll bite. Who?"

"How the hell should I know?"

Celia noticed the woman when she came in simply because she was so striking. She stood at the steps to the dining level, beside a huge pot of flowers. She wore a gray silk dress with a beige sash riding low on her hips. Her shoulder bag was soft natural leather, her hair black and tousled, her features strong, decisive, handsome. She scanned the room, motioned the hostess away, went quickly to Cunningham's table and sat down before he could say a word.

"Wow. Now who the hell is that?" Greco said.

"She's not your type."

"Woman like that, she's anybody's type, kid."

"She'd never be seen dead with a guy in a warm-up jacket. But she's not Mr. Z."

"I'd change tailors. Maybe she's Miss Z. Drink your tea and watch."

The woman was clearly imperious, impatient with the situation. Her hands flicked hair away from her face; she folded her arms across her heavy bosom; she assumed a fixed posture while listening, then exploded into another when she spoke, as if her power lines were overloading. Cunningham made matters worse by knocking his water glass over when he reached across to light her cigarette. She looked pointedly away, disassociating herself from the scene when the waiter came to sponge away the mess. Cunningham was flushed, trying to smile nervously. As soon as they were alone again she bore in on him once more, pointing a finger at him, her lips so tight it seemed miraculous she could speak at all.

"Maybe she's the Director," Greco said. "I'd help

him kill her if it turned out that way. Still, look at her. . . ."

Celia shook her head. "She's not the Director. They're lovers. No woman would dare give that kind of hell to anyone she wasn't sleeping with. Believe me, I know these things. She's probably married to someone else and their affair is causing her some problems. Maybe it hasn't anything to do with killing the Director—"

"It has to connect. Believe me, everything old Charlie does now has something to do with killing the Director. The meter's running. He can't think of anything else. I know these things."

The woman suddenly pushed her chair back, stood up with a shake of her black mane. Cunningham wasn't allowed to finish his drink, and she'd never ordered one. She shook her head again, this time at the approaching waiter, and stalked up the abbreviated stairs, down past the checkroom and back out to the street, leaving Cunningham just far enough behind to miss getting the doors for her.

She stood with her feet wide apart, listening to him. She nodded, went across the street to a white Rolls-Royce Corniche convertible with a tan top that looked fat with expensive padding.

"Woman looks like that, now I think about it," Greco said, watching her through the large window at the end of the bar, "she's gotta drive the perfect car. Survival of the fittest, right?"

"Give us all a break. And anyway, what about the way she behaves?"

"Guy'll put up with a lot from a woman who looks like that."

Celia made a face that Greco missed.

The woman went around past the familiar chrome slab of grillwork, got into the car, slammed the door. Cunningham bent down to speak to her at the window but she started the engine and pulled away from the curb, accelerated down Twelfth.

Cunningham stood at the curb staring after her. He was swearing and his fists were clenched. He looked around to see if there had been any witnesses to his humiliation, then slowly let his face relax into its normal blandness. He shook his head philosophically and trudged away.

"Not a very frightening-looking murderer," she said.

Greco was following his own train of thought. "Real man would treat her rough. She'd love it."

"Greco," she sighed, "you hold no surprises for me."

"You never know," he said. "Come on, we might as well make one more stop."

"Where?" She chewed the last ice cube from her glass.

"Miles Warriner. We'll take him by surprise."

Chapter Ten

❧

The cab took them up First Avenue, darting among the potholes, past the United Nations, and dropped them in the Fifties. They walked over to Sutton Place and began checking numbers. A doorman who looked like he was wearing an admiral's uniform from Gilbert and Sullivan clearly didn't approve of Greco's jacket and jeans, so Greco was happy.

Miles Warriner's home had window boxes full of very self-satisfied flowers fighting for attention, lots of red and yellow and pink. The brick and trim looked old and classy but freshly scrubbed, as beautiful and perfectly anonymous as a London club in St. James's. There was a cast-iron security door swirled with flowers that could stop a tank. It covered a heavy, paneled oaken door, which was shiny and lovingly oiled. Even the small bronzed numbers discreetly screwed in place, virtually invisible to the passerby, looked slightly embarrassed, as if they might be causing too much of a stir.

Celia lifted a gorgon's head, let it fall on the brass plate a couple of times. A dog began yapping somewhere within, a small but fierce creature by the sound of it. She looked around, back down the empty street, insulated from the rattle and bang of the city. She felt as if she were being watched.

Greco said: "Hello up there."

He seemed to be speaking to a hanging plant. He didn't appear the type who communed with greenery, and sure enough he wasn't. Behind the drapery of vines, set into the faded brick, was a tiny electronic barrel pointing at them. A television camera.

The vine spoke. It was a lady vine. The dog had stopped barking. "May I help you?"

"Yes," Celia said. "We're here to see Miles Warriner. Charlie Cunningham sent us."

Greco winced and closed his eyes.

"One moment, please," the vine said.

"Nothing like showing our hand," he muttered.

"We had to give him a reason to see us, didn't we? Stop picking on me. And anyway, you think a famous mystery writer like Miles Warriner's in on Cunningham's lousy murder? Come on, Greco, use your head—"

"He called Cunningham M.M. in the inscription—"

"Of course. That's probably how Warriner came to meet him in the first place, as Mr. Mystery. Think, Greco, think—"

"Why?" he asked tolerantly. "When I've got a heavy hitter like you to do my thinking for me?"

He patted her fanny and she jumped.

"Surprised you, toots," he said.

The door began making unlocking sounds and swung open. A Japanese woman of indeterminate age, wearing a black maid's dress, stood back and ushered them in. She gave them a distant, haughty once-over. "A Yankee fan," she murmured, as if chatting with her most honorable ancestors.

"Yeah," Greco replied. He fixed her with the glittering eye. "You don't approve?"

Celia almost gasped, but pretended she hadn't heard.

"Oh, but I do approve. I go back to the days of the mighty DiMaggio, young man. The most awesome Gehrig, the nimble Rolfe, the fleet Crosetti, Ruth who truly blotted out the sun—"

"So you've got seniority. Let's get down to cases.

I'm the dauntless Greco, this stringbean here is Slats Blandings, good hands, goes to her right in the hole like Rizzuto in his prime. . . ."

The maid giggled girlishly, won over.

"Now where is the deft and facile Miles Warriner?"

"Follow, please," she said, giggling again, covering her mouth with her tiny hand. "Slats Blandings," she murmured, casting a glance at Celia. "Charming, charming . . ."

She led them through rooms crammed with opulent objets d'art, futuristic Italian furniture, Aubusson carpets, full bookcases, TV sets masquerading as eighteenth century escritoires, past a dining table of burled wood six inches thick resting on a boulder of peach marble. Before opening French doors she said: "Mrs. Bassinetti is on the porch."

"Mrs. Who?" Celia asked.

"Bassinetti," Greco said.

The first thing Celia saw were six Italian deck chairs she'd admired the previous summer at Jensen and Lewis. Eleven hundred bucks apiece to sit out in the rain. There was a forest of lofty palm trees, a glass table the size of any one of a number of small European principalities. And an extraordinarily beautiful woman she'd seen before. She stood at the railing looking out at the cruise ships on the East River, glinting brightly in the late afternoon sunshine. The porch, as well as the woman and the scowling, determined little dog at her feet, was in the cool shade, serene.

Celia saw that she was more than beautiful. The woman was possessed of an uncommon, radiant sensuality. Fires smouldered in her eyes, her lips were full and furled. She was wearing the same dress, only now Celia saw the tinge of lilac in the

gray. The beige sash was draped across the faint
swell of her belly as provocatively as before. It was
the same woman, and the Corniche sat on a ramp far
below them, cantilevered above the FDR Drive. Celia
felt as if she'd been caught in the middle of act one
without a line in her head. A violent shiver cascaded
down the back of her neck, worse than any stage
fright she'd ever experienced. This woman was
Charlie's girlfriend.

"Mrs. Bassinetti," the maid said, "Miss Blandings
and Mr. Greco."

She retired soundlessly and Mrs. Bassinetti turned
to face them. A smile of curiosity played across her
full, deep purple mouth.

"How do you do?" Her voice was deep and soft,
with a sandpapered edge. "What can I do for you?
Charlie Cunningham sent you to see me?"

Celia looked at Greco. Greco said: "Take it, Slats."

Her mind was racing back and forth like a maddened actress in search of a speech. Everything was
different, as if she'd started out in *Charley's Aunt*
and suddenly found herself doing Lady Macbeth.
What would Linda Thurston do? A swoon seemed to
be the most reasonable option. They'd come to see
Miles Warriner, to ask him what he might tell them
about his pal Charlie, like did he know if maybe
Charlie was planning to kill anyone. But as usual,
unlike life on stage, nothing had been rehearsed,
nothing was what it was supposed to be. Miles
Warriner was nowhere in sight, and she was confronted with an earthy predator called Bassinetti
who was Charlie's girlfriend, and one of the Furies to
boot. And the heroic cop says, Take it, Slats, whatever that was supposed to mean. Linda? Oh, Linda.
She couldn't seem to stop the gooseflesh rippling up
and down her arms. She was certain Mrs. Bassinetti
had seen it.

"I'm terribly afraid we're wasting your time, Mrs.

Bassinetti. There's been some mistake. We were told . . . well, that is to say, we came here looking for Miles Warriner. The mystery writer? Inspector Littlechild?" Her voice was shaking and she felt as if she were caught in a spotlight, naked, vulnerable. At a loss.

Nobody was saying anything. Greco had dipped into a silver bowl of mixed nuts on a rolling drinks cart and was crunching, blandly watching the ships like toys on the water while the dog licked his fingers. Celia watched him. The man had no nerves. She pressed on.

"And, well, we don't actually *know* Charlie Cunningham—I mean, look, I feel like a fool barging into your home. . . ." Remember, Celia, she cautioned herself: she doesn't know you know about her and Charlie Cunningham. But the whole situation was impossible; she couldn't keep it all straight. She looked at Greco, wondering if she had enough psychic energy to will him over the railing to a horrible death.

"Excuse me, Miss Blandings, but there's been no mistake." She smiled like the Dragon Lady. For the moment she seemed to be enjoying herself. Either that or her self-control, following her performance at the Gotham, was spooky. "Oh, dear Charlie didn't make all this clear, did he? But then you don't actually know Charlie, do you? Well, in real life I am a simple housewife, as you see." Her eyes lingered on Greco for a moment. He wiped salty fingers in the dog's beard.

"But your publisher," he said, "thought a man's name was more salable?"

She shook her head. "Not entirely. It's more a matter of my husband, and you know how stubborn husbands can be. Bassinetti didn't like the idea of being the unknown husband of the Mystery Writer, do you see? Very old-fashioned but," she shrugged,

"Bassinetti is not a great devotee of women's liberation. He doesn't mind my doing it, he just wants me to do my thing as quietly as possible. Anyway, enough about me. I am curious as to how you found out who I am—"

"Just a friend in publishing who happened to know—"

"Well, isn't that the way? You think you have a secret, and of course you don't." She glanced at a small but very serviceable gold-and-diamond Rolex. "I mustn't keep you while I chatter away. You did want to see me, I take it?"

Celia said: "Oh, I was really trying to reach this Cunningham. I found something of his and wanted to return it. It's not all that important—" Her mind raced ahead: Should she be giving anything away to this woman? Where did she fit in? She heard herself talking, tried to stop.

"What is it?"

"Just a book—"

"A book? You've gone to a great deal of trouble just to return a book. But why come to me?"

"It's one of your books."

"Inscribed to him from the author," Greco said. "We couldn't find him, we figured you might know him."

"How terribly clever of you! But, alas, I can only give you a general idea of where to reach him. I think he lives on Bank or Perry or Jane, one of those picturesque, funny little streets in the Village. Or he could call you, perhaps? Are you in the phone book, Miss Blandings?"

"Oh, I must be," Celia said with an idiotic laugh. She cringed inwardly.

"We'll be on our way, then," Greco said. "We're running late and have imposed on you enough already. We gotta catch the train up to the Stadium. Twi-nighter tonight. The Pale Hose, as they say."

Mrs. Bassinetti looked at him quizzically, as if he'd just broken into an Urdu dialect. "I'll have Nancy show you out." She pressed a buzzer on a cord and the maid appeared in the doorway.

"Thank you for your help," Celia said.

"The pleasure was mine," Mrs. Bassinetti replied.

Back on the street Greco breathed a boisterous sigh. "Now that was right off the wall! Today's been just full of surprises. I'm losing track of all the angles, Slats, but that lady's in the big leagues, murder or not."

"You are such a bastard! You left me hanging there—"

"You hung in, what are you complaining about? By the way, *are* you in the telephone book?"

"No," she said. They turned the corner and headed back toward First Avenue.

"That's a relief. We can't let 'em find you."

"I hardly think Mrs. Bassinetti is plotting a *real* murder—"

"Doesn't matter once she tells Mr. Mystery how to get hold of you. But if you're not in the book . . ." He shrugged. "Then you're okay."

"Greco, you sound sort of funny."

"I feel funny, Slats. I feel like maybe we should give all this one helluva hard second look. I'm feeling like you'd better butt out—"

"After one day? I'm still in the clear—"

"Exactly my point. Thing is, we've been too far out front in all this. You play chess? Well, we're out here with too damn many things undefended. Like your ass, Slats—"

"Leave my ass out of this!"

"Watch my lips. We want to keep you in the clear, whatever these people are up to. They still don't know who you are, we can drop it and you're none the worse for it—"

"While the Director gets killed in the middle of Dan Rather—"

"What the hell's the matter with you? What are you trying to prove?" He hailed a cab that slid over to the curb, cutting off two or three hundred cars slogging their way up First.

They climbed into the cab. Celia gave the driver her address. Greco wasn't kidding. He thought they should get out of the whole thing. Maybe he was right. She couldn't get over the shock of seeing Mrs. Bassinetti on the terrace with the white Rolls down below.

"We gotta talk," she said.

"Okay. But I didn't sign on for night work."

"You really going to Yankee Stadium?"

"Naw. That was just clever repartee."

"But you're busy tonight?"

"Look, you're growing on me in sort of a weird way, Slats. But I am tied up tonight."

"Got a hot date?"

"Gotta shoot some pool," Greco muttered, and looked out the window at the shops and restaurants whizzing by.

Chapter Eleven

❧

Spending the entire day alone had put Ed-the-Mean into a crummy mood. A contrary beast, never overly chummy in the best of times, he nonetheless was emotionally delicate, prone to finding the imagined slight. He resented neglect. Combined with his customary aversion to strangers, his resentment by the time he heard the key in the door had gone well off the meter. When Celia opened the door, Ed's sixth sense warned him of an alien presence. His blood was up. He struck.

There was a blur of purple blue feathers, a streak of yellow like the arc of a tracer bullet, a terrible beating of feathers, and a strangled cry.

When she spun to look, helpless to intervene, she saw that the strangled cry had emanated from Peter Greco who, arms semaphoring frantically, was pirouetting back through the doorway. He kicked the door shut at the last moment.

It was too late for Ed to peel off. He slammed into the door. With the sound of splintering wood his beak sank into the door. For a moment he cast a puzzled eye toward Celia as he hung by his black beak. Then he yanked himself backward, disengaging the beak, spitting out shreds of wood, and flopped with little or no dignity to the floor. Like a cat preserving its self-respect he staggered to his feet and strolled into the bedroom, as if that had been his clever intention all along.

"What in the name of God was that?" The muffled

inquiry came from beyond the damàged door. "Slats? You all right?"

She opened the door. Greco's arms flew up again to protect his remaining eye. He spread his fingers and peered through the spaces.

"Jealous boyfriend. Ed. Should have warned you. It's okay now, I've got him calmed down in the bedroom. Come on in—"

"You're sure it's safe? This is no joke. I'm a guy who worries about his eyesight, right? So cut the crap—"

"No, it's safe, really. Come in."

"Oh, shit! There he is!"

Ed had meandered back into the hallway. A bit of the door still hung from his beak. Suddenly he took wing and fluttered back to the living room. He landed atop his cage, pointedly turned his back to them, and began flexing his muscles.

"Funny, some women you figure for a Rolls convertible. Other women, I'm naming no names mind you, have like, y'know, giant goddamn *condors.*" Greco snorted. "Look better in a stew pot. You really oughta keep him tied up if you won't just kill him and get it over with. Really, I'm serious. Somebody could sue you."

"You're just jealous. He's tougher than you. He's jealous, Ed."

"What's all this?" Greco asked, gesturing at the box of index cards, the notebooks and folders that were scattered on one end of the couch.

"It's a book I'm working on," Celia said, as she swept the stuff aside and sat down. "A Linda Thurston mystery. Sometimes I use her to help me figure things out."

Greco paced the room, watching Ed from the corner of his eye. He was checking out the bookcases and the pool table. He stood back and admired the massive carved legs and the detailing on the sides.

He lifted the wooden platform from the top and stood it against the wall. He whistled softly.

"This baby looks like an Orenstein, pre–World War One. Made in Kansas City. How does it play?"

"Like a dream."

"Mind if I . . . ?" He nodded toward the rack of cues.

"Not at all."

He looked at the cues, chose a two-tone Bradwell from England and chalked it. "Bird comes at me again, I break the cue on him."

"Just shoot pool."

"Okay, okay." He looked at the casual arrangement of balls on the table, stroked a few shots to check the mat, the roll, the tendencies. "So, you think we should talk. The more I think, the more I think. It's like Zen. So talk to me." He didn't show off with the cue, nothing fancy. He'd retrieve the white ball and take the same shot again and again.

"I keep trying to get it clear. There's a lot going on here, it's frustrating." She grabbed a file card, put it on a book and poised a Bic over it. "Charlie Cunningham is M.M. and he's involved in Z's plan to kill the Director. We know he's lost the written plan Z gave him, because we found it. Right so far?" She watched him lean over the table and smoothly stroke the balls, heard the gentle, precise clicking as they smacked one another.

"We know he knows he lost it," Greco said, surveying the table, moving around it calmly and quickly, "because we saw him run to the Strand like a maniac. But he's too late, the book and letter are gone. He doesn't know where. So what does he do . . . and here's where it begins to come apart. He calls his girlfriend, who is Mrs. Bassinetti, a rich married lady . . . who is also Miles Warriner, author of the book he mistakenly sold, the book in which he'd stuck the murder plan. *Now why the hell*

did he call her?" He made another shot, then leaned
on the cue, staring at her.

"It's a puzzlement," she admitted. Ed rearranged
himself on top of his cage, so he could see them. She
gave him a warning look.

"Where does she fit? What does he tell her? That
he's just lost his plan to murder somebody? Unlikely.
But still, she runs to him fast as she can, and what
does she do? Sympathize with his problem? No, she
gives him holy hell about something, and with her
feathers ruffled—if you'll pardon me, Ed, you asshole—she splits. What's her role? I'm telling you,
Slats, once you know where Mrs. Bassinetti fits in,
you know what's going on. She's the key."

"You're smirking."

"I am not."

"You think you know where she fits, right?"

He nodded grinning. "You're not gonna like it—"

"I was afraid of that."

"It just hit me in the cab. Right when I was
beginning to worry about everything . . . it hit me
head on. The obvious solution that fits all the facts
and is completely logical." He finally made a rather
flashy shot and turned his back on it before the ball
plopped into the leather strap pocket.

"I'm going to *hate* this."

"It is a plot, all right. For one of her novels. It fits. It
fits with his being a mystery critic *and* her lover.
She'd naturally consult him about her plots . . .
particularly with a husband who isn't all that en-
thusiastic about her career. Plus—"

"But—"

"Plus this whacked-out personality of hers. All
sweetness and light when we see her, but a nightmare with Charlie. Why? Because he's carelessly
disposed not only of her notes on the plot, but a book
she inscribed for him. Her husband won't take her
work seriously and now her lover pulls a dumb

stunt . . . and the lady blows her top, her ego
explodes. Face it, Slats! It's a perfect fit." He put the
cue back in the rack.

"I don't know," Celia said.

"Think about it. It fits. Well, look, I've got to hit the
road."

She got up and walked him to the door. He
frowned at the splintered indentation where Ed had
met his match. He pushed his finger into the hole.
"That bird is hard to believe. Look, I'll call you
tomorrow." From the top of the stairs he winked his
eye and smiled. "Sleep tight."

The thought that he might be right took the wind
out of her sails. She sat on the couch as the light
outside dimmed. In retrospect the danger seemed
fun. Danger! She felt like a fool. What danger? Maybe
she really was someone with an overactive sense of
the dramatic. An actress. Maybe she had gotten
carried away with Linda Thurston and had confused
fiction with reality and, well, the fact was Debbie
Macadam had called Linda an escape route. . . .
Maybe Celia had been using Linda for the wrong
kind of escape. She wasn't Linda. Linda didn't exist,
except in Celia's imagination. The more she thought,
the more foolish she felt. Maybe it came from being a
loner. Celia had always been a loner, never happier
than when she was lost in a book or a movie or a
play.

Ed went to the kitchen with her when she made
coffee. She filled his water cup and feeder and
brought a huge mug of coffee back into the living
room. She put *Double Indemnity* on the VCR and
there was Fred MacMurray with the Santa Ana
blowing, having no idea what he was walking into.
Just a guy trying to sell some insurance.

She curled up at the end of the couch, picked up

one of the Linda Thurston notebooks, and began writing down everything that had happened in the last twenty-four hours, since she'd found the murder letter. She held the letter in her hands again, pored over its meager contents trying to see something that had eluded her before.

Rolls.

Hmmm. Not a croissant, not a kaiser, not a Parker House. But how about *a* Rolls? As in Rolls Royce? Mrs. Bassinetti drove a Rolls. . . .

Trunk. A Rolls had a trunk.

You could make a Clean getaway in the Trunk of a Rolls.

If you didn't do anything STUPID.

How about M.M. in the Trunk of the Bassinetti Rolls?

She felt her interest quickening, but she tried to fight it. Forget the dramatic, Celia. She heard Greco's argument again, all perfectly reasonable. It fit. He was bound to be right, because life was prosaic. A bitchy adulterous wife gets mad at her careless lover. Happens every day, on every block in New York.

But half an hour before he'd become so reasonable and so wet blankety, Greco had seemed genuinely worried, going on about chess and undefended positions and being too far out front. Mrs. Bassinetti had scared him.

What was it with him?

Had he been trying to talk her out of something he felt was just too dangerous for her to play with?

Well, she was dead sure of one thing: Linda Thurston would never have fallen for Greco's new theory. She'd have gone with her instincts. Celia knew Linda Thurston better than she knew herself, and no man could have waltzed Linda sideways and out of the picture. No way. Linda wouldn't let herself be *protected* . . . while a man got killed. Linda would know her own mind, would trust her own mind. She'd have listened to Greco and thought it over and said . . . nonsense!

Nonsense! She felt it in her guts, and like Linda Thurston, she was going to trust that gut feeling. At least for a few minutes. . . . Just look at things a little differently and what could you find?

Z, the unknown, is masterminding the murder of the Director, also unknown.

Charlie Cunningham, for reasons unknown, is important to Z's plan, may indeed be the lucky lad chosen to do the killing for him. Which means that Z is not an experienced murderer, since Charlie has all the earmarks of a singularly unqualified killer.

Charlie loses the murder note, tries to get it back, and discovers that it's fallen into the hands of someone unknown, who is in fact our own Celia Blandings.

Charlie calls his girlfriend and *someone else:* Who?

The girlfriend drops everything, comes to meet Charlie, and blows up at him. Why?

And the girlfriend turns out to be Mrs. Bassinetti, who is Miles Warriner, mystery novelist.

So you have Charlie, you have Charlie having an affair—Celia was sure of that, she could tell—with a rich woman married to a rich man with old-fashioned values . . . and this woman has a temper like a blowtorch.

Now was that a triangle or was that a triangle?

Whom do lovers murder?

Rich, old-fashioned husbands.

And innocent bystanders who find out too much.

She was staring at MacMurray and Stanwyck meeting accidentally on purpose in a grocery store.

God in Heaven! What were they doing? They were planning to kill Barbara Stanwyck's husband for the insurance!

Money. Bassinetti's money? Maybe. Charlie Cunningham didn't seem very well-heeled. And who knew what was Mrs. Bassinetti's and what her husband's?

But money was one of the reasons for murder. What were the others? Power? Love? Sheer cussedness. If Ed ever killed anyone it would be sheer cussedness—

The telephone rang.

It was Claude, her ex-actor pal, now full-time at the Strand.

"Darling, I hear you came in search of me. So sorry I missed you. Offering free food, were you?"

"Really just wanted to say hi, Claude—"

"Well, my dear, it shows you the power of coincidence, that's what it shows you."

"What are you talking about?"

"You want the long dramatic reading or the short facts?"

"Short, please."

"You're just no fun." Claude's lisp was getting worse the further he got from the stage. "But I was upstairs—any more time spent in the dungeon and I'll begin to look like a gopher—and I was talking to Henry when this regular comes dashing in, apparently sold us a valuable book by mistake, valuable to him I mean, and he wanted it back. Matter of hours was all. Henry says My God, what a small world, she was just in looking for the guy whose book she had. He described you, five-ten, lanky, lovely to look at, delightful to know—"

"This is the short version?" She felt a cold wind raking across her: fear again. Damn it. This was all too real.

"Okay, cut to the chase. I heard the description and knew it was you. Lucky girl! And I was able to tell this Charlie Cunningham where he could find his book."

She felt her knees start to go a little rubbery. She'd known it was coming. "What are you saying, Claude?"

"So I gave him your name and address. He said he didn't want to just drop in on you and, you know, he seemed very nice, your type, Celia. Sort of an intellectual. And utterly hetero." She could imagine Claude smirking on the other end, as if he knew her nasty little secret.

"Celia? Celia? You there?"

"Sure, Claude. Look, I've got to run."

"The thanks I get!"

"Thanks a million, really," and she hung up.

She stared at *Double Indemnity*, not seeing it.

Charlie knows now. Reality was back, and she wasn't liking it. Maybe Greco had been right after all. . . .

Suddenly she found herself hoping so.

The problem was, Linda Thurston didn't think so.

She called Hilary Sampson once the movie was over. She'd thought it through again and again, dealing with the various unknowns, substituting a variety of possibilities for each. One scenario after another. They all made sense, none of them made sense. She'd also considered her own resources, as if she were setting up a defense perimeter with herself at the center. Her resources didn't amount to all that much. But knowledge was important, particularly in light of all the unknowns. And Hilary Sampson made her living as a researcher at the *Times*.

She was in luck. Hilary was home. Celia ran through the day's activities, a recitation satisfyingly accompanied by Hilary's gasps of excitement.

"What are you going to do now that he knows who you are? I think you'd better camp over here tonight—"

"No, it's okay," Celia said, wondering if it was. "But you can be a big help—"

"Anything!"

"Work your research magic. Get me anything you can on the family Bassinetti. I need to know who her husband is. There's always the chance he's not only rich but has some kind of public record. Also, Mrs. Bassinetti or Miles Warriner. Can you do that?"

"Sure, no problem. Are we looking for anything in particular?"

"If I only knew—but I don't. We'll just have to go with whatever we find. But there are too many blanks in the equations. I'd like to fill any of them. Hilary, we're really up against it. We've only got until Dan Rather comes on with the news tomorrow night—"

"I know, I've been paying attention. So how'd you like Greco?"

"He's a real con man, a real smartass, he keeps calling me Slats—"

"That means he likes you. You like him, right?"

"I said nothing of the kind—"

"I can tell, you like him!"

"Hilary, find out about the Bassinettis, okay?"

"I *knew* it! You like him!"

"Later, Hil. We'll talk about that later."

"For sure!"

She forced herself to accept the idea that Charlie Cunningham knew where to find her. If Greco's theory was right, Charlie naturally enough wanted to recover the keepsake-inscribed book as well as the plot notes. If Linda Thurston's theory was correct, she didn't want to think about it.

She was in the shower washing off the accumulated grime of the day. She stepped out and ran naked and dripping to the extension beside her bed. She shook the water out of her right ear and said hello.

"Miss Blandings?"

"Yes."

"My name is Charlie Cunningham. I believe you have something of mine. I want it back, Miss Blandings." He coughed into the mouthpiece while she stood rooted to the spot, shivering from the whiff of fear. "Miss Blandings? Are you there, Miss Blandings?"

Chapter Twelve

❧

Peter Greco stopped at the Jefferson Market and went
home with one of the big glossy blue shopping bags
full of milk, grapefruit, broccoli, anchovies, tuna,
shelled walnuts, parmesan cheese, chopped garlic in
oil, red pepper flakes, hamburger, corn flakes, and
orange juice. He was thinking about Celia Blandings,
wondering if she'd bought his explanation of events.
He'd made it up on the spur of the moment, and as
he'd listened to himself it sounded fairly plausible,
almost ingenious. It seemed to take her off guard. At
least she hadn't burst a blood vessel arguing.

He stood in the kitchen unpacking groceries,
putting away what he wasn't going to use for dinner.
He had his preparations down to a system. He filled a
large pot with water and put it on to boil. He took a
saucepan, ran an inch of water into the bottom of it,
then put it on to boil. He cut the tops from the
broccoli with a handy knife he'd gotten in France
years ago and put them in the folding steamer. When
the water in the saucepan was boiling, he placed the
steamer in it. He took the enameled red colander
from the cupboard and put it in the sink, got a small
flat saucepan down and put it over a very low flame.
He poured some olive oil, extra virgin, into the pan
and forked some garlic bits into it. He sprinkled it
lavishly with red pepper and a bit of oregano.
Carefully he peeled back the top of the tin of rolled
anchovies and capers and dumped them with their
oil into the olive oil mixture. He opened the can of

solid light tuna and broke it into chunks on a plate.
He opened the packet of walnuts and the fresh
parmesan. The water was boiling, so he slid half a
pound of #10 spaghetti into the bubbles and steam.
He pulled the cork from a half bottle of Chianti,
sniffed it, poured some into a mug because he
couldn't see any glasses, and took a sip.

He waited for the spaghetti to cook and kept
sipping at the wine and wondering about Mrs.
Bassinetti. He wondered if she really was having an
affair with Cunningham, who looked like a pleasant
enough guy but not quite in her weight class when it
came to the sexual championships. Still, you never
knew about things like that. He had a difficult time
seeing Charlie as a killer, while Mrs. Bassinetti
looked as if she were cut out for the job. So who the
hell was Z?

He drained the spaghetti in the colander, shook it
over the sink, dropped it back into the empty pot. He
poured the olive oil mixture over it, tossed it with
two forks, then ground black Tellicherry pepper over
it. Then he put the steamed, brilliantly green broccoli in, the tuna, and sprinkled walnuts over it all.
He tossed it thoroughly again, doused it liberally
with parmesan, left it in the pot, and began eating.
He took another satisfying drink of wine, turned on
the kitchen's small black-and-white television, and
listened while Dan Rather told him what horrors
President Reagan had in store for the lame, the halt,
the blind, and the elderly, without regard to race or
religion. They were all equal-opportunity sufferers,
as far as the administration was concerned.

He ate his way through the suffering farmers, the
suffering parents of kids who could no longer get
college loans, the suffering elderly who were scared
half to death that the nation's oldest President, for
whom they'd voted in vast numbers, was about to
take the axe to their Social Security benefits. When

the suffering for the night was done and Dan Rather
had wished the nation a good night, Greco fixed a
piece of plastic wrap over the pot and put it into the
refrigerator. He dropped the Chianti bottle into the
trash, rinsed the mug in hot water and put it into the
wooden drying rack. He went to the bathroom,
brushed his teeth, put his Yankee jacket back on, and
walked two blocks to the garage where he occasionally ransomed his car, a four-year-old Chrysler Le
Baron he'd bought from his former wife's ex-brother-
in-law, who'd married her step-sister in Passaic.
He'd wound up liking him better than he'd liked
Phyllis, and the car was a dandy.

Tuning in the Yankee–White Sox twi-nighter, he
drove uptown to Sutton Place. He pulled over, cut
the engine and turned off the lights, but left the game
on to keep himself awake. There was a dim light on
above the Bassinetti doorway. The lights were out
inside, or the draperies had the density of blackout
curtains. She was either in the back of the house or
out; it didn't make any difference. He was prepared
to wait quite a while. He had no idea what to expect.
Maybe Charlie would show up. Maybe somebody
else would show up. Maybe Z would appear in a
clap of thunder and a puff of smoke.

The sounds of the horses in the stables floated
across the dark green expanse of lawn as the Director
sat on the spacious back porch watching the sun sink
behind the Jersey countryside. His wife's horses
were one of the best things about her. He hadn't been
much of a rider even before his accident, but he had
then, as well as now, enjoyed visiting them in their
stalls, chatting with them, soothing them, making
friends, feeling their great rubbery mouths taking
sugar from his palm. He wasn't altogether sure what
the beasts represented for him, but in soothing them

he inevitably soothed himself, no matter what pressures he'd been feeling. Now the stable boy and trainer had departed for the night, and he drew comfort from the sounds of their settling down to sleep.

Finally he guided his wheelchair up the ramp and into the kitchen. From the refrigerator he took eggs, an apple, and a wedge of Gruyère. He melted butter in the omelette pan while he whisked the eggs and a few dashes of nutmeg in a copper bowl. While the eggs set up in the butter, he slivered the cheese and the apple, then laid them in on the eggs, waited, slid the eggs around, and gently flopped them over. He had something moist and perfect for his dinner. He drank a half bottle of a jaunty little Riesling. While he had his dinner, he watched Dan Rather and let his mind turn the corner and contemplate for a moment what might be going on tomorrow at this same time. He smiled to himself, patted a bit of melted cheese from the corner of his mouth. It was all a game, of course, and he enjoyed the game. The higher the stakes, the better he liked it. The odd thing was, he doubted if he'd ever have pushed things quite this far if he'd still been a whole man, walking around on his own two legs. There was surely a lesson embedded in what had once seemed the tragedy of his life. The tragedy had liberated him from the rat race, had left him free to think. He felt as if he'd been possessed by the spirit of mischief.

At the appointed time he called the General.

"Did you enjoy the manuscript, General?"

"Enjoy is not precisely the word I'd have used, my friend. I certainly found it interesting. I wonder who wrote it?"

"I too. But other data has reached me, and I feel obliged to tell you. Those who intend to kill me have made a blunder—"

"No kidding. Whattaya know? A blunder—is that like a mistake?"

"Your usual amusing self." The Director chuckled. "Apparently their intentions have become a matter of public knowledge—"

"No!"

"Some person, a woman, seems to have learned of the plan. She's an unknown quantity. What will she do? Perhaps she will rescue me. One never knows. I certainly don't, but I do know this: I *hate* variables."

"Who is this woman?"

"Her name is Celia Blandings."

"We wouldn't want her to be hurt, would we?"

"Perish the thought."

"Maybe we could reach her. . . . Do you know how?"

"I think I might." The Director gave the General her address, knowing he was being recorded in Virginia.

"How the hell do you come by all this information?"

"Why, General, you surprise me. It's my job to know things. Everything." He couldn't resist another chuckle.

Chapter Thirteen

❧

She sat on the couch staring at the telephone she'd just finished with. Then she called Hilary's number again and there was no answer. All right, it was time to become Linda Thurston.

Cunningham had suggested that they meet somewhere public, at which time she could return his property. He'd thrown out the name Area, the trendy environmental disco in TriBeCa.

"Not a chance in the world," Celia had said.

"Why not? Who's calling the shots here?"

"I am. And I was there once. People were fucking in the stalls in the ladies room. I'm not going back. They wouldn't notice a dead body, they'd think it was part of the decor—"

"Who's talking about dead bodies?"

"That, Mr. Cunningham, would seem to be your field of expertise." It was a peculiar sensation, hearing Linda Thurston take over.

"I don't want to argue. I just want my things—"

"What's going on? Before we start hanging around together, just who are you trying to kill? Who is the Director?"

"Oh, shit," came across the line muffled. "Look, you don't understand what's going on here. Nobody's going to get killed . . . it's a long, very complicated story. Whattaya say you just give me the stuff back and forget the whole thing? I'm just a guy, believe me. I got more problems than I can count, and you're making it a helluva lot worse—"

"Does Mrs. Bassinetti know what you're doing?"

"What? What are you saying?" He sounded like he'd just walked into a bear trap and had noticed he was missing most of his leg. "You haven't told her!"

"I went to see her—"

"Oh, God, tell me you're kidding, tell me you're making that up—"

"I'm not kidding—"

"Oh shit, oh shit," he whined, as if he wished he'd never gone into the woods after the bear. "You didn't tell her some cockeyed story like me murdering someone—"

"Well . . . no."

"Oh hell, it doesn't make any difference. Look, you've gotta give it back, forget you ever saw it."

"All right, Bradley's on University Place. Right near the D'Agostino's—"

"I know Bradley's, for God's sake, I wasn't parachuted in yesterday. Okay, twenty minutes."

She took the murder letter and hid it in the best possible place. Safe. She put the book in a bag, put on a jacket, and left the brownstone. Linda Thurston wasn't scared, she was curious. And she wanted to save someone's life.

Mason and a clone named Green pushed their way into the crowded room that was Bradley's. The tables were full, they were standing three deep at the bar, and a trio was playing first-rate jazz toward the back. The saxophone player sounded a little like Stan Getz but the pianist wasn't Jim McNeeley so, though he couldn't see through the crowd and the haze, it probably wasn't Getz.

Mason sent Green into the crowd at the bar with orders to get a couple beers. He was looking for Celia Blandings, who'd entered the crowd only minutes before. It took a little looking, and then he saw

Charlie Cunningham standing back in a corner, fading into the surroundings. He was nursing a beer of his own. Mason followed Cunningham's line of sight and saw Celia. A tall bald guy was already putting some moves on her, getting her a drink. She was good-looking, all right, if you liked them tall and dark, with a sense of humor around their mouths. She was turning this way and that, trying to pick Cunningham out of the crowd, but wasn't coming close. The General had given Mason a great deal of latitude in keeping Celia Blandings out of the Director's problems. But the job, like a stain, kept spreading.

Green came back with the beers and Mason said: "Drink up. I've got a job for you. Cunningham and Blandings are both here. It's a perfect chance. Go check out Cunningham's place, find anything that could tie him to the manuscript that's bugging everybody. Thoroughness is your watchword, Greenie. We've got to find out who wrote the damn thing, that's first priority. Now get going. The General will love you for it."

Green dutifully chugged his beer while Mason watched, disgust mingled with primitive envy of the stupid college trick. Then Green left, and Mason worked his way closer to the music, moving like a crab, keeping an eye on Celia Blandings. Damn, she looked intriguing. He wanted to get close enough to hear her voice. The trio was doing justice to "Airmail Special." The piano had a drive to it, like Dorothy Donegan's up in Boston one night. Blandings had put away her drink and Mason wedged himself in next to her. She'd drunk it fast because she was nervous. He read it in her face, her eyes. "Excuse me," he said, brushing against her. "Hard to get a drink in the crush." He smiled at her, she nodded. "You're empty," he said. "Can I fill that up for you?" She looked down at her glass.

"Sure, one more. Gin gimlet with ice."

He got her the drink and pondered the sin of mixing business with pleasure. "Waiting for someone?" he said.

"Why?" She sounded surprised.

He shrugged. "Keep looking around."

"Yes, I am. Not having much luck."

"Boyfriend?"

"Not in a million years," she said.

"I just come for the music," he said. His sense of responsibility got the upper hand, and he worked his way back toward the other end of the bar.

Charlie Cunningham was gone.

Charlie Cunningham was very nervous.

The conversation with this Blandings horror show couldn't have been worse. How she'd wormed Mrs. Bassinetti out of the book and the letter, he couldn't imagine, couldn't be bothered to worry about. Somehow she had, and whatever she'd told her was bound to have made matters worse, a turn of events he hadn't believed possible.

Then he'd set out to follow Blandings to Bradley's, just to get a feeling for the kind of woman she was. That had proved pointless, but he'd seen two other guys get out of a car and start following her as soon as she'd come down the steps of the brownstone. He'd ducked into a narrow trash alley running alongside her building and watched as they fell into step behind her. He had no idea who the hell they were, but he didn't like it. There was something wrong with those guys. They didn't look quite like other people.

He was tired at the end of an indescribably bad day that kept getting worse. He'd run ahead on the other side of the street and gotten to Bradley's first, found the darkest corner, coerced a beer out of the hassled

barman, and waited a few moments until Blandings
arrived. He assumed she had no way of identifying
him, but the other guys made him worry.

They arrived looking serious, and he tried to hide
behind his beer. After one of them left, he'd watched
the other one close in on Blandings. His head was
swimming, and then he'd had a wonderful idea. He
slipped out of the smoke and din and headed back
toward the Blandings place.

He checked to see her apartment number on the
buzzer box, then found the narrow, dank trash alley,
and giving what he supposed was a uniquely suspi-
cious look around, he ducked into the darkness. And
banged into a shadow-hidden trash can. He stifled a
yelp of pain, closed his eyes and felt gingerly for the
blood seeping from his injured shin. Par for the
course.

He felt his way along the side of the brownstone,
which stretched about the length of six football
fields. Finally he came to a chain-link fence continuing along beside the brownstone's garden. A dog was
barking somewhere in one of the apartment build-
ings looming above the garden. *Rear Window*, for
chrissake. The lighted windows looking down at
him were clearly unblinking, watchful eyes. Still, a
man had to do what a man had to do.

The fence gave a little when he began climbing
and seemed to make a deafening amount of noise.
However, upward and onward. He hung on the top of
the fence, calculating the distance to the fire escape
ladder. He would jump. He could make it.

No, as it turned out, he couldn't.

Aarrrrghhhhh!!!

It was just like a comic book.

Celia waited nearly an hour at Bradley's before
deciding that Cunningham wasn't coming. It didn't

make any sense to her. Meeting had been his idea. Why would he stand her up? The man who'd fetched her the second drink seemed to have disappeared, and the first man had gotten to talking about those Mets with a redhead, and the trio had finished the set, and she felt like a fool.

Then it hit her—he'd suckered her out so he could search her apartment! He'd known she'd never bring the letter to the bar. . . .

She was halfway home before it occurred to her that getting hold of the letter and the book wasn't the point. Once she'd read the letter and figured it out, even in part, he had to convince her that she'd misunderstood the implications. They had to talk.

Unless, of course, it was simpler, surer, and far better to kill her. If he really had murder on his mind, he had to make sure she wouldn't go to the police. Talking would help him only if he weren't going to kill anyone . . . and if he didn't have murder on his mind, why would he care what she thought?

There had to be a murder for Celia to be of any importance to him at all. . . .

And if there was a murder, Cunningham couldn't risk taking her word that she wouldn't tell.

Which meant he really had no choice at all. He'd have to kill her. And once he had the book and the letter, who could tie him to Celia Blandings?

Well, quite a few people, actually. The Carling woman at Pegasus, Penzler, the people at the Strand, Mrs. Bassinetti—

So why was she so sure he wasn't thinking about them?

Because he didn't know about them.

He must be thinking, kill Celia and I'm safe again.

But where was he?

Thinking like Linda Thurston again, she looked at the door lock to see if anyone had jimmied her building's front door. Of course no one had. She went into the hallway and climbed the long single flight to her own door on the landing. The bulb had burned out several days before and she hadn't gotten around to replacing it, but there was enough light from below to find the lock. She swung the door open and waited. "Hello? Hello!" Ed made one of his macaw noises. She sighed with relief and went in.

It was almost one o'clock. She was exhausted. There were no messages on the answering machine. She slipped out of her clothes, left them on the floor where they fell, and climbed naked into bed. Ed was quiet, snoozing in the safety of his cage. The apartment was quiet.

On the tiny deck beyond the French doors at the end of her living room, Charlie Cunningham had finally gotten his nose to stop bleeding. He was quite sure his wrist was sprained. After all, he had fallen about ten feet, head first into somebody's goddamn garden furniture. A foot to the left and he'd have killed himself on the barbecue. Lucky he wasn't dead. Some luck . . .

His face and beard were sticky with blood. His shin was stuck to his sock with blood. He felt like he might need a transfusion at any moment. He couldn't seem to bend his left wrist. He leaned against the wall, watching the lights going out in all the apartment windows rising around him as one o'clock came. He wondered in this moment of quiet how he'd come to such an absurd place, and the answer wasn't long in coming.

Zoe Bassinetti.

He was not a violent man, but at the thought of her, his hands began shaking. It was all her fault. How could he possibly have known when he'd first seen her at the Algonquin that she was the Princess of Fucking Darkness?

He looked at the French door and considered how he might get in.

He didn't know yet that Celia Blandings had never locked that door in all the years she'd lived in the brownstone.

Then it began to rain.

Hard.

Chapter Fourteen

～

At first she thought it was a dream. One of those
nightmares you suffer through but are simultaneously able to identify as just a bad dream. It was raining
and she could hear the steady metronomic beat of
breathing. She turned in the bed, kicked at the
comforter, trying to free a leg. It was her own
breathing, obviously. She switched onto her back,
felt her eyelids fluttering on the edge of conscious-
ness, hearing the rain dripping and the breathing.
Panting. More like panting. All she had to do was
hold her breath and prove it was the sound of her
own breathing filtered through her dreams.

She held her breath.

The panting went on, harder if anything.

Then she felt a large wet drop of water land on her
forehead.

She came awake, eyes wide, and saw the hulk
above her, a shape almost shrouding her in the glow
from the streetlamp outside her bedroom window. It
was dripping on her.

Adrenaline began squirting like blood from a
severed artery. She turned like a dervish, spinning
across the bed, tangling herself more thoroughly in
the sheets and comforter. She tried to scream but
there wasn't much result. She fell out of the bed,
kicked out of the mummy casing, grabbed at the
lamp on the bedside table, knocking it off and
turning it on simultaneously.

The light from the floor wasn't all that flattering,

but no amount of light could have improved what was standing on the other side of the bed.

It was soaking wet.

It wore a beard, and the face and hair were covered, matted, with blood that looked pink because it was diluted by rain.

It was holding a butcher knife high in the air.

It looked at her and said: "Hey! Relax!"

Which was when she realized she was naked.

It said: "Look . . . I'm Charlie Cunningham. . . ."

"Oh, my God—"

"Ah . . ." He looked up at the knife as if he hadn't noticed it before. "Ah . . . this is your letter opener. . . ."

She wanted to say something but nothing seemed quite appropriate and her mouth was too dry anyway. She wanted to run, but being naked made her wonder where she wanted to go. She made a feint, and like a mirror image he tilted with her, the bed still between them.

"Give me the goddamn stuff," he growled, coughing. He waved the letter opener. "I don't want to hurt you, but I'm telling you, lady, I'm right on the goddamn edge! I'm about to stop giving a shit whether you get hurt or not! Say something!"

She made another darting motion, felt so horribly vulnerable in her nakedness, and stopped, holding her breasts to her with a forearm.

"I'm wet and I'm bleeding and I've broken half the bones in my body and . . . aw, shit! Have a little consideration for chrissake! I haven't done anything to you—it's my stuff, just give it back!"

"Why didn't you meet me, like you said you would—"

"I tried but there were some other guys following you. They got out of a car and followed you—who the hell were they?" Rain was dripping from him, like something dredged from the sea.

"What are you talking about?" She was quite suddenly colder than she'd ever been. Thunder rumbled softly. The rain drummed on the windows.

"You brought reinforcements—"

"I did not!"

"Look, it doesn't matter." He was trying to be patient. His nose had begun bleeding again. He wiped the hand with the letter opener in it across his nose, smearing blood. "Give me the book and the paper and I'll get the hell out of here—"

"No you won't, you'll kill me once I give—"

"I will not!"

"Yes, you will—"

"This is nuts!"

He leaped onto the bed and came at her.

She made a dash to get around the bed and felt his cold wet hand on her ankle as he slipped in the bedclothes and sprawled facedown. He held tight. She turned and hit him in the head, dragged her nails across his scalp. He shrieked and she yanked away, made a run for the hallway.

He'd recovered with an alacrity born of desperation and was right behind her, panting like a locomotive. She reached for the door into the hallway but the locks were too complicated. She slipped away from his grasping fingers again and plunged into the darkness of the living room. She got the pool table between them again and stood gasping, almost unable to breathe at all.

He stood silhouetted in the hallway entrance. The only sounds were both of them trying to breathe and the rain splattering on her narrow balcony. She heard a faint clicking noise behind her, almost drowned out by the wheezing and panting.

"Please," he gasped, "please just give me the—"

"You must think I'm crazy!" She felt for the

telephone. Then she knocked it off the table. It made a hell of a noise.

"Okay, that's it! That's really it this time!"

He charged across the room in the dark, managed to skirt the end of the couch. The corner of the pool table slowed him down. Celia backed up, tripped over the telephone cord, fell down, scrambled forward in an attempt to get back over the couch and into the bedroom, where she might be able to barricade the door. Instead she ran afoul of Linda Thurston's cardboard boxes and scraped some skin from her left wrist and forearm.

The situation didn't look good.

He was standing over her sniffling. He wanted the stuff. He couldn't kill her until he had the stuff. . . .

She hit him as hard as she could with a packet of file cards, catching him in the shin.

He howled.

And in the howl she heard the ominous fluttering of the old winged avenger.

Ed-the-Mean, doubtless overcome by yet another chance to exercise his badass attitude, this time stemming from being rousted from a sound sleep, took his best shot at an unsuspecting Charlie Cunningham.

The scream was unearthly.

She'd never heard anything like it. She clapped her hands over her ears. She felt herself splattered with something.

Charlie Cunningham crashed over her, over the couch, onto the floor, where he landed with a considerable thud. The letter opener banged off the wall, bounced somewhere. Cunningham was babbling incoherently, staggered to his feet, struggled to get to the door. He kept ducking, waving his arms, shouting things that weren't words, wrenching wildly at the locks on the door.

Ed swept through again. Cunningham fell down in the hallway, clutching the side of his face.

The door swung open.

He crawled through.

She heard him falling down the front stairs, heard the door to the street open and shut.

He was making terribly pitiful sounds.

She sat on the floor waiting for her heart to stop pounding. Finally, after being very glad at the thought that the Clemons family downstairs was in Europe, after wondering just who had been following her to Bradley's, Celia got up and slowly padded around the edge of the couch.

Barefoot, she stepped on something soft and slippery, like a tongue. She leaped back, turned on the lamp, and looked down. Ed had joined her, perched belligerently on the back of the couch.

Part of Charlie Cunningham lay on the floor.

Slippery with blood.

An earlobe.

Celia got to the bathroom in the nick of time.

And then she called Peter Greco.

Greco listened while the Yankees swept both games from the White Sox. Just as the final out was recorded, the large soft raindrops began spotting the Le Baron's window. It was thundering very softly off to the southwest, moving toward the city. He yawned. Maybe this had been a dumb idea, after all. The evening on Sutton Place had been almost supernaturally quiet. Nothing had happened at the Bassinetti place. He looked at his watch. Eleven-thirty. He yawned again. It had been a long day. When he'd gotten up in the morning, he'd never heard of Celia Blandings and was thinking about the money he'd won the night before and the fun he'd had keeping it from the bozos. Now he was knee deep in something that might be murder. A long day. He hoped Celia had put it all out of her mind and

gone to bed. Then he began thinking about Celia in
bed and realized he liked the thought. She was a
little taller than he was, but what the hell, he'd make
allowances. . . .

A car pulled up about twenty yards behind him
and its lights went out. At night in the rain its color
was indistinguishable. It looked like a Chevy. He
watched in the rearview mirror. A man in a raincoat
got out and dashed through the rain, down the shiny
sidewalk, hands clutched in the pockets. He knew
where he was going. He rang the bell at the Bassinetti
house and stood shifting from one foot to another,
waiting in the steady rain. The door opened, a few
words were exchanged, and he went inside.

Greco didn't think it was Charlie Cunningham,
though it was hard to tell for sure. So Mrs. Bassinetti
had a visitor, though he hadn't actually glimpsed
her. On the radio the post-game scoreboard show had
ended and a talk show had begun. It would keep him
awake. He listened while a caller wanted to talk
about old-time railroad trains. Greco didn't care
about old trains. He was trying to find something else
on the radio when he heard something that could
have been a gunshot. He flicked the radio off and
listened. He heard a similar sound come again, a
muffled crack. He'd heard enough in his life to
recognize a gunshot when he got two quick chances.

The street stayed as quiet as ever, rain drenched,
no pedestrians. He sat waiting, expecting someone to
come out the front door. He didn't want to commit
himself to getting in any deeper. Mrs. Bassinetti was
all trouble, the kind of woman the farther away you
are, the happier life you'll lead. She was also the
kind of woman it was hard to stay away from.

Ten minutes crept wetly past.

He sighed, got out of the car, ran across the street
and up the walk, splashing in the puddles. The door
stood ajar.

He pushed it open and stepped inside, stood still, listening. Music was playing softly on a radio somewhere. The lights were low. Mainly he heard the rain. He closed the door to within a couple of inches of shutting, leaving himself a fast exit route if needed.

The house seemed deserted, but he smelled the gunshots, hanging in the air like bad memories.

He moved down the hallway into the living room. It was unchanged from the day's earlier visit, with one exception. A woman's bathrobe lay across the couch.

Something moved and he looked up.

Mrs. Bassinetti stood in the doorway to the deck where she'd received them that afternoon. She wore a nightgown that clung to her, rain soaked. The black mane was dripping. Cradled in her arms was a bundle of bedraggled fur. Her nightgown was smeared with blood. She was crying, her face running with tears and rain.

"My dog, he killed my dog . . ."

Greco went to her, saw indeed that the dog was dead, its head lolling, tongue out.

"He tried to save me. . . ."

She stared at Greco, her eyes fixed on his eye patch. Slowly she turned toward the deck. She hugged the dog to her breasts.

Sitting with his back to one of the potted palms was a man with a great big mess where his chest had been. He was staring at Greco. A nine-millimeter pistol lay beside him. The rain was hitting him hard, but he was long past complaining.

Greco took the dog gently from Mrs. Bassinetti and laid the body on the floor. When he stood up he saw that underneath the dog she'd been holding a .45 automatic, which accounted for the inert gentleman on the deck. Slowly she let the hand drop to her side.

"What happened?"

She shook her head. "He came in, began threatening me . . . Pepper was barking, nipping at his ankles . . . he kicked her out of the way . . . took out his gun . . . Pepper didn't know how to be afraid, she kept at him . . . he shot her, and I took the gun from the silverware drawer in the dining room . . . when I saw Pepper all bloody I shot him. . . ."

"You'd better sit down," Greco said, leading her back to the living room. "I'll take a look at this guy."

He left her alone and went back to the deck, knelt beside the corpse.

There was a wallet in the inside jacket pocket. He had to yank it to dislodge it. There was a driver's license, some credit cards, a check-cashing card on a bank in Washington. He went through them and somewhere behind him heard a sound on his blind side. "Well, Mrs. Bassinetti, it looks like you've killed a man by the name of Irwin Friborg—"

He heard her hiss: "Hit him!"

There was a shock, a sharp pain exploding in the back of Greco's head, the pain rippling through his neck and down along his spine, and just like Philip Marlowe in the old days, he took a nosedive into a bottomless black pool. . . .

Chapter Fifteen

❧

Charlie Cunningham was in the grip of one of the oldest of mankind's notion, atavistically alive even in the grip of the plastic cynicism of the twentieth century.

He wanted to die at home.

He was sure he was going to die. There was so damn much blood . . . all his. He was going to die, and it didn't even seem like such an unattractive idea. Death. The big sleep. The long good-bye. Dying was fine by him. Save a lot of trouble.

It was dying on the street he wanted to avoid. It would be like dying in the desert with the vultures circling lazily overhead. Only here in the city the vultures would be human, at least barely human, and they'd be thorough. He couldn't bear that. They'd take everything. His Phi Beta Kappa key . . . Damn, he'd always thought he'd be buried with the stupid key.

It was impossible to calibrate the pain in the different parts of the body. As he hobbled along in the rain, his blazer soaked, his pants clinging, his shin on fire, his ankle swelling, one finger probably dislocated, holding a dirty old handkerchief to what was left of his ear . . . as he staggered along, his whole body was crying out for the blessed relief of death. His nose was probably broken, first from the fall over the fence, then in the fall down the stairs from her apartment. His ear throbbed like the kidney stone he'd never had.

He'd never be able to look another bird in the eye!

Christ, it had been like something born in the fevered mind of Stephen King in a vengeful mood. A creature from the stench and fire of the Bottomless Pit.

He hobbled onward, homing in on Perry Street.

Thunder crashed. Sheets of rain hung in the glow of the streetlamps. The streets were slippery with oil and water, lights reflecting like comets.

He stopped and vomited into a trash can near St. Vincent's Hospital, and the violent cleansing of his guts seemed to clear his head. It wasn't far now. He could make it.

He slipped and fell on his knee going up the stairs to the front door, but in the symphony of pain, his knee added only another random note. It was late, and he was stranded in the anteroom of Hell, knowing that he'd overreached himself and had been brought low in this insane attempt to . . . to . . . well, whatever he'd thought he was accomplishing. Fuck it, he had to do something about his ear. . . .

He got the door to his apartment open and fled to the bathroom, turned on the light and almost fainted when he saw himself in the mirror. He dabbed at the sheared edge of his earlobe and it didn't feel so hot. He took four aspirin and wiped the blood and rain off his face. He ran a comb through his beard, then went back to inspecting the ear. The bird's beak seemed to have cauterized the wound to some extent. If he didn't look at it too closely, he might be able to keep from vomiting again. He made a bandage of gauze from the medicine cabinet and taped it on with adhesive. It took a lot of tape, and he wound up with a bigger bandage than Van Gogh. He took two more aspirin because the first four had had a vaguely pleasant effect. Then he washed his other wounds and limped to his closet for clean slacks, shirt, underwear. He changed in the bathroom. Maybe he would live. But now he had to start thinking about the unholy mess he was in. He needed a drink for that. There was no way things could get worse.

He went into the living room and turned on the light.

He made a funny little noise. He'd made a good many that evening. But this was the funniest.

He was staring directly into the eyes of a man—middle-aged, short gray hair, wearing a suit—who was sitting on a love seat with a bullet hole in the center of his forehead.

Charlie Cunningham sagged onto a chair and bit his sleeve to keep from crying out loud.

There was no point in spending the night staring at somebody who just stared back. For fifteen minutes, or forty-five minutes, whatever it was, Charlie Cunningham sat and thought. Everywhere he looked he felt utterly out of his depth, yet his basic plan seemed secure still. He could still do what he'd set out to do.

But what was all this razzmatazz around the edges?

It all started with this damn Blandings woman. . . .

Now he was missing a piece of his own personal ear, the murder plan was no longer a secret, he felt like a man headed for a body cast and traction, Celia Blandings was bound to go to the police with his earlobe as evidence, and there was a dead man sitting in his favorite chair.

And who were the two men who'd been following Blandings?

It had gone way, way beyond the bad dream stage.

He girded himself, got up, and went over to the corpse. How in the name of sweet Jesus was he going to explain this?

Naturally the man's billfold was in his hip pocket, which necessitated a prolonged bout with the dead weight in order to extract it and learn his unwanted guest's identity.

Vincenzo Giraldi. Of Queens.

It meant nothing to him.

He needed help. There was only one place to turn, like it or not.

Well, he didn't like it. He didn't like the feeling of his brain unraveling. His nervous system was fraying. When he thought about things, his psyche began to hurt as much as his body. Impossible. Who was this guy? He frowned at Vincenzo Giraldi. Why wasn't this idiot home asleep in his own bed? Why couldn't anything—ever—be easy?

He called Lefferts, who sounded sleepy. Cunningham had some trouble making himself understood. Finally the editor had grasped the essentials. "You sound funny, man," Lefferts said. "Hey, you know, it's the middle of the fuckin' night—"

"You're right, I do sound funny. You'd never believe how funny I feel. You get the manuscript?"

"Yeah, sure, fine, no prob—"

"Well, everything's going crazy. People are getting killed. Just sit on the damned thing and . . . well, if anything happens to me, go for it, publish the damned thing, call press conferences, call Walter Cronkite and the *Times* and whoever owns CBS this week."

"Boy, you really sound weird, Charlie. You on something or what?"

"Listen to me, asshole, I've got a dead guy I don't know from Adam sitting in my favorite chair, and he's staring at me. I gotta get outa here. Tell Julie Christie my last thoughts were of her."

"Hey, you better get some sleep, man—"

Charlie Cunningham hung up on him. He put on his raincoat and took an umbrella from the closet doorknob. He sighed and said good-bye to poor Vincenzo Giraldi, then limped into the street in search of a cab.

The door to the Bassinetti house stood open, the rain blowing in across the entry hall carpet. Cunningham stopped at the last moment, his finger poised above the bell. Why was the door open? He closed his umbrella and pushed through into the hallway. He heard some music. He went quietly down the hall and stood in the doorway.

She stood by the couch, watching him. She'd been crying, but had apparently stopped. She put her finger to her lips and motioned with her other hand to be quiet, beckoned him into the room. She handed him a heavy statuette of the Goddess Kwan-Yin, which usually decorated an end table. "Hit him," she whispered, and nodded toward the deck. A man was kneeling beside a body. Hell, just another body. Her voice was insistent, almost hypnotic, commanding him. There was something smeared across the front of her nightgown, but all he could see were her large erect brown nipples poking through her wet nightgown. He had no idea what was going on, but nothing seemed to make any difference anymore. He felt her hand on his back pushing him across the room. The kneeling man hadn't looked up. She kept pushing until he stood beside him.

"Hit him!" she hissed.

He lifted Kwan-Yin above his own head and brought it down as hard as he could in his weakened condition. Just before impact the man's head turned a fraction of an inch and Cunningham saw that he wore an eye patch.

There was a solid thud as the statuette whacked into the head. The man slumped forward and sprawled across the body of the evening's second corpse.

Cunningham sat down while she got him a brandy. It didn't seem like a good time to tell her that he had a corpse of his own waiting at home. He socked back the brandy and she poured him another. She stood before him, hands on hips, waiting for him to shape up. She'd slipped into gray wool slacks, a silk blouse, and a heavy sweater that hung below her hips.

"Who's the dead man?" he asked, throat and belly on fire with the brandy. "Who's the other guy, for that matter? Who killed Pepper?"

"The dead man killed Pepper," she said. Her eyes bored into him, as if she were looking for cracks in his nervous system.

"And who killed him?"

"I did."

"Jesus! Who did I hit?"

"A man called Greco. He was here this afternoon with a Miss Blandings." Her voice was festooned with sarcasm. "Ring a bell?"

"Oh, God . . ."

"I have no idea what he came here for tonight, and I certainly didn't have time to find out. But he had to be nosing around for the same reason they were here for this afternoon. Now listen to me, Charlie. We've got to stick to our plan . . . and we'll have to get rid of this body. We must get it down to the car and dump it somewhere—"

"What about Greco?"

"I don't know, I'm thinking. He doesn't look awfully good at the moment. You probably fractured his skull. First, we get the other body out of the way—"

"Christ, how can you be so calm?"

"Because I'm a homicidal maniac, you fool. Now let's get moving before Greco wakes up."

The corpse provided a considerable challenge. With his various injuries, Cunningham found himself unable to carry or drag him for any distance. There was no strength in his wrist. And the damned woman had looked at his ear bandage and refused to ask him what happened. Cold-blooded bitch . . .

"This isn't working," she said. "You're hopeless. We'll have to drop him—"

"What? Drop him where?"

"Over the railing, of course. Quickest way."

Cunningham shuddered. He peered over the railing. Far below, the rain bounced and danced on the shiny bonnet of the Rolls.

"Come on," she said, "hurry up." She was tugging at the corpse of Irwin Friborg. He reached down, got the dead weight under the arms, hoisted, then slid his grasp down to the hips and lifted. His ankle gave way under the weight, he slipped forward into one of the huge pots and lost control of the late Mr. Friborg, who plummeted over the railing. His arms flailed in the rain like a bottom-heavy bird trying to take flight. Then his descent was abruptly interrupted by the driver's front fender of the Rolls. Friborg bounced sluggishly and landed on his back in a deep puddle, one arm outstretched. He looked like he was waving good-bye.

Cunningham slowly followed her down the back stairway, trying to ignore her orders to hurry up. The rain was heavier, if anything, and he was getting soaked again.

"My God, look, just look at that fender!"

"I didn't aim him," he shouted back, still trotting carefully behind her.

"If you had, you'd have missed!" She unlocked the trunk and ducked back out of the rain. "Come on, what are you waiting for? Get him into the trunk!"

He pulled and tugged, and dripping with sweat as well as rain, finally lifted the legs up into the cavernous interior and slammed the lid. The traffic on the FDR was so loud it seemed to be running in one ear and out the other. He came back to her, leaned against the wall, out of breath.

"What about Greco?" he asked.

"Come back upstairs . . ."

Gasping, he followed her. "What are we gonna do?"

She stood in the kitchen, dabbing at her face with a fresh towel. "Kill him," she said.

"I won't do it," he said, shaking his head.

"He knows about us. He knows everything—why do you think he came here? Now don't argue with me, you'll bloody well do as you're told."

She went into the dining room, picked up the .45, held it out to him.

He took it. He watched her go to the deck.

"Oh, damn!" she said, stamping her foot.

He went to the deck and looked down and sighed with relief.

Greco was gone.

Chapter Sixteen

❧

For a while he saw two of everything, which made it all a little dicey on the drive through the rain to the Village. Once he got to Fifth Avenue he was all right. It was just past three o'clock and there wasn't any traffic. It was like having the city to himself, and he needed every damn inch of it.

He parked in front of a fire hydrant and looked up at her windows. It hadn't occurred to him to go anywhere else. Now that people were getting killed, it was a whole new ball game. First thing you did, you made sure your partner was all right. So, why did she have all the lights on in the middle of the night?

He leaned on her buzzer. His legs weren't too good yet, but that was to be expected. Just so he didn't start throwing up. He buzzed again and left his finger on the button. He heard a window opening, and stepping back out into the rain, looked up.

"It's me," he called. "Greco." The sound of his voice felt like a wedge being driven into a frontal lobe. "Lemme in, Slats, I'm gonna keel over out here."

He heard her answering buzz, lunged unsteadily through the door.

She found him sitting on the steps halfway to the second floor. "Are you all right? What are you doing?"

She sounded okay. She was okay.

"Praying. Waiting for a St. Bernard. I don't know

what I'm doing." He stood up, grabbed the banister and pulled himself the rest of the way.

"You look awful—"

"You're a vision. I gotta sit down. Keep that goddamn bird away from me."

"Come in," she said. She'd never been so glad to see anyone in her life. She took his arm and felt him lean on her. "What happened to you?"

He laughed, winced, and collapsed on the sofa.

"What is that?" he said, pointing, squinting.

"Oh, well, that's a piece of ear—"

"Of what?"

"Just an earlobe. I thought I ought to keep it as evidence—"

"Works for me." He looked up at her. His vision was blurring again. "You're strangely beautiful. Both of you."

"Are you drunk? You don't smell drunk—"

"Tell me, whose ear is that?"

"It's a long story. Oh, God, you've got blood all over your neck. What happened?" She knelt on the couch beside him and peered at his head. "You've been sapped!"

"Please don't make me laugh."

She touched the matted hair and he jerked away, flinching. She stood up and cinched and knotted the belt of her robe. "I'm going to clean your head, you just stay put."

"Who used to be connected to this ear, Slats?"

"Charlie Cunningham." She headed off to the bathroom.

Greco closed his eyes. Somehow that only made things worse.

He sat quietly while she washed the wound with warm water. She brought him a glass of water and

two Advil. He gulped them down and leaned back
on the couch, smiling up at her.

"That's good work, Slats. I feel a hundred percent
better." He took her hand and squeezed it, held on
for an extra moment. "Thanks," he said. "Now sit
down. It makes my head hurt to look up."

She sat down at the other end of the couch. She
couldn't stop smiling. "I'm so glad you're here, Peter,
really I am. I've been calling you and calling you. Are
you all right now?"

"I'm fine. Now tell me about this ear—"

"In a minute. What happened to your head?"

He told her. Then she told him. It was four o'clock.

"I don't get it," she said, mystified by the pattern
that had to be there but remained resolutely hidden.

"It's a mosaic," he said. He shrugged. "I just keep
trying to see the picture but it won't come clear.
Thing that worries me now is time. And old Charlie
doesn't sound like he's in very good shape. Mentally
or physically. I mean this is one desperate guy . . .
that's the kind of guy really scares me—"

"So that little buck and wing you were doing when
you went off to shoot pool was just an act! I don't
need protecting from the harsh realities, Peter—"

"I guess not." He tried not to look at the earlobe,
which was wrapped in a baggie. "I promise not to
protect you anymore, okay?" He smiled crookedly,
his lip curling up, joining a thin scar below the black
patch.

"Okay," she said. "I'm a full partner in this, the
senior partner, in fact. Now, about Charlie Cunningham—he really seemed sort of crazy, like he wasn't
thinking straight at all."

"What bothers me is there's too many shooters in
this game, you need a scorecard. We got a dead man
Mrs. Bassinetti says she killed—who was he? He
breaks in, shoots her dog, but what did he want from
her? Does it have anything to do with Cunningham?"

"It must!"

He nodded slowly. "Sure. But what? It's a violence matrix, but what does it mean? Then someone sneaks up behind me and knocks me for a loop, but it wasn't Mrs. B. She had to know who it was, she was standing right there . . . but who was it? Cunningham was ready for a hospital when he left here, by the sound of it . . . so who and what else is she involved with? Then I wake up and the body's gone, Mrs. B is gone, the guy who hits me is gone, I'm all alone with a dead dog. I get up seeing at least two of everything and walk out the front door and drive away. Getting back to you, Cunningham says he saw two guys get out of a car and follow you to Bradley's. Who would be following you? Who could have a reason? Cunningham knows you've stumbled into the murder thing, let's say he did tell Mrs. Bassinetti—but when he came out of the Strand he made *two* calls. Who did he call besides Mrs. B? Did that call produce two guys tailing you? Was it Z? And these two guys are still out there. If they were watching you a few hours ago, they're watching now. Which means they now know I'm in this too. Yet they haven't made a move. They're just watching . . . but why? What do they want? What do they know about you that makes them watch?"

"It's got to be the murder plan," she said. She was too tired to connect any of the dots. "My brain is tired," she said in a Gumby voice.

"We need some sleep. I'm trying to think about tomorrow but I'm drawing a blank. Let me crash on this couch, Slats. I don't really want to drag the wreckage home—"

"You're supposed to stay here."

She went to the bedroom and brought back a blanket and a pillow. She was fussing over him when he put his hand on her arm. "Go get some sleep. I'm just fine."

"Look, it's been a weird night. I got pretty scared and . . . well . . . could I sleep out here with you? Boy, I feel like a wimp—I just don't want to be alone. Can I?"

He grinned and made a space for her.

She tucked her robe tight and lay down beside him. "Am I an idiot? Am I crowding you?"

"Relax. You're not an idiot, you're not crowding me."

She burrowed down against him, her back to him. She felt his arm resting across her. "Sometimes I snore."

"I can outsnore you any night." He sighed deeply.

The rain kept drumming on the deck.

"You know, Peter, you really do jump in with both feet, don't you? I mean, you didn't have to go to Bassinetti's tonight, you went on your own. You could have gotten yourself killed—"

"Don't romanticize me, Slats. I didn't know anything was going to happen . . . it was just something to do—"

"Sure, sure, something to do." She lay quietly for a moment, listening to the rain, watching it streak the windows. Ed shifted on his perch. Cunningham's ear had apparently satisfied his killer instinct for the night. "You still awake?"

"Yeah, My head aches. I'm tender. Be very gentle with me, okay?"

"Who are you really? And what happened to your eye? Do you mind my asking?"

"Nope."

"You don't seem like a cop, you don't strike me as much of an organization man."

"Ah, now you begin to see the essential Greco," he said. She felt his breath whispering at her hair. "I'm not much of an organization man, I'm a trouble-maker, they've been telling me that all my life. I guess that's why I've got only one eye. It all comes

down to ego. I've had plenty of time to think about it
the last few years. Thing is, I've got way too much
ego for my own good. See, I spent most of my career
undercover, I wasn't just your everyday cop. Undercover," he mused, "it's a strange, kinda unreal life,
right on the edge of something bad happening all the
time. You can understand better than most people,
maybe—it's a little like being an actor. You pretend
to be someone you're not, but the play is always
changing without warning, everybody's always im-
provising . . . sometimes the line begins to blur,
you start becoming the person you're pretending to
be. Anyway, you gotta have a real king-sized ego
problem to go undercover. You gotta believe you can
handle anything, no matter what goes down—you're
most alive when it's most dangerous, because nothing's too tough, nothing's too dangerous, not for you,
'cause you're the best there is—and that's all ego,
pure ego, whatever you think you're proving.

"But that wasn't enough for this guy—oh, no, not
for Greco. I found out I was in the middle of a big
narcotics scam going on within the department, cops
stealing confiscated drugs and dealing them, sometimes back to the Mafia and sometimes through their
own connections. Get it? Real sleazy.

"Now you gotta understand, I was a good cop, I
was liked, y'know. I did a damn good job. I was a
cop's cop, one of the boys. So I saw this real bad
thing going down—not the penny ante stuff every
cop was in on back then—this was major and I went
along with it, a major drug ring—cops wasting guys
with big shipments, Colombians, Mafia, anybody,
and selling their goods. I even made some money
and got myself a broker down on Wall Street. But
then a coupla kids got hit by a coupla cops I knew,
guys I drank beer with and went to the ball games
with, but they blew these two kids away like it was
another day at the office. And my ego got into the
game, see?

"I coulda just looked the other way, figured what the hell? But I couldn't. I had to do something, push myself into the foreground. It takes a huge ego to betray your fellow officers, the guys who were your best friends, your family. That's what these guys were, these cops—they were my family, I *loved* these guys. But I went to a couple reporters I knew and got the story to them—once they knew the names and dates and places, I had my insurance, so I wasn't scared to go to Internal Affairs, and I gave them all the same stuff. They didn't have any choice, they *had* to do something.

"So they wired me and I went in, in return for immunity, and I nailed a lotta guys, guys I knew and liked and had depended on for my life more times than I could count . . . I nailed 'em, Slats. It takes a helluva lot of ego to betray people that close to you—"

"But you did what you knew was right," she protested.

"That's a matter of opinion, once you get into questions about where your loyalties lie. I wasn't a white knight. I was reinforcing my ego. It's always ego. Ego makes the saint what he is, makes the villain what he is, makes the traitor what he is . . . made me what I am."

"I like what you are," she murmured, felt him stroke her hair.

"Which brings us to my eye."

"You don't have to tell me, if it bothers you—"

"Takes more than that to bother me. When I had two eyes, I was just another guy. With the eye patch I got charisma. It was a miracle. Drove chicks wild, it was worth it." He laughed darkly. She could feel it move her hair.

"So tough," she said softly, "such a macho man."

"Well, here's what happened. Somewhere along the line, deep in the belly of Internal Affairs, somebody high up leaked word of what I was doing, let 'em know the fit was about to hit the shan if I got before the grand jury. Well, a couple of the lads—not guys I knew—had a talk with me one night. They were not your average Rhodes scholars, they didn't quite know what they were doing, gettin' down and dirty with the boss. I killed one of them with a brick wall, put the other one in the hospital for a year or so. But in the course of our discussion I wound up with one eye hanging down my cheek, four broken ribs, a skull fracture, a broken leg, damn near a broken back. Easy come, easy go, right?

"About forty cops went down on my testimony, including my old partner, the guy who broke me in. I remember one time he said to me, 'Pete, Serpico's one thing. Nobody really holds all that shit against Frank. He was never one of us, he had a beard for chrissake, and in those days the only guys with beards were the ones throwing rocks at cops. Serpico was never one of us, so what he did, well, what would you expect from an asshole with a beard? But you, Pete, you were one of us, none better than Pete Greco, and you took us down . . . you're the guy none of us will ever forget or forgive. Too bad the lads didn't kill you, Pete, too damn bad.'

"So ego cost me that eye. And now what do I do? I got plenty of money, but I love to hustle a little pool, play the ponies. I'm a hustler . . . and what's that? It's all ego, my dear. And that's why I'm in this thing with you, Slats. I can't resist. It's another chance to prove I can handle any damn thing. . . ."

She was asleep.

"Good night, Ed," he said into the darkness.

He leaned over and very gently kissed Celia, felt her smile. He closed his eye and in a minute or two, with the sound of the rain lulling him, he was fast asleep.

Chapter Seventeen

❧

Hilary Sampson woke them at eight with a telephone call. She'd be over for breakfast in half an hour, and that was that. Snap to it, she'd be on her way to work. Celia didn't get a chance to say much of anything. Hilary was on one of her efficiency kicks and was running by the clock.

Celia was in and out of the shower in five minutes, dressed in another five. Jeans, a gingham checked red-and-white blouse, beaten-up white Top-Siders she'd worn for ten years. By the time she'd come back and headed for the kitchen counter, Greco had opened the door to the deck and was stretching, groaning, taking deep lungsful of the heavy gray mist hanging in the courtyard trees.

"Your turn," she said, getting out the carton of Tropicana orange juice. "Hilary's on her way over. You'd better hop to it. Clean towels are on the rack next to the tub. You take orange juice?"

"Sure, sure," he muttered. He moved slowly across the room, scratching his head, shuffling. "Don't be alarmed," he said over his shoulder. "Age tends to show first thing in the morning. In my case, all forty-five years. I get better as the morning goes on."

Celia split several bagels and toasted them, wondering about Peter Greco. She'd slept—actually slept—with him last night, and she'd felt so comforted and protected and so . . . what? So happy he was there? Hmmm. She found lox, cream cheese, strawberry jam, butter. She put the works on a tray, which she carted over to the pool table. She went back to the counter, ground Gillies coffee beans and got the coffee brewing. Why had she been so happy? He hadn't done anything—in fact, he was the one who needed protection, with his head practically in pieces. But there was something about him. Hmmm. Maybe it was the ego thing he'd been talking about while she slowly let herself drift off to sleep. Maybe the sheer ego of his contention that he could handle anything had fortified her feeling of well-being. . . . Hmmm.

She was perched at the table finishing her juice when Hilary arrived, threw down a voluminous leather shoulder bag, looked at breakfast, and said: "You think this is enough for the two of us?" She shook her head, the red hair snapping. "Or were you expecting maybe the Mormon Tabernacle Choir?"

"Well, the fact is—"

"I'm the one with the facts," Hilary interrupted. She took a sheet of notes from the pocket of her raincoat and drained a glass of juice. "You left your shower running."

"Oh, no, that's—"

"Okay, so, let's get down to cases here. I was up at the *Times* until one o'clock this morning, finding out about this Bassinetti bunch and," she announced proudly, "I'm going to knock your socks off for you. First, where's the murder letter?"

"Ah. I hid it."

"Well, come on, get it. What's the matter with you, anyway? You look sort of glassy-eyed—"

"I was up late too." Celia turned to Ed and unlocked the cage. Ed gave her a discouraged look and backed away along the perch. An unwarranted intrusion. "Excuse me, Eddie boy." She lifted the newspaper in the bottom of his cage, felt around, and withdrew the murder letter. Hilary was staring at her, bemused. "Best hiding place I could find," Celia said. "Ah, here it is." She spread it flat on the table.

"Hi, Hilary."

Hilary frowned, spun around and saw Peter Greco. He was standing in the hallway, his face covered in shaving cream. "Lucky you had some of this stuff, Slats. I'm gonna have to use your cute little razor, okay?"

"Be my guest. You *are* my guest."

Greco went away. Hilary turned back to Celia, a smile slowly spreading across her freckled face. "You devil," she whispered. "You cunning devil! I mean, so fast! But you heard what I said, I was right—you do like him!" She grinned her battle-of-the-sexes grin at Celia.

"It's not what you think—"

"Of course not. I always say if it looks like a duck, walks like a duck, and quacks like a duck, chances are it's a duck. I knew you'd like him, he's not a run of the mill guy—"

"Hilary! He almost got killed last night working on my case—"

"Ha! I'll bet! You've got to be gentle—"

"Mrs. Bassinetti killed a man last night and Peter showed up and somebody broke his head open, knocked him out, and he came here practically ready to collapse . . . and then I told him about Ed biting off Cunningham's ear—"

"Whoa! I think I've missed most of this story. Just what's been going on since last we convened?" Hilary started piling cream cheese and lox on one of the toasted bagels.

By the time Celia had summarized the previous day, Greco had reappeared, looking reasonably chipper for a man who'd survived one very arduous day.

"My head still hurts like a pisser, I must admit," he observed in his favorite classical style, pouring himself a cup of coffee.

Hilary just stared, chewing.

By the time they were all munching away, and Ed was looking hungry and more than a little peevish since he coveted lox, Hilary got to the results of her researches. It had taken a good bit of digging, which was what Hilary, fortunately, did best.

"In the first place," she said, pointing at the murder letter, item by item, "I've got your Director for you. Emilio Bassinetti, Director of the Palisades Center. He's got to be the intended victim, right?"

"What's the Palisades Center?" Celia asked.

"Sounds like a racquetball complex," Greco said.

"The truth is a little murky, but on the surface it's a very low profile, high intensity think tank, right across the Hudson in the Jersey Palisades. From what I could find out from reading between the lines and talking to some of the guys on the night shift, it's chock full of political experts working out endless scenarios. You know the kind of thing—from planning to melt the polar ice caps to invading and annexing Central America to calculating the effects of meltdowns in nuclear power plants, particularly if we could make that happen in other countries' plants. Get it?"

"Sure," Greco said, "but do they know the only player who was active when Babe Ruth hit his last home run and when Hank Aaron hit his first?"

Hilary looked at him as if he were an unruly student. "I don't know if they do, but I certainly do. It was one of the all-time great Cubs, Phil Cavaretta. Now could we get back to business, please? Or has the beating you took completely deranged you?"

Greco tried not to look surprised. "Sure, go ahead. How did she know that, Ed?"

"Research is my business. Now, the rumors at the *Times* have it that Palisades is in bed with the CIA, the FBI, and if not them, with the National Security Agency. In other words, tied in with the government in a big way. Right at the top levels. With a special interest these days in some of our friends south of the border . . . which could mean just about anything from exporting revolution to importing drugs." She stopped to refill her coffee cup and grab another bagel.

"What about Bassinetti personally?" Celia was jotting down notes. Linda Thurston certainly would have. While she kept listening, her thoughts replayed the incredible events of the previous day. It was pure Linda Thurston, even down to spending the night in the arms of the wounded warrior.

"Strange guy. He was a professor at Duke, then at Georgetown, in political science. Specializing in Third World countries, or as they were known then, Emerging Nations. But that was quite a while ago, late sixties, early seventies. Then he dropped out of sight in Europe for several years. My people think he was probably working in intelligence for the United States. Then, about ten years ago, he married the present Mrs. Bassinetti, whose name—da-da, get this—is Zoe Madigan, the daughter of an American diplomat in London and a Spanish mother he'd married while serving in Madrid. She became the mystery novelist Miles Warriner shortly after she married Bassinetti. She's in her late thirties, a knock-out, but then you know that already. Sort of social too. At present they maintain homes in Manhattan, in the country in New Jersey, a flat in London, a ranch in Argentina. We're talking very heavy money, folks.

"And, a final note of interest, the Director is a cripple. His horse threw him while he was riding with his wife a few years ago—he was already running Palisades—and he's been in a wheelchair ever since. Can't walk at all. Otherwise he's in good health but has a weight problem. He lives mainly in the country in Jersey, his wife mainly in the city."

Hilary took a deep breath and went back to eating.

"Amazing," Celia said, awed by Hilary's performance.

"I'd say so," Hilary agreed.

Greco stood up, nodding his damaged head gingerly, and went to the bird cage, fixed Ed with his one-eyed stare. "Whattaya think, killer? Zoe, for God's sake. So now we've got that big blank filled in. Zoe is Z. Zoe Bassinetti is behind the whole thing. She wants to off her crippled husband, get the money and four places to live, and she picked a halibut like Mr. Mystery to help her do it." He shook his head in astonishment. "I'd be hesitant about putting my IBM stock on Charlie Cunningham's chances for getting out of today alive. Zoe's gonna kill the Prowler— that's Charlie—right after he puts paid to poor old Emilio. I can see it now, the brave little wife, working her fingers to the bone in the west wing, whipping up her new book, hears a shot from Emilio's study . . . hark! She thinks, could that be a vicious prowler who has just blown my poor crippled hubby's head off? I'd better get my nifty little Smith and Wesson and go see. . . . Egad, it is! Shriek, shriek, bang-bang, Mr. Mystery bites the dust and Zoe is free and rich." He looked at the two women. "It's simple, classic, I like it. Except it's all screwed up now because we've got the letter . . . and if anyone knows she's screwing Charlie, that would cast some doubt on her innocence. But," he reasoned, arguing with himself, "she could say yes, I made a girlish mistake with this dashing fellow and I do have this impotent husband, sob, sob, but I saw the light, broke off my affair, and he came here in a rit of fealous jage to have it out with my husband, la-di-da-di-da. It could work ladies. Or it could have worked . . ." He nodded at the piece of paper on the tabletop. "If we hadn't come up with this."

"But what about the Rolls and the Trunk and the Clean getaway?" Hilary consulted the paper, rapping it with a finger.

"That's easy," Celia said. She was getting the hang of the game. "All that's window dressing for Charlie's benefit. He doesn't know she's going to kill him—so his getaway route is important to him. He's got to think she has a great plan. Right, Peter?"

"That's the way I see it. She has her real plan, and the plan she's made up for Charlie Cunningham's sake—"

"But what's in it for Charlie?" Hilary asked.

"We've seen Mrs. Bassinetti," Greco said.

"Sex? You mean Charlie's in this 'cause he's that crazy about her?"

"Hilary," Celia said, sounding like an expert, "sex is the main cause of murder in the family."

Greco came back to the table. "So tonight's the night, Charlie shoots him right in the middle of Dan Rather. All we have to do is warn him."

"Then why do you look so perplexed?"

"There's funny stuff going on, that's why. Like the guy Mrs. Bassinetti shot last night. Friborg. Where does he fit in? Everytime we learn something, like Z is for Zoe, we get a new unknown. There's something about Friborg . . . swear to God, I dreamed about him last night. I know him from somewhere, or I've heard his name, something. Irwin Friborg. I'm gonna have to make a call about him. And then there are the two men following Celia. Where did they come from?"

There was a long pause, which didn't solve anything.

Celia finally said: "When you look at this one way, it's really pretty crazy. I mean, the Director sounds like a scary and important guy because of his place in the intelligence community—but it seems like he's a murder target for purely domestic reasons. If such a man were going to be murdered, you'd think it would have something to do with the kind of work he does. . . . Think how much he must know. Think how valuable he must be. But it's his wife who's planning to kill him—"

"One of life's little ironies," Hilary said. She finished her coffee, looked at her watch, and said she'd better be on her way.

"What I can't figure out," Celia continued, "is why the Director doesn't have all kinds of bodyguards around him. You'd think his bosses, whoever they are, would have his life under a microscope. What if he sold secrets? Or defected to the Russians? You'd think they'd know all about his marriage and his wife having an affair. A man confined to a wheel-chair with a beautiful wife, that sounds like a prescription for disaster. So where's his protection? He's a sitting duck and nobody but us seems to care—"

"We don't know that," Greco said. "He may be surrounded by guys from the Outfit. We just don't know. We're still in the dark about an awful lot of this, and it makes me nervous. And I keep thinking about Friborg. . . ."

Celia got up and started loading the tray.

"So what are we waiting for? Let's get the show on the road!"

Greco looked at her and smiled. She didn't know enough about stuff like this to know how easy it was just to lose your life before you even noticed it was going anywhere. She didn't know enough to be scared. She wanted to save the World. Well, if not the World, at least the Director. Greco lit a cigarette and wondered if the Director was worth saving.

Chapter Eighteen

❧

Jesse Lefferts sat at his desk in the Pegasus Building and stared at the gray smudge hanging like bad breath over the city. The wooden water tanks on rooftops were sodden and streaked with rain. He was exhausted, but there was enough adrenaline rushing around to fuel the National Football League.

Before him on the desk lay the briefcase with a newly broken lock and the forbidden manuscript Charlie Cunningham had entrusted to him for the interim before publication. He truly hadn't intended to read it until Charlie gave him the go-ahead. He'd thought he'd go along with the letter of his instructions just to keep the whole thing kosher and in one piece.

But the midnight call from Charlie had cancelled all his obligations and good intentions. He'd lain there, slowly coming awake once Charlie had hung up, and reality had begun dawning. If people were getting killed, as Charlie said, then all bets were off. He was going to read the manuscript. First thing in the morning he'd cancel his meetings for the day, his lunch date, and devote all his attention to the manuscript.

He got up to get a drink, went back to bed, and realized there was no way he could get back to sleep. It was hopeless. He got back up and dressed quickly, with his heart beginning to race and his palms moistening. People getting killed? What the hell was in the pages in his office?

Eight hours later he turned the last page and his breath, which he felt he'd been holding the whole time, slowly escaped from a very dry mouth. He kept seeing little black dots and stars at the corners of his vision. Dead ahead was his coveted senior editorship. At last. And the publishing event of the decade. At least.

It was bigger than the Pentagon Papers. Bigger than Watergate . . . No wonder people were getting killed.

He put the manuscript back into the ravaged briefcase, took the elevator down to the lobby, and went to a nearby coffee shop for breakfast. He kept the briefcase tight beside him on the booth's seat, hidden by newspapers. He ordered an omelette and fries and a Danish and coffee, and when it came he couldn't eat it. His stomach wouldn't let him. His belly felt like it had been hot-wired.

So far as he could tell from his reading, the book would destroy the presidency of the sitting incumbent, leave the careers of a great many cabinet members, senators, and representatives in flaming ruins, demolish the intelligence community as we knew it . . . while making Jesse Lefferts, if he managed to live through it, the hottest editor of the year. The book would finance Pegasus House's entire list, and sure as hell would have the book clubs kicking themselves around the block in the competition to get it. The paperback advance would be astronomical. The serial rights, the foreign rights . . . and the ecstasy at the new ownership, the Omega/Conclave Group, would be unprecedented. And Jesse Lefferts would be golden.

He paid the bill and went back to the office. He refused to look in the men's room mirror. It would be awful and he would lose his nerve, and doubts as to his course of action would set in. Instead he took a deep breath and called the office at the top of the tower, where Admiral Arthur T. Malfaison, USN (ret.), served as the chairman and chief executive officer of Pegasus. He had been on the job less than a year but his impact on company morale had been enormous. Admiral Malfaison, fifty-nine years old, had given Pegasus a strong new presence in the world of publishing. Which meant he was a go-getter; he went-and-got with the heaviest of the heavyweights. Gloria Vanderbilt, Prince, Michael Korda, George Steinbrenner, Richard Gere, Jack Kemp, Barbra Streisand, Steven Spielberg, George Bush, Ed Koch—the Admiral was everywhere. He was also customarily in his office by seven-thirty. He was a party-goer and a party-giver, and he lunched with Marvin Davis at "21" and was always in the columns, devoting his presence to one worthy chari-table cause or another, and sometimes seen standing next to a Guest or a Whitney or Jackie O. in the society-page photos. He had grasped the publishing world by the throat, shaken loose and gathered several hugely successful authors whose contracts had run their courses with other houses. He had resurrected the career of a faded movie starlet with a workout book, rescued another from oblivion with her tome on breast enlargement through self-hypno-sis, and had seen to the publication of *Tripe*, the trashiest and hottest selling novel/miniseries deal of the year. In an acquisitive firm, the Admiral led by example. He saw, he liked to say, his duty to the public and stockholders and Omega/Conclave, and he did it as best he could. He was going to be amazed at what Jesse Lefferts had for him this dark, dreary morning.

Chapter Nineteen

❧

Mason watched Green drinking coffee from the Styrofoam cup. Mason was sitting behind the wheel of the Chevy, holding his own cup to warm his hands. The coffee Green had fetched on command from a coffee shop on Sixth Avenue was scalding, impossible—in Mason's view—to drink as yet. But somehow Green was slurping it down. How did he do it? Mason watched the unconcerned Green and decided there was something wrong with him. Maybe he was impervious to pain. That was frightening. It was all right to be resistant to pain. You were supposed to resist it, master it. But nobody was impervious. Impervious was crazy.

It was a dirty, dishwatery, dispiriting morning, if you were prey to such fluctuations in the weather. Fortunately Mason wasn't. But the rain was steady, washing muck out of the atmosphere, and Mason didn't have an umbrella. Which was another reason why Green had to go get the coffee. That, and because Mason was senior.

Neither of them seemed to need much sleep. Green had been all pumped up when he'd come back to the car after killing the man who'd walked in on him at Cunningham's place. He had wanted to sleep. His motor had been racing when he told Mason what had happened. Mason had calmed him down, thinking to himself that Green seemed to have enjoyed the killing too much. Some guys got off on killing people, said it was better than the best lay of their lives. Mason thought maybe Green was one of those guys. That was crazy too. Mason was pretty uninvolved when it came to killing somebody. If you had to do it, you did it and forgot about it. He'd even regretted it once, when he'd had to do a job for the IRS. He'd killed a man who had too much inside dope on an IRS operation involving heavy skimming by a couple of top regional collection people tied back into Washington. Mason hadn't wanted to do it. He hated the IRS more than he'd have believed he could have hated anything. As far as he was concerned, they were the only *really* bad guys.

Green smacked his lips noisily and turned his gaze on Mason. "Good coffee. Don't you want yours?"

"Yes. I want it."

Mason wondered about Cunningham's absurd departure from Miss Blandings's apartment. Something horrible seemed to have happened to the man, but Mason couldn't tell what. He'd looked like a threshing machine had driven over him.

Greco's arrival had taken him by surprise. Who was this guy with the eye patch? When he didn't come out, though he'd passed across the front windows of her apartment, Mason decided he must be her lover. Maybe she'd stay in bed with him all day and forget about the Director. It would be so much easier that way. All Mason wanted to do was keep her out of the picture without revealing himself. He tried to recall the last time things had gone easily. He couldn't.

The woman in the raincoat. She meant nothing to Mason. And when she eventually left, he hadn't been sure she'd even visited the Blandings apartment, though he thought she'd pressed that button.

Once Miss Blandings and Eyepatch left, Green said: "Shouldn't we follow them?"

"The apartment must be empty now," Mason mused.

"Weren't we supposed to keep an eye on her? Keep her out of this?"

"Don't worry. It's my hindquarters, not yours. The Director's right where he should be, everything's fine."

"I don't know," Green said doubtfully.

"I do, Greenie. Relax."

"I guess you're the boss."

"Nice you remember that. Now let's go take a look in there."

"What for?"

"Maybe you'll find somebody to shoot."

"What?"

"Maybe we'll find the manuscript the General's afraid might be floating around. Maybe she wrote it. Maybe the guy with the eye patch wrote it. Let's just go see, Greenie."

A few minutes later Mason was staring into the cold eye of a very large bird who had ostentatiously stalked into his cage and slipped the bolt into place when the two men had entered the room. Mason regarded the beak and thought, There is a bird with one hell of an edge.

"Polly want a cracker?" Green said softly.

The bird stared hard at him, then relieved himself on the newspaper in the bottom of the cage.

Mason spoke to the bird. "Manners, manners." The bird cocked an eye at him and came closer, recognizing a kindred spirit.

Green was looking through cardboard boxes full of what might be the manuscript in question. He was kneeling beside them when the front door swung open again. Mason heard the clicking of the latch and turned to see who'd come in.

Two men came quickly into the room. One of them already had a pistol out of his pocket. There was a clunky, tubular silencer on the barrel. He heard the puffing sound and the slug digging into the plastered wall behind him. The big bird started squawking. Mason hit the deck, rolled behind the bulk of the pool table.

Green was very good with a gun. So was Mason, but there was a difference. Green was the fastest with a gun Mason had ever seen.

The man who had missed Mason with the first shot had done all the shooting he was going to do.

Green was still on his knees but had the nine-millimeter Baretta out. There were three quick puffing sounds, whoof-whoof-whoof, and Mason peered around the massive carved leg of the pool table to see one man fall sideways into a stereo cabinet, knocking a lamp onto the floor. The other man sagged back into the hallway, dying as he squeezed off a final shot that took a chunk out of the ceiling above the pool table. The sprinkling of plaster drifted down on Mason's hair and glasses and made him sneeze. He had finally gotten his gun out of the shoulder holster, and there was almost no one left to shoot.

Green stood up. He wasn't even shaking. One of the men he'd shot made a dying noise from behind the couch.

Green looked at Mason and smiled.

"You're a dangerous man, Greenie."

"Yeah."

Green's smile broadened.

Mason raised his gun and shot Greenie square in the middle of his smile.

Chapter Twenty

❧

Teddy Birney was a short fat man in a sportcoat that looked like last night's leftovers. He walked fast, talked fast, thought fast, and bounded into Costello's at a breakneck clip. He looked around with slow, circular eyes that missed nothing, and saw Greco waving from one of the booths in back. Herbie, New York's most famous and worst waiter, gave Teddy a dirty look. Teddy brushed him away and settled into the booth beside Greco.

Greco introduced him to Celia as the *Daily News's* top crime reporter. Teddy blushed as he always did when confronted by a pretty woman, and sucked the foam from a beer Greco had waiting for him. Teddy had a column that all the research said was money in the bank.

"So how's the underworld, Teddy?" Greco asked.

"Same old stuff. You got your Satanic cult killers, you got your slasher who's in love with little old ladies, you got your wealthy wife in a permanent coma while hubby is chasing skirts through the after-hours scene, you got your seventy-year-old choir-master diddling the boy sopranos in the organ loft, and you got your shopping-mall ghoul leaving pieces of cheerleaders in trash cans. Same old stuff." He sounded like the winner of a fast-talking contest. His face was getting redder. "How are your sunset years?"

"Soothing, Teddy, very quiet and soothing."

"So what's on your mind? You hawking a tip or

what? The Police Commish is a secret child molester? Old news, old news." He lit a cigarette and coughed something wet and thick in his throat.

"No, nothing like that. I need to pick your brains—"

"Good luck. If you find anything, let me be the first to know." He grinned at Celia and drank some more beer.

"I got a name. Strikes me as somebody I've heard of before, but I'll be damned if I can place him. Friborg. Irwin Friborg."

Teddy Birney pulled his lower lip like a rubber band and let it snap back into place. He dribbled ash onto the table. "Why? What'd he do?"

"He died."

"And how did that happen?"

"Do you know the name?"

"I'm thinking. How did he depart this vale of tears?"

"A woman shot him."

"The woman in the case. You don't sound retired."

"Who was Friborg?"

"I'm working on it. Who's the woman?"

"This is off the record, Teddy—"

"Whatever you say, sport. Who is she?"

"Lady's name is Zoe Bassinetti."

"No kidding? She the wife of that think tank character? Eduardo . . . whatever his name is?"

"Emilio. Yeah, she is."

"Murder, I take it?"

"Maybe self-defense. Friborg offed her dog—"

"Doggie defense? That's novel—"

"Who was Friborg?"

"Hey, you oughta remember Friborg. He was the liaison in the old days between the Commish and Internal Affairs. That's where you must of come across his name, back in your fink days. Maybe even met him—"

Greco shook his head. "I don't think I ever met him, but you're right, that's where I heard the name. So Zoe killed a cop—"

"No, he's not a cop anymore, not the NYPD, anyway." Teddy lit another cigarette off the first, sucked until he got it going. "I don't know where he is now." He pulled his lip again, revealing a set of yellow-stained teeth.

"Try and remember," Celia urged him. "You look like a man who's got a computer bank in his head."

"Well, I am pretty good, come to think of it. Let's see, he left New York, but where the hell did he go? When did the lady kill him?"

"Last night," Celia said.

"Where?"

"Her home. Sutton Place—"

"So why haven't I heard about it?"

"Come on, Teddy," Greco interrupted. "We don't know. I saw the body. She and her boyfriend must have stashed him somewhere. We just want to know who Friborg was working for."

"Well, seems to me I heard Mr. Friborg went to Washington a few years back. I could be wrong, so don't hold me to this. But I'd say he went down there and hired on with the CIA, the FBI, maybe even the IRS. He had a nasty streak, did Irwin. Oughta been right at home down there. Some enforcement agency or other. That's the best I can do, Pete." He finished his beer and wiped his mouth on his sleeve. "Make any sense?"

"If it does, it's bad. I hope to hell you're wrong."

"Whatever. Quid pro quo. Tell me what's going on. Just background me and I'll take it from there. Your name never comes up. You know damn well you can trust me. You trusted me with your life once upon a time."

"Okay, Teddy. But this story is just the tip of a big mean iceberg, you read me?"

* * *

Greco stood in the rain staring at the Le Baron, which had a wet ticket stuck under the windshield wiper. He'd left it by the fire hydrant. Now he grabbed the ticket, crumpled it up, and jammed it into his Yankee jacket pocket.

"Give it to me," Celia said. "Please. You came here for my sake. The least I can do is pay the ticket."

"Can it, Slats," he growled. "I'm not mad at the ticket, I'm mad at what Teddy had to say. Forget it. Let's just get outa here."

"We're going to Palisades right now?"

"Sooner the better."

"Do you think they'll just let us see him?"

"Gotta be resourceful. Think like this Linda Thurston of yours. She'd think of something. We'll just have to make them understand it's a matter of life and death, that's all. But," he cautioned her, "once we warn him, we're out of it, understand? If people like Friborg are involved, then the serious side of the Washington bunch is involved, and that's where you and I had better bail out. Got that?"

"I'm not going to run away, Peter."

He sighed and unlocked the door for her, and she got in. When he was behind the wheel he reached under the dashboard. She heard a metallic thud, and he pulled his hand out with a gun in it.

"Oh, God, Peter! What's that for?"

"It's a Walther PPK for intimidating people—"

"Isn't that a little melodramatic?" She blinked. "I hope—"

"Look, I found a dead man last night and got half brained for my trouble. That may not rile up your blood, but it sure as hell does mine—"

"Okay, okay. Look, before we go, I think I'd better use the bathroom. I don't want to make you start looking for a gas station at the crucial moment—"

"Right, go then. Hurry up. I'll wait down here and shoot anybody who tries to tow me away."

He was smiling to himself, watching her bound up the stairs from the sidewalk. She wore a yellow slicker jacket and jeans. She had long legs and a high, firm rear end, and it was fine by him. He wondered about the men in her life, who they were and where they might be. She hadn't mentioned anyone in the slightly more than twenty-four hours he'd known her. He remembered the smell of her hair as he'd fallen asleep last night . . . or rather this morning. She smelled just fine, and he was wondering if he was about to commence making a fool of himself.

Then he heard her screaming.

The sound pierced the closed doors and windows of the brownstone, and he knew it was Celia. He was out of the car with the Walther in his hand and up the steps, where he was stopped by the locked door. He began pushing the buzzer through the wall, finally heard the answering buzz and was through the door, hurling himself up the narrow staircase, knowing he was making himself a hell of a target, knowing he had to get to Celia.

She was standing outside her doorway and the screaming had stopped. She was staring at him, her wide mouth open and her large dark eyes full of fright. She was pointing into the apartment, shocked into silence. At just that moment, in one of those crazily inappropriate mind tricks, she looked like Mary Tyler Moore doing a very long take.

The top half of a man extended through the doorway onto the hall carpet runner. He was staring the walleyed stare of the dead. His face was terribly pale, showing a thick black overnight growth of beard, and looked like he'd seen a ghost and died of fright. But Greco knew there had to be a bullet hole or two somewhere. Even as he looked quickly at the corpse, he was thinking ahead, recognizing a full-blown nightmare when he saw one.

He stepped across the man and went into the apartment with his Walther ready to go to work.

Another man was stretched out behind the couch. A lamp with its ceramic base shattered lay beside him. Some records had been swept off the stereo cabinet as he fell. An eyelid flickered, the eye came into view like a bloodshot marble.

Greco knelt, felt for a pulse in the throat. Celia gasped behind him, covered her mouth with one hand. There was faint throbbing in the man's throat. The eyes were halfway into eternity and had given up any hope of getting back to shore. He'd lost a lot of blood from a chest wound. His white shirt was soaked with it. He was almost gone, bubbles of pink saliva expanding, bursting on his gray lips.

Greco leaned down. "What is it, man? Who did this? Why were you here?" He put his ear close to the lips and felt the last frail breaths.

"Pete . . . for chrissake . . ."

"Louie. It's bad, Louie," Greco said.

"No shit . . ." The man struggled to swallow, as if it made a difference anymore.

"Why, Louie?"

"Some . . . book or something . . . the General . . . funny, I don't hurt anymore . . . Pete . . . whatta mess . . ."

"What book?"

"General's . . . scared . . . shitless . . ." He sighed heavily, and Greco thought for a moment he was gone. "Everybody . . . dyin' for a . . . for a stupid . . . book—" He coughed, licked weakly at his lips.

"Who did this? Who shot you?"

"Sy . . . sy . . ."

"Say it, Louie. Time's almost up—"

"Psycho . . ."

"Psycho?"

"Psycho . . . Branch . . ."

Then he gave a gentle little cough, like an apology, and died.

Celia was leaning over, close to Greco. She smelled the blood. "What did he say? Could you hear him?"

Greco sighed and nodded. He closed the man's eyes with his fingertips. "You know what Teddy said about Friborg? CIA, FBI, IRS, all that?"

She nodded, trying not to look at the dead man.

"Well, Teddy was almost right. He just left out Psycho Branch."

"What's that? Sounds like a joke."

"If it's a joke, it's the absolute worst. Psycho Branch works for all the alphabet agencies—the worst, the dirtiest jobs, the stuff other people won't touch. When you start talking about bad dudes, you start with Psycho Branch. It doesn't have a real name, it isn't funded openly by anyone, it doesn't even exist. The funding is hidden in twenty different budgets. It just *is* . . . it's just Psycho Branch."

"He just told you that?"

"Yeah."

"Did he call you Pete?"

"That he did. I knew this guy a long time ago. Louie Manfredi. Mafioso. Hit man, general muscle, works mainly in the drug trade. Knew him from the undercover days . . . used to shoot a little pool with old Louie here."

"The Mafia's in my apartment," she said weakly. Her voice trembled and she started to stand back up. Her legs weren't all that steady.

"Seems so. Mafia here, Psycho Branch at Bassinetti's." He rolled his eyes and made a helpless gesture with his hands. "Slats, we're up to our asses in alligators. We're in the middle of a Hitchcock movie he never got around to making—'The Woman Who Knew Too Much.' You're the woman."

She pushed herself up on the back of the couch and felt her breath catch in her throat, her stomach drop away.

"Oh, no," she whispered, "there's another one. He's right in the middle of Linda Thurston."

Greco got up and looked across the couch at the body huddled against the cardboard boxes. He circled the couch and didn't have to check to see if the guy was alive. Also, he wasn't Mafia. He had the Friborg look, all that calm, neat, weird control that hallmarked Psycho Branch. "Well, he didn't bleed on her. . . ." He stared down into what had been a man's face. The back of his head was all over the wall. He didn't want Celia to see the mess. "Come here," he said, taking her arm and leading her to a chair. She sat down with her back to the wall.

"You okay, Slats? You look a little peaked—"

"Oh, Peter, I don't know." She felt sick to her stomach. It was like finding Cunningham's ear. Worse. Only now she had Peter. "I don't understand any of this. . . ." She couldn't stop shivering. "Psycho Branch, the Mafia, I don't know . . ."

He took her cold, clammy hand in his. "It all comes back to Palisades."

"Hold me a minute, will you?"

He knelt in front of her. Her eyes were blank with shock.

"I want to be brave about this, like Linda Thurston, but I've got three corpses in my living room and I don't know their names or why they were here, and I don't know what Linda Thurston would have done because I've never actually written a book and they wouldn't be scary like this anyway because she's sophisticated and goes to opening night parties and this is all so horrible and I can smell the blood and—"

He took her face in his hands. "You want a kiss from a one-eyed tough guy?"

"Oh, God, I do, I do . . ."

He pressed his mouth against hers, his fingertips tracing the line of her jaw, willing her to be still, slowly pulling her to him.

She began to cry, but he didn't stop kissing her and didn't stop holding her. She'd been alone and on the road for so damn long, and all of a sudden she felt as if she were home. Real life, a real person kissing her. It wasn't like being on stage. It wasn't like being with an actor. It was just like being with a one-eyed tough guy. Peter Greco.

Chapter Twenty-one

❧

"You've got to listen to me, Slats. We're way out of bounds now, a couple of lost balls in the high weeds. We've got to get the police in here—you can't just ignore the bodies in the apartment—"

"Peter! I'm not an idiot! I'm perfectly well aware they aren't going to get up and go home when the curtain comes down!"

"You understand the implications of Psycho Branch and the Mafia? This is now a world where they make the laws—and they don't tell us what they are. Got that?"

"And there's also," Celia said stubbornly, "a man about to be killed by his wife and her lover—I can't see that that, which is where we started out yesterday, has changed at all. I don't want to get in the way of these maniacs, I just want to keep this man from being killed."

"Aw, Slats, get with it! Whether or not you want anything to do with the maniacs is totally irrelevant—they're in it, they're in your life, and you'd better accept it!" He turned in frustration and stared at someone who might be reasonable. "Right, Ed?" The intrusions into his apartment seemed to have left Ed jaded and content to stay in the safety of his cage.

"I'm not arguing, Peter. I'm just saying that the reason we got into this still holds." She wasn't trying to be difficult. She just didn't want to leave a job undone. Neither she nor Linda Thurston could have done otherwise.

"This isn't a nutty woman wanting to knock off her rich, crippled husband anymore—"

"Peter, I *get the point*. What it is, even I can see, is wholesale murder, and some crazy think tank that's into God only knows what. I know all this—"

"Well, lemme tell you something else. If the Director gets killed at this point, I'm prepared to say his number was up and forget it."

"Forget it! What are you talking about? Aren't you just plain mad? Me, I'm goddamn mad!"

"Don't tell me—'And you're not gonna take it anymore.'"

"Laugh if you will." She drew herself primly to her full height. "But they've invaded my life, my house, I'm surrounded by corpses and mental cases, present company probably excepted—"

"Probably. That's beautiful."

"And I can still do my best to keep this man from being killed!"

"Sort of all-in-a-good-cause, don't-tread-on-me. Is that about right?"

"Exactly! Now you've got it!"

"There's something you haven't thought of. . . ."

"Oh?"

"The Director may be the innocent victim in the game Zoe Bassinetti is playing but . . . but there's another game being played. The General, the Director, Friborg, these guys scattered all over your floor, the Psychos and the Mafia—they're all playing a game, and *the Director may be the bad guy*. . . ."

Celia gnawed at a hangnail, frowned. "But that's a maybe," she said, brightening, "and maybes are a dime a dozen. Anyway we cannot go this far, wading through bodies, and suddenly just turn our backs—"

"Ed, the girl has spirit. She has spunk. As Lou Grant used to say, I hate spunk."

Celia laughed.

Greco looked at her appraisingly. "Is it you talking? Or is it Linda Thurston?"

"I don't know, Peter, I really don't know."

"Maybe it doesn't make any difference," he said. "Maybe there isn't any difference."

In the end they decided not to run the risk of wasting time on a trip to the Palisades Center and having the Director be gone. Getting the telephone number was no problem, and Celia made the call, asking to speak with the Director's office. Then she asked for the Director himself and gave her name. There was a pause and then a click.

"Miss Blandings, this is Emilio Bassinetti speaking."

"You don't know me," she said, having to take a deep breath to calm her nerves, "and I don't know how to say this, but there is something I must tell you—"

"Excuse me, Miss Blandings, but I know who you are and I have been expecting your call."

"*What?*" she gasped. "You've been expecting—"

Greco turned away from the window, his eye glittering.

"I know a bit more than you imagine. I want to speak with you. But I cannot speak to you now about this matter. Do you understand what I am saying?"

"Well, I don't know . . . look, what do you mean you know about me?"

Greco whispered: "You're kidding! Damn, damn, damn!"

"Mis Blandings, I'm just leaving for my home. I most definitely want to hear what you have to say. In fact, it's imperative that I do."

"There isn't much time—"

"Please, hear me out. We both understand how very serious this situation is. We must speak as soon

as possible, I agree. Can you possibly come to my
home?" The oily ease of his voice had developed a
touch of urgency. "Let me assure you, you will be
entirely safe and I will be . . . shall we say, deeply
in your debt."

"All right. I don't know if you realize it, but people
are getting killed—"

"Please. Not now. I'm aware of your present . . .
inconvenience. We will speak of that when we
meet." He gave her the directions and she noted
them on her pad. She handed the sheet to Greco. "I
look forward to meeting you," he said, and the line
went dead.

The West Side Highway was slick with the blend
of oil and rain, and even in the early afternoon the
clouds hung low and claustrophobic over the Hudson, resting atop the thickening fog. There was a
clinging shroud of darkness, as if the day had given
up on itself. The wipers flicked steadily as Greco
threaded his way toward the George Washington
Bridge.

"I don't like it one damn bit," he groused, eyes on
the road. "Everybody seems to know all kinds of
things we don't. I *hate* that."

"So you've said." Celia was trying not to think of
all the unknowns in the various parts of the equation. Everytime she did she got scared, and she
couldn't deal with any more fear than she already
had.

"The Director," Greco mused. "First I figured Z
was at the center of things, but now I'm beginning to
think she's as far from the center as we are. She
doesn't know a damned bit more than we do—
namely, that she's engineering her husband's death.
Now I look at it and I think it's the Director, he's the
spider at the center . . . he knows—and God only

knows how—about you! I can't figure that. You got
into this yesterday. Well, you bought the book with
the letter in it the day before, okay. And already the
Director *knows* about you. How the hell can that be?"
He shook his head with a tight, angry jerk. "And then
he tells you he's aware of your present inconvenience. Inconvenience! A living room full of bodies!
Now how the hell does he know that, I ask you?"

"Two ways," Celia said quietly.

"Oh, two ways, she says! Not one but two ways!"
He was beating a tattoo on the steering wheel.

"Either he ordered the killings at my place—"

"Listen, two of those guys were mafiosi, the other
one—well, the way it sounds from the late Louie, the
other guy was Psycho Branch—"

"Or, two, a survivor told him what happened. Two
ways."

"Hmmm. A survivor . . ." He gave her a sidelong,
perplexed glance. "That's good. I hadn't thought of
that—somebody just might have gotten out of your
place alive. But who? One of the Psychos? Or one of
the Mafia lads? And who would be more likely to run
to the phone and call the Director?"

"I'm trying to work that out." She was following
her instincts, letting the thing take shape as if it were
a plot—a simple plot—for Linda Thurston. A simple
plot made impenetrable by keeping certain pieces of
the plot hidden and dribbling the others out piece-
meal. The General . . . a manuscript . . . a Miles
Warriner manuscript? That was the first question
you'd ask, but then you'd ask why would someone
called the General—as well as the Mafia, according
to Louie—be so fascinated by an Inspector Littlechild novel? No, that made no sense at all. So,
some other kind of manuscript . . .

A manuscript needed a writer . . . and there
were two writers in the equation. Poor Charlie, who
was just a pawn . . . and Zoe Bassinetti, but not as

Miles Warriner. What might she write, not about
Inspector Littlechild, that would interest the General
and Psycho Branch and the Mafia?

Zoe Bassinetti. A writer. Also a wife. Wife of the
Director of a think tank. And maybe the Director was
connected in some way either to the Psycho Branch
or the Mafia . . . since he already knew so much.

The plot was hanging together. It all meant something. The answer was in there somewhere. . . .

She imagined her Linda Thurston notebooks, all
the pages of tight, legible script, working out the plot
lines of possible novels. Celia had done the same
thing building a character for a play she'd been
doing, fitting the character snugly into all the
nuances of the role as written. It was different, of
course, dealing with these violent, chaotic events.
Different but the same. You had to get up high and
see the whole picture, the pattern.

The murder letter had seemed impenetrable at
first. How could you have expected to track it down
to its source? But it had taken no time at all. The new
puzzle would yield, too, she was sure.

But now there was literally almost no time left.

The bridge had materialized at the last moment
out of the fog, and driving across it there was a time
when they could no longer see where they had been
or where they were going. The fog enveloped them,
sealed them off, and Greco was gripping the wheel
with both hands, checking the directions while she
read them aloud.

The fog and rain intensified as they headed out
into the countryside with its hints of velvety green
glimpsed through holes blown in the soft grayness.
Traffic thinned out as they passed through a couple
of fogbound, dreamlike villages, and Greco turned

off onto a secondary road with picturesque wooden fences running alongside the shoulders.

"Shouldn't be too far now," he said. "Two miles after the turn off. Damn fog . . ." He slowed as a thick blanket swept across them. When it lifted momentarily, there was a huge gray horse standing at the fence, staring at them as they rolled slowly past. "Horses," he grunted. "An outmoded form of transportation."

"Good in fog, though," she said. "They've got a sense people don't have."

"You're an expert on horses, I suppose."

"No, but I've ridden them in California. I rode one in a TV movie once. I got killed—"

"Thrown off the horse, no doubt."

"No, a sniper got me. I was the wife of this horsey millionaire, the horse got kidnapped and I found it but got shot—maybe you saw it?"

"Missed it."

"Oh, well, lots of people miss TV movies," she said.

"No. I missed the turnoff." He managed to back the car around in the fog, and they weren't killed by traffic. It was that kind of lonely road.

"There it is," she said.

Two rows of poplars lined a narrow gravel driveway that ran off into the fog before it reached any sign of habitation. The trees were as Bassinetti had described them. The gate was supposed to be half a mile up the drive. Greco hung a sharp left and burrowed into the fog.

Slowly the outline of a high, dramatically arched iron gate took shape. It reminded Celia of the camera dolly up to the gate in *Citizen Kane*. A nondescript brown sedan sat off to the right side of the road beside a formidable stone gatehouse.

"I feel like the Green Knight arriving at the portcullis." Greco sighed. Celia looked over at him and grinned. You never knew what this guy was going to say next. "What are we supposed to do, climb over?"

He stopped ten feet short of the gate. The rain seeped out of the fog like a sponge being squeezed.

The door of the gatehouse swung open and the barrel of a shotgun came out, followed by a man. Celia watched him closely as he came toward them across the wet, crunching gravel. He was a medium man. Medium height and weight, a pleasant medium face with medium blue eyes. He looked like a prototype average man, a new generation of robotic, all except for the tiredness that showed. His blue eyes were red rimmed and sunk deep in sockets that had begun to discolor with the purple of exhaustion. He wore a business suit. There was mud on the cuffs and on his shoes. He carried an umbrella that looked like it had been hanging on a hook in the gatehouse since 1920. He cradled the incongruous shotgun in the crook of his right arm.

Greco rolled his window down. "We're here to see the Director," he said.

"Names, please."

"Miss Blandings, Mr. Greco."

Celia strained to see the man's face. Something familiar . . .

"Of course, you're expected. I'll open the gates, but would you mind hanging on once you're through? I'll hitch a ride up to the house with you." He used a button on a device like a garage door opener. The gates swung slowly open and Greco eased the car through, stopped. The man followed them and pressed the device again, waited for the gate to lock. He came to the car and got into the backseat.

"Straight on," he said. "He wiped his damp face with a handkerchief. "My name's Mason," he said.

Chapter Twenty-two

❧

The house was a gray stone affair not as large as a football field but three stories high. It had all the majesty that went with the commercial barons of the early part of the century, who knew what they were doing when it came to erecting monuments to themselves. Greco brought the car all the way into the paving-stone courtyard between the house on one side, the horse barns on the far back side, and a vast greenhouse and garage on the third. He pulled to a stop where Mason pointed and cut the engine. The sudden quiet surrounded them like the fog. The snorting of horses came from the barn. A hay-strewn ramp led up from the court, into the barn's darkness. Swallows and wrens darted through the fog. The smell of earth and rain and horses was everywhere.

"We'll go in now," Mason said. "Over there."

They went across the flat wet stones, under the slate roof of the porte cochere, and inside through a small side door. A hound was barking somewhere behind them. The horse barn had already disappeared in the fog, as if it had sunk.

"Just straight ahead, all the way down the hall, then take a right."

Mason followed them the length of the chilly corridor. The damp had invaded the house, bringing the inevitable scent of mildew. They reached a vast baronial foyer full of carved paneling, tapestries hung from a two-story height, polished tile floors, and a chandelier that in a pinch would have lit Yankee Stadium.

"Mr. Greco, I'll have to relieve you of your gun. You understand, we can't be too careful where the Director is concerned." Mason still cradled the shotgun casually, but the twin barrels were pointed at Greco. "Please. Just put it on the table."

Greco took the Walther from his jacket pocket. When he placed it on the marble surface the sound was loud and final.

"Fine. Now let's go into the library." Mason nodded toward a doorway where mammoth sliding doors stood partially open. "More comfortable in there," he said. "Certainly warmer."

Celia's first thought was that she'd walked into some masterpiece of the set designer's art. The walls of the large room were lined with books, and several hunting prints on a grand scale. A huge fireplace was bordered with more elaborately carved wood, and the better part of two trees burned extravagantly within. The room was warm, almost stuffy, with the aroma of the flaming logs and a residue of smoke. The heat had scorched the dampness away. Tall French windows formed the outside wall, giving on to a wide stone balustrade decorated by man-size urns dripping with bright spring flowers, the colors softened by the fog encroaching from the billowing void beyond. Centered in enough leather furniture to stock the Harvard Club was the most beautiful pool table Celia had ever seen. The green felt looked like a putting green scattered with the polished balls.

Mason slid the doors shut. "Make yourselves at home, please." He gestured to a low table covered with countless bottles, glasses, an ice bucket. "If you'd like a drink . . ."

"Look," Greco said, "this is a very nice little routine but I don't know you from Rasputin. All I know is that you've got my gun on a day when most of the people I run into are newly deceased—"

"I told you, my name is Mason." He smiled apologetically. "Not Rasputin, rest assured."

"Where is Bassinetti?"

Celia heard the edge in Greco's voice as she warmed her hands before the fire. Mason was certainly polite and concerned for their comfort, but he was clearly overtired and strangely remote. And he had that shotgun. He still seemed vaguely familiar, but she couldn't quite place him. She thought she recognized his voice, but more than likely it was as medium and nondescript as everything else about him. Greco, on the other hand, was sounding like his mainspring was wound too tight.

"The Director isn't here yet. We'll just wait for him."

"Sure, sure. Have a drink, admire the first editions, shoot some pool while you point a shotgun at us. Do you work for the Director?"

"In a way," Mason said.

"Or do you work for the General?"

"I beg your pardon?" Mason swung slowly back from the drinks table where he'd been checking the ice, and the shotgun swung with him.

"You heard me. Now you're trying to think of an answer. The General. Just who is the General anyway? I keep hearing about him. And there's some book, a manuscript . . . maybe you could brief us. Hell, you work for the Director. In a way—"

"I'm afraid you're asking the wrong man."

"Don't be afraid, Mason, old sock. You're the man with the blunderbuss, after all. I'm the one who should be afraid, isn't that right?"

"Mr. Greco, there's no advantage to be gained by being disagreeable."

"For all we know, the Director's here now. He could be dead . . . sort of a pre–Dan Rather surprise. How does that sound?"

"It sounds like gibberish to me. I've told you, we're waiting for the Director—"

"Then you wouldn't mind if we just looked around, toured the joint. Am I right?"

"I'm afraid that's just not possible."

"Aw, what the heck, relax! We're all friends, trying to come to the aid of the Director. I'd love to see this house, y'know? Last time I saw a place like this, it cost me three quid to get in and some clown had lions playing on the lawn." Greco smiled sharkishly and headed for the door. He yanked the handles and came face to face with a large but otherwise medium man on the other side. The man shook his head silently, a gun in his catcher's mitt of a fist.

"Mr. Arnold," Mason said, "would like us to stay put for the moment." Mason shrugged as if he deplored the situation but rules were rules and Mr. Arnold was to be obeyed.

Mr. Arnold slid the doors back together.

"Hey," Greco said, his smile broadening beneath the eye patch, the scar on his cheek a little pinker than it had been, "that's hospitality."

"Why don't you just make this easy on yourself?"

"I want to know what *this* is, old sport. Old gun toter." Greco came back to the center of the room and leaned against the pool table.

"Can I get you a drink, Miss Blandings?"

Celia was staring into the fire when Mason spoke. Without looking at him she made the connection. Bradley's, the crush around the bar, the man who'd gotten her another drink. The man who came to Bradley's for the music.

Mason.

Mason must have been watching her then. Last night. But why? Was he the link to the Director? The Director had found out about her somehow . . . why not Mason?

"No, that's all right," she said.

"Well, help yourselves if you get thirsty."

Greco took a cue from the walnut rack. "Shoot some pool, Slats?"

She shook her head. He caught her eye, then glanced into the fire. He turned back to the table and made a bank shot, then began prowling about the table, with Mason staring at him as he banged in ball after ball. There was something hypnotic about the perfect clicking and the sound of Greco moving quickly, efficiently around the table. He ran the table, racked up the balls, broke them and began again.

"Six ball side pocket . . . four ball corner pocket . . . nine ball cross corner . . . three ball side . . ." It was like listening to a metronome.

Mason couldn't take his eyes off the display of shot making.

Celia moved slowly toward the fire. The brass-handled tools sat in their stand. She didn't want to make a sound, didn't want to break the spell. Click, click, click. Rack 'em up again.

Slowly, carefully, she grasped the handle of the poker and slid it from its notch. She held it at her side, afraid to take her eyes from the flames. Nothing to break the spell Greco was weaving at the loom of the pool table. He was good. Better than good. He hadn't missed a shot, had held the rhythm in his hands and never let it get away from him. The fire crackled, spit sparks up the flue.

She was uncomfortably close now, felt the heat burning at her through the jeans. Across the room fog, like ghosts, scurried inside the windows.

Then she leaned forward with the poker, as if she were closing in on a uniquely bothersome fly, and hooked the poker into the loose bark of the immense top log. She applied enough pressure to gauge what she had to do.

With a quick, decisive gesture, she yanked back with the poker.

The fiery log and the one beneath it came at her

like an avalanche of flame, showering sparks and
flying bits of burning bark. The logs tumbled out
across the Oriental rug, burning it through in an
instant.

She screamed and leaped backward, as if she were
an innocent bystander. Smoke swirled around her.

"Good Christ!" That was Greco yelling.

Mason said nothing, was around the pool table in a
flash, heading for the conflagration.

Celia cried: "I was just standing here and it
. . . came at me!"

Mason grabbed the poker from her hand and began
pushing at the heavy log. The carpet was burning,
the smell of the smouldering material acrid and foul.

The log was a twenty pounder and tough to move.
Mason's hand slipped and he fell forward on hands
and knees, his palm slamming down on a glowing
red coal.

He didn't cry out. He pulled his hand back, staring
at the raw, sizzling palm. He tried to pick up the
poker with his other hand. The shotgun lay at his
side.

Greco arrived at his side. "Here, let me help. . . ."

Mason was trying to get the logs back onto the tiles
of the hearth.

Greco broke a pool cue across the back of his neck.

Mason pitched forward, his face at the edge of the
burning carpet. The smoke was suddenly thick.
Mason moaned. Greco leaned forward. Celia saw the
flash of color, his fist closed around the seven ball,
and the first smashing down at Mason's cheekbone.
Mason flattened out on top of the shotgun.

Greco grabbed Celia's hand and pulled her away.

There were sounds coming from the sliding doors,
where Arnold, having heard the commotion, was
fumbling with the catch.

Greco pulled her almost off her feet, heading for
the long bank of windows. He found a handle,

yanked it down, pushed the door open. The cold wet air rushed in as they stepped outside.

The sliding doors behind them slammed open. "For chrissake!" Then Arnold began coughing in the smoke.

Greco held her hand tightly in his own. They were across the wet stone of the balustrade, found the steps leading down to the lawn; deep grass, soaking wet, Greco tugging her along.

And then, like Jonah in the whale, they were swallowed by the fog.

Chapter Twenty-three

❧

Smoke was pouring, funneling out of the French doors, swirling like a tiny tornado into the fog. Celia stopped, wiped rain from her eyes, smelling the smoke, which added yet another rich smell to the wetness and the grass. A city person, it had been a long time since she smelled the natural world, and it gave her a high, sent her heart pumping while she stood gasping from the run, a stitch in her side. Greco leaned over, hands on knees, fresh air being gulped into his lungs.

"Way to go," he said, nodding back toward the house. "We got telepathy, Slats. Great trick with the fire . . ."

"But what about now?"

"Got any good ideas?"

"Yup," she said, "I do."

The angry beeping of a tardy smoke alarm floated toward them.

"Mason and Arnold . . ." he panted. "They're waiting for the Director. Looks like everybody in the world wants to kill him. . . ."

"I'm not so sure. I can't figure out Mason at all—he's working for Mason, I think. I wonder if any of them knows what's going on. . . . They're going to come after us, you know that . . ."

As she spoke they saw the figure of Arnold lurch out onto the balustrade, batting away smoke that seemed to cling to him. He looked out into the fog. She'd have thought he was bound to see them, but he stood still, trying to will the mists to part. Mason, a smaller blur, joined him. He had the shotgun again.

"First," Celia said, "we can try to get to the car. Have you still got the keys?"

Greco nodded, patted his pocket.

"Okay," she said, "let's move it."

Staying far enough away, wrapped in fog, they began circling the house, careful not to let it slip away, using it as the center point of their compass. It was dark now, though somewhere up above them, above the fog and the rain and the clouds, the sun had to be shining. The yellow lights of the house hung like distant flares, diffused on each drop of water. The grass was long and slippery underfoot, treacherous if they moved too quickly. She was beginning to wonder if they'd somehow gotten turned around, when suddenly they reached the gravel of the driveway, felt its reassuring crunch. Holding hands to keep from losing one another, they moved toward the house along the gravel.

"They're not gonna try to get out the driveway."

It was a voice so close she felt she could reach out and touch it, and she heard feet on the gravel, stopping.

"You're right. If they try to run their car through the gates it'll be like going through a shredder."

Celia felt her heart come to a full stop.

The voices of Mason and Arnold were right on top of them. Footsteps edged closer to where she stood. She felt Greco drawing her away, deeper into the fog.

"The fog does funny things to sound." Greco was whispering at her ear. "Bounces it around. They can't see us. We can't see them."

"But they're right, Peter," she breathed. "The car won't do us any good. I forgot about the fence—"

"Yeah, me too. Any other ideas?"

"Sure. Plan B," she whispered.

The footsteps on the gravel faded away, back toward the house.

Celia pushed off into the murk, Greco holding on tight. All she could do was try to judge distances, knowing that she'd seen a huge old oak beside the driveway, just before the greenhouse and the garage. Find the oak and you'd find the greenhouse and know where you were. You'd be halfway to the destination she had in mind.

But somehow the oak never did reveal itself. She didn't see the greenhouse until she ran into it, reached out and touched the chilly, water-streaked panes of glass. She felt her way along the side of the building and reached the end, where she turned left and kicked a bucket and hoe across a cement sidewalk. The sound was deafening, and she instinctively drew back, bumping into Greco, who grunted and swore.

"What the hell was that?"

The voices echoed from farther away this time, from the courtyard, trapped by the fog and the walls of the house, barn, garage, and greenhouse, all bouncing sound back and forth. "Where did it come from?" That was Arnold.

"I can't tell. Where are you?"

"Over here. By the cars . . ."

"I think"—that was Mason—"they're by the greenhouse now. Blandings? Greco? We're not going to hurt you. . . ."

Celia pulled Greco forward, moving along behind a low shed and stacks of pots, tools, flower tubs, discarded lawn furniture. The greenhouse, now twenty feet away, was gone, but she had it locked in memory and was sure they were moving parallel to it. They were behind the garage when they heard clanking from inside, then an engine coughing into life, a motor revving.

They were past the garage and Celia was jogging

through the fog, looking for what she knew must lie ahead. There it was, the second ramp to the horse barn, leading not into the courtyard but out the other end, into the fields beyond. The motor was racing in the garage, then it dropped back into gear and some kind of vehicle rattled out into the courtyard.

Suddenly, glimpsed between the corners of the barn and the garage, a powerful yellow fog light swept across the courtyard, probing, casting a kind of chartreuse glow into the fog.

"Up the ramp," Celia said, pulling Greco behind her.

"What the hell for?" He stood panting at the top of the ramp, straw clinging to his wet shoes, to the knee of his pants where he'd fallen down.

"Look, we've got to get as far away from these bozos as possible, somewhere safe. Right? We've got to be able to strike—"

"Strike? Jeez, Slats, commando talk—"

"Strike at seven when the Director settles down to watch Dan Rather. That's a little over an hour. We've got to assume the original plan is still in effect— Cunningham to kill him, on schedule—"

"But what about Mason and Arnold?"

"We don't know about them, they're not on the scorecard. First we've got to get away, and then we've got to be able to get back, so what does logic tell us?"

"Oh, no, I know what you're thinking."

"The noble horse. Now let's take a look."

The voices came from the courtyard again. "Point that thing at the greenhouse, damnit!" Then the sound of the shotgun clattering on the paving stones, a sharp cry right behind it.

"Are you okay? What happened?"

"What the hell does it sound like? I fell down. Shit! Damn slippery stones . . ."

"I can't ride a horse!" Greco insisted, panicking.

"You can ride a horse to save your life," she said, moving ahead into the barn. "It's amazing what people can do when they have to. Now be very quiet and easy, don't spook these big guys."

Fog had infiltrated the barn. Horses blew and snuffled at them as they passed between the stalls, their great rubbery nostrils and lips reverberating. Birds cooed and twittered in the dark upper reaches. Hooves stomped and rattled against the wooden slats of the stalls, thumped on the straw.

"What about a saddle?"

"I rode bareback in the movie—"

"But I wasn't in the goddamn movie!"

"Shhh."

"I don't like this."

"It's the only way they can't get us. We're unarmed, all we can do is get away, hide."

She found a big chestnut that was watching them amiably over the gate to his stall. She leaned across and began talking to him, trying to do what she'd remembered the wranglers on the movie doing. She stroked the long nose, whispering the news that he was a very nice horse, wasn't he? For better or worse she climbed over the gate and threw a leg over the huge back, settled down on him, stroking the powerful column of neck. "Nice horsey, we're going for a ride. . . ."

"Listen, why don't you just go ahead? I'll make the best of it here—"

"Get on, you oaf. This is a nice horsey, aren't you, Roger?"

"Roger? You know this horse?"

"His name's on the gate. Good, Roger, nice, Roger . . . come on, climb up."

Greco climbed up. Roger gave him a slightly bemused nudge with his muzzle. "He doesn't like me—"

"He adores you."

Greco settled in behind her. "I'm gonna fall off the minute he moves." Roger stamped one foot impatiently. "I'm too old, I've only got one eye, I'll get another concussion—"

"You all set back there? Put your arms around my waist, get down low, head on my back . . ."

She leaned forward against the muscular neck, fingers of one hand laced into the mane. She stretched and lifted the latch, pushed the gate away. She coaxed Roger out of the stall, tugged the mane, pulling him to the left. Here, she thought, goes nothing. "Thatta boy, that's a good Roger." Roger ambled toward the rear ramp. Greco was clearly holding on for dear life.

A man, indistinct in outline, appeared on the ramp, fog blowing past him in shredded wisps. He peered into the darkness of the barn and for an instant didn't recognize the horse for what it was.

Celia turned to Greco. "Don't let go now." To Roger she said: "Go, honey, go," and jabbed her heels into his ribs.

Roger liked the idea, a break in the day-to-day routine. With a blustery blowing of his nose and a shake of his head, he broke into a trot. Within a few strides he was bearing down on the man in the doorway at the top of the ramp.

It was Mason, his face reddened and scorched on one side, a pad of gauze wrapped around one hand, his mouth skewed open in surprise and anger and fear as he stared up into Roger's flaring nostrils and wide eyes.

The shotgun swung up, almost in self-defense, and Roger pranced sideways to miss Mason, but Celia kept telling him to go, go, go, baby. Mason tried ducking sideways, tripped in the straw, and plunged off the side of the ramp, disappearing from view.

The shotgun discharged as he fell.

Wood splintered in the eaves of the barn.

The air was suddenly filled with terrified birds, including a few bats roused from their day's sleep.

Someone else—it must have been Arnold—came pounding and thrashing out of the fog behind them. A pistol shot cracked and a bullet sizzled past Celia's head.

"Run, goddamnit!" Greco shouted. He, too, dug his heels into the ribs, massive as barrel staves, but Roger had already flicked his tail and taken off into the fog.

Greco prayed old Roger came equipped with radar.

Chapter Twenty-four

❧

Emilio Bassinetti's specially-equipped 1978 Mark V, which he firmly believed was the last of the truly distinguished domestic motorcars, nosed slowly through a world that had begun to remind him of his favorite gray cashmere muffler. Since his legs were useless, all the controls were hand operated, a fact that amused him, made him feel that his favorite car was an immense toy.

He was generally amused at the moment, even with the fog and rain, because everything was taking shape so beautifully. Not too smoothly, but that had made it all the more amusing. When one lost the power to be amused, it was indeed time to rethink one's priorities. This whole business was, indeed, amusing, had been so ever since he woke up in his hospital bed unable to walk or copulate and began planning a modicum of revenge. Ever since he'd fallen off one of Zoe's goddamn, rotten, and malevolently stupid horses at one of her goddamn, rotten, malevolently stupid weekend "hunts."

Recuperating to the extent possible, going through the physical and attitudinal rehabilitation, he began to contemplate his future as a cripple . . . and his future with Zoe. He wasn't going to be much use to her, certainly not in the only way that mattered to her, and he hated her for what she'd led him to, but there was no question in his mind that she'd manage to gut him in a divorce proceeding. He had a great deal to lose, but the only thing he really wanted to

lose was Zoe. They had outlived their mutual
usefulness. Now the trick became how to outlive
Zoe. . . .

Of course, he could have had her killed, stuffed in
an industrial grinder somewhere, then incinerated in
the Jersey landfill—sure, no problem. A man in his
position, at the top of Palisades, knew how to make
people disappear without so much as a smidgen of
dental bridgework left behind.

But Emilio had another problem that needed solv-
ing.

It wasn't just Zoe. It was the General down in
Virginia. It was Arturo Tavalini up in Scarsdale and
the whole horrifying Tavalini "family." It was all that
money passing through his hands, figuratively
speaking, and the thought that only a lousy million a
year was sticking to him.

The Director was no greedier than the next man.
Which meant he'd have slain his sainted granny if
there was enough in it for him. Granny, wife, it was
all the same thing. A poor cripple wondering how to
insure the future, the quality of life in his sunset
years. Wondering how to buy the kind of restaurant
to which he might retire in contemplation of life's
better, gentler, nobler pursuits.

Zoe. The General. Tavalini. The money.

Get rid of Zoe. Neutralize the General and Tavalini, and then squeeze. And come out with a little
money. Ten, twenty million. Nothing too piggish.
But there were bound to be certain risks.

It was a lovely problem, and the solution had been
in the works for two years. It was like a Bach fugue,
building, repeating, turning in upon itself, growing,
endlessly enriching itself. Everyone had cooperated
so painlessly, all because Bassinetti knew them,
understood how their minds worked. In a way it was
simple. You figured out what each one would betray
his own code for and then you went to work. They

all operated the same way. Everybody, in Bassinetti's
view, operated the same way. Everybody was eager
to practice the fine art of betrayal, if only they were
given the proper opportunity.

Zoe. Cunningham. The General. Mason. All of
them.

Which was where Celia Blandings came bumbling
into the picture. She was the glitch in the program.
She was what had made it all so interesting here at
the climax. Only a couple of days, but it had been
quite thrilling, actually. Having to improvise. He had
known nothing could possibly go quite so smoothly
as this had for two years. Somewhere there had to be
a glitch. In this case it had come right at the end.
There had to be a Celia Blandings, and she'd turned
up at the last minute—the unknown quantity. He'd
have been disappointed if she'd never materialized.

Having turned Mason a couple years before, thus
having his own man inside the General's operation,
had been his insurance. Now, with the Blandings
woman almost wrecking the delicate balance, Mason
had been the one he'd called on.

And now it was all going to pop.

He was smiling, listening to *The Barber of Seville*
on his tape deck as he passed the great oak tree and
slid beneath the porte cochere slates.

Mason stood like a specter in the swirling fog and
the blur of the Lincoln's headlights. The Director
pulled into his customary parking spot, swiveled the
driver's seat and pulled his collapsible wheelchair
across from the passenger seat. But before he as-
sembled it, Mason had come to stand before him,
looking as if he'd just had an unpleasant encounter
with the world's largest exploding cigar. An alarm
began going off in the back of the Director's very large
brain.

"What has befallen you, Mason? And, more importantly, where is the Blandings woman?" He looked into Mason's eyes and hoped very sincerely, for Mason's sake as well as his own, that what he was seeing in them was neither fear nor defeat.

"We had a little accident," Mason began, and paused, searching for the proper approach.

"Oh? I thought maybe you'd suddenly gone all punk." Bassinetti fixed him with an increasingly steely stare. He began unfolding the wheelchair.

"The library," Mason said, waving his bandaged hand at the house.

"The library—yes, I'm familiar with my library."

"The library caught fire." Mason looked away, as if to disassociate himself from the sad story. "Here, let me help you with that." He took the wheelchair and began locking its various joints.

"The library . . . my library . . . caught fire," Bassinetti repeated.

"I take full responsibility, sir—"

"I daresay you do. Please explain yourself." He grabbed the chair back from Mason. "Here, give me that, you don't know what you're doing." He finished unfolding and making the wheelchair ready.

"It was the burning logs that did it . . . the Blandings woman dragged them out onto the rug—"

"You're talking about the rug in my library?"

"Yes, sir."

"The rug in my library is worth forty thousand dollars—"

"Not anymore, sir."

Bassinetti hoisted his immense bulk out of the driver's seat and into the wheelchair, impatiently brushing Mason's offer of help away. "And once my rug was nicely aflame, what happened?"

"They got away while Arnold and I were putting the fire out."

"They?" The glitches were multiplying.

"She has a man named Greco with her. Used to be a cop in New York. I disarmed him."

"I see. And where are they now, as we speak?"

"We lost them in the fog. They got away on horseback."

"Horseback?" Bassinetti looked up at Mason from his wheelchair. "Forgive me if I find this all rather difficult to believe. You mean she and this man are still at liberty?"

"Yes, sir."

"And still determined to save my life?"

"I suppose so, sir. She's a very resourceful woman."

"Well, take the Land Rovers and try to find them. We mustn't have her barging in saving my life, Mason. You understand?"

"Yes, sir. We've got the Rovers ready to go—"

"Fine, fine. Keep track of the time too."

"Yes, sir."

"And Mason?"

"Yes, sir?"

"You're looking a little ragged. In pain, are you?"

"I can handle it, sir."

"You're looking rather the worse for wear—"

"I am rather the worse for wear, sir."

"Yes, well, buck up. I'd better go in and look at my worthless rug. You know, Mason, if you didn't look so ragged, I'd have to think about docking you the forty thousand." He began rolling toward the doorway beneath the porte cochere, then turned back. "And Mason?"

"Yes, sir?"

"Don't let that woman save my life."

"Right, sir."

"I kid you not, old man." He'd reached the doorway with its little wheelchair ramp when he turned back and called to the limping, bandaged, and burned figure retreating in the light of the

Rover's fog lights like a man out in the middle of the twilight zone. "Oh, Mason?"

The figure turned slowly and heaved a sigh worthy of Job. "Yes, sir?" The voice came weakly, muffled by fog.

"Do keep things quiet, will you? My wife will be with us soon. I'd rather she didn't know you were here. Understood?"

"Yes, sir."

Mason trudged away.

The General was talking into the speakerphone on his desk in Virginia. The sun was setting in a brilliant red fireburst on the western horizon, and the shadows were long and soft, reaching across the lawn toward his study. The General was in a bad mood, even for him. His wife was giving a dinner party and he'd have to be on his good behavior, just a retired old crock farting away his life in the Virginia countryside. The man at the other end of the line was in his White House office, three minutes walk from the Oval Office itself.

"We've got a situation, Ben. Whole damn thing's out of control—"

"Now, General, I'm sure it's not so bad—"

"Bullshit, Ben. It's so bad I've taken all my calls in the bathroom since noon. I'm dealing with Tavalini's crew and you know what that's like. Manicotti with blood sauce. And the Admiral—he couldn't find his asshole with both hands and a map. He's at some goddamn tea dance with Gloria Vanderbilt and Calvin Klein. So—"

"Now, General, let's relax—"

"You relax, sonny. That's the trouble these days, everybody's too goddamned relaxed and the world's in the crapper. Now get this—I've lost Green completely. The NYPD found Friborg decorating a gravel pit just off the Brooklyn-Queens Expressway today. I figure that was Tavalini's thugs, but I can't get hold of Bassinetti, and he's the only one who just might know. . . . And, lessee, there's something else—oh, Mason! He hasn't checked in either, and he could be living at the bottom of the East River, the way things are going."

"Hmmm."

"Your damn right, hmmm. The Admiral calls and tells me about some idiot editor at Pegasus, of all places—you getting this, Ben? We *own* Pegasus. This editor brings him the manuscript that's got everybody rending their goddamn flesh—can you believe it? This guy brings it to the Admiral *to publish!* I mean, what the hell's going on? Not one of these shows is listed, Ben, not a damn one!"

"But that's swell, General. We control the manuscript now. We're in luck—"

"Sure . . . but how many copies of this damn thing are floating around? Maybe Random House and Putnam and the goddamn Literary Guild have all got copies. Hey? And how about the Russians? Maybe that numbnuts in the Kremlin is getting a big haw-haw now reading about what Palisades was created to do? Sure, relax, Ben, nothing to worry about . . . and we don't even know who wrote the goddamn thing! Maybe he's working on a sequel—you like that idea? Relax? Bullshit!"

"Well, I don't know what to say, General—"

"How about you waltz into the Oval Office and tell the President we're all about to get flushed down the Great Toilet? Tell him that Nixon'll look like Abraham Lincoln next to him. If I were you, I'd make a tape of that little chat for posterity—"

"General, it's really my duty to point out to you that Palisades is your responsibility. We know nothing about it."

"Ha! You kill me, Ben, you really do! I knew you'd

get to that eventually—gee, General, it's all your
fault. Well, maybe, but the Commander-in-Chief goes
up against the wall too. Sleep well, Ben."

The Rovers were gone and the courtyard was quiet
as the grave when the white Rolls-Royce convertible
purred up the driveway, drew to a halt in the
darkness beside the Director's Mark V.

Zoe Bassinetti was tense from fighting the fog all
the way from the city. She sat quietly for a moment
behind the wheel, then took a Valium from her
pillbox and swallowed it without benefit of water.
Nestled in her purse was a .22 caliber pistol for
which she had a permit, registered in New Jersey. It
was for self-protection at the country house which
was, after all, remote and secluded and a perfect
target for uninvited guests.

She sighed, wondering if one four-grain Valium
was enough for what promised to be an evening full
of strains and constabulary and God only knew what
else. The problem, of course, was that she was
surrounded by men who were idiots, and she knew
perfectly well that far too many variables had come
sprawling into the picture. There were traps everywhere now, where two days ago there had been
none. But it was too late to turn back. No matter what
happened, she had to tough it out. Stick to her story.
Stonewall it.

She didn't know what was going on with the
Blandings woman and her one-eyed friend: she
knew only that they never should have gotten
involved, and it was entirely Charlie Cunningham's
fault. She didn't know who Friborg was or what he'd
thought he was doing. But he was gone now, out of
sight, out of mind. Cunningham was an idiot, but
she'd gotten him back in line a few hours before with
a sexual performance that had been extravagant even

for her. She had to get him ready for the night's work and that was the best way to get him thinking straight. All he had to do was make it through the next hour. . . .

She got out of the car, patted the trunk as she went past, and entered the house.

She went to the library, where lights were burning. Her nose was twitching at the unusual smell. Her husband was in his wheelchair by the fireplace. It smelled terrible.

"Darling," she said, crossing the room and kissing him.

He turned his reptilian smile on her. "My turtle dove." His hand caressed her hip, squeezed her.

"What in the world has been going on in here? Look at the rug! Oh, dear! What a mess!"

"An accident, I'm afraid." Bassinetti sighed. "The cleaning people were in . . . a fire carelessly laid . . . a log rolls out." He shrugged. "One of those regrettable little things, eh?"

Zoe Bassinetti shook her elegant head. "I suppose we should be glad we had a house to come home to and not a smoking ruin. Still, this rug is one of your favorites! Poor Emilio." She rested a hand on his shoulder. "Well, we'll have a nice quiet weekend."

"Indeed," he said. "I've sent everyone home. We're quite fogged in. I thought you might even decide to stay in New York with the driving so bad."

"Oh, no, I've been looking forward to this weekend. So cozy, just the two of us."

"Ah, so have I my dear."

She took a closer look at the burned rug and murmured more words of sympathy. Standing up, she said: "I have some typing I must do to put my mind at ease. I'll join you after Dan Rather and we'll find something for dinner in the kitchen. Does that suit you?"

"By all means."

She kissed his forehead and he smiled, noticing that she smelled like sex. It was something she exuded after a lively session, and she couldn't get rid of it for hours. How fitting, tonight of all nights . . .

Chapter Twenty-five

❧

Roger was familiar with the lay of the land, a fact of which Greco was particularly thankful. The ride was bumpier and more harrowing than he'd imagined any human could withstand, but he hung onto Celia, who kept saying it was going to be all right. Greco wasn't sure if she was talking to him or to Roger, but as an article of faith he believed her. He hung onto Celia, closed his eyes, and figured it simply had to be over soon.

Roger took them down a path that led into a thick stand of trees. The leaves and branches brushed them, water cascading down upon them, a deluge. The fog hung like ancient, forgotten bunting from the black branches. Roger slowed to a walk, glancing back for more pats of approval from Celia.

"Is it over?" Greco panted. He wondered how you could get so tired when the horse was supposed to be doing all the work.

"I think we're out of harm's way," she answered. "Let's just see where he takes us."

The path wound through the trees. If being lost meant they were safe, then they were, at least for the moment, safe. If it didn't, then they were just lost. Finally Celia did something that made Roger stop. Greco assumed she knew arcane horse language. Which was fine, but his mind was racing ahead. He wished to God he still had his gun.

"So how do we get down?" He thought the ground seemed incredibly far away.

"You could just slide off the back," Celia said.

"Okay, but don't watch. You've probably never noticed, but dignity is my middle name." He let go of Celia and she heard a grunt. Roger looked back and shook his head.

Greco appeared, mud on the seat of his pants and the back of his Yankees jacket. "Okay, okay, get down." He was wiping his wet, muddy hands on the front of his pants. Celia dismounted and Roger followed them as they set off through the muck and found a fallen tree to sit on. They looked down on a long sweep of meadow that fell away toward the house. The roof poked up through the top of the fog, which filled the space between.

The rain was falling harder, pattering angrily on the leaves. They were hidden by the tree line as well as by the fog and the gathering darkness. Slowly the bright yellow pairs of fog lights pierced the fog, crisscrossing the wide meadow.

Greco said: "Those must be four-wheel drive vehicles, Rovers or Broncos, something that can handle that long wet grass. They're just gonna keep combing the fog, I suppose. They'll have to get right on top of us to find us. Unless they get a break. Hell's bells, it's getting cold. You okay?"

"I'm wet, I'm cold, I'm scared. Otherwise, everything's fine."

"It's ten past six." Greco sneezed. Roger sneezed. "We're all gonna die of double pneumonia. This is nuts."

"I know this Mason," Celia said. "He's been following me. He followed me to Bradley's last night when I went to meet Cunningham . . . he's got to be Bassinetti's eyes and ears on this thing, which means that he's the Director's man. But how could he have known of any reason to follow me? You don't think the Director knows Zoe's trying to kill him, do you?

But that wouldn't make any sense, he'd just stop her—he wouldn't wait for it to happen, surely—"

"Stop, stop," Greco said. "It's hopeless, we can't figure it out anymore than we have. Too many people, too many angles—"

"But one more thing," she insisted. "The other dead man in my apartment, the one in the boxes with Linda Thurston? Well, he was with Mason at Bradley's! So . . . if your friend Louie was right and it was Psycho Branch versus the Mafia—that means Mason must be Psycho Branch too . . . and it means he was probably in my apartment killing people! Oh, Peter, it gets worse and worse."

"Yeah, well, I recognized Mason too, and I think he knew me. I saw it in his eyes. Goes back to what Teddy called my fink days. Mason had been a homicide dick, but there was a story about him—he killed a guy, or a coupla guys, during an investigation, and there was another investigation of him." Greco sneezed again and dug a handkerchief out and blew his nose. "He wound up on the Rubber Gun Patrol—"

"The what?" She wiped rain from her forehead and eyebrows.

"Cops take guys who get trigger happy, give 'em desk jobs, issue fake guns—years ago they were made of rubber—so they became the Rubber Gun Patrol. Sometimes they're the Bow and Arrow Brigade. Funny thing, Mason was one of my bodyguards when I was testifying. Not for long, and I never talked to him but it *was* him, I'm sure—"

"So that makes three of them in Psycho Branch." Celia couldn't believe it: she was getting used to all this. "So that must mean—"

"Forget it. We don't know what the hell it means."

"So all we can do is warn the Director and try to stop whatever's going to happen down there." She nodded past the moving fog lights, toward the house.

"You're sure you don't want to just wait until it's all over and then try to go home?"

"Funny man. We've got to get back to the house. And soon. Thank God for the fog. . . . How do we do it?"

The fog lights were probing closer, turning, sweeping in golden, blurred arcs. Closer, closer, as if they somehow knew where the hiding place was. The sound of the motors carried toward them like whining beasts looking for dinner.

Greco said: "Okay, here's the plan. First, I'm not getting back up on that horse again, that's a given. Second, you can ride, so I'd say you make a diversion for me, make some noise on that horse, then get back into the foggy woods. But, Slats, listen to me—don't let 'em catch you, okay? Everybody's playing for keeps—"

"While I'm risking my life, what are you going to be doing? Assuming I'm willing and foolhardy, that is."

"I'm going to make a run for the house." Greco blew his nose again.

"Doing what when you get there?"

"Get some aspirin. My head's killing me."

It was dark and damp and cold and cramped in the trunk of the Rolls-Royce. It didn't do any good to recall that his immediate predecessor in the trunk had been dead as a skunk. Charlie Cunningham was sick to his stomach from the bumping and swerving and skidding and stopping and starting, and for good measure, from the effects of all the aspirin he'd taken for his ear. Now the aspirin had worn off, and as the pain took hold of him again, he began wondering if he should have had a tetanus shot. Goddamn bird . . .

The luminous paint on the wristwatch face had

lost its power at least ten years ago, so he didn't know what time it was. The trunk lid was wired shut, and in addition to being stiff and sick and in pain and not knowing what time it was, Charlie Cunningham had to take a leak. He felt around for the wire, found it with numbed fingers, and began to unwind it. It took forever. He cut his finger, of course, and sucked it, tasting blood. Finally he felt the wire come loose and he pushed the lid up six inches or so and peered out into the darkness and the fog. For a moment he thought he'd gone blind, then realized that there just wasn't anything to see.

He felt around for the gun Zoe had given him. It felt cold and clammy and heavy. He stuffed it into the pocket of his windbreaker, pushed the lid all the way open, and struggled into a kneeling position, listening to bones crack. Most of the bones not already broken from earlier misfortunes now broke. Gingerly he got one leg out of the trunk, felt around with his toe for the ground, then crawled out and managed to stand upright, much like a man. His knees were weak. He stood wobbling. Getting his bearings. Good God, he had to find a bathroom!

However, it could have been worse.

For the first time since he'd realized he had sold the wrong book at the Strand, he felt he knew what was going on.

He didn't like it. But at least he had a clear picture of the situation. No dead dogs, no dead men scattered from his living room to Zoe's terrace, no guys with eye patches, no big fierce birds. He tried not to think about why there had been a body in his favorite chair.

He sighed. Now it was all clear, for a change.

They were alone in the Jersey countryside. Just the three of them. Himself, the Director, and darling Zoe. The eternal triangle, as it were. After all the confusion, the end was so simple!

He wondered if just maybe he should pee right there in the courtyard. Maybe against the house. Or Zoe's Rolls. He was sick of the damn Rolls.

No. You just didn't pee in somebody's courtyard. He'd find a bathroom in the house. Zoe was up in the west wing. The Director was in the study. He had time. He yawned nervously. There was a dim light under the porte cochere. He walked into the penumbra of light and checked his watch. Just past six-thirty. Plenty of time.

He headed for the side door, remembering all the instructions Zoe had given him about the layout of the house.

There was supposed to be a bathroom off that first long hallway. There might even be some aspirin. His head was killing him.

Chapter Twenty-six

❧

Mason realized he was wasting his time out in the middle of nowhere when he lost sight even of Arnold in the other Rover. There was nothing but fog. No horse, no Miss Blandings, no Peter Greco, and now no Arnold. He was beginning to see himself as Field Marshal Rommel in the middle of the North African desert, disappearing in a sandstorm, looking for the key to Rebecca.

Then the fog lights of Arnold's Rover came out of nowhere, swept past him up ahead. Mason wheeled off to the right, angling up across Arnold's path, making yet another X through the fog. Not having a walkie-talkie connection with Arnold was bad. He slowed, leaned forward, vainly trying to see where he was going. It was idiotic. They'd never find anybody, and the fog was getting thicker. He was soaked to the skin. The rain felt like blood running down the burned side of his face.

Without warning he saw the horse.

It was a flash of the huge eyes, the flicker of a mane, on its back a figure crouched low, then a glimpse of hindquarters, a jerk of the tail . . . then, in a flash, the horse was gone, like a ghost, like the Headless Horseman dashing through the night.

Mason yelled, "Arnold! Arnold, over here! I got 'em!" The hell with Bassinetti's order of silence. The hell with all of it. The horse was dead ahead, he knew it. "God damn you, Arnold!"

It was pointless to try to make himself heard.

He couldn't even hear his own cries. The engine was roaring. The blood was pounding in his temples. Arnold's lights cut across in front of him again. Christ! He must be right in line with the horse!

He gunned the accelerator, making a hole like a bullet in the fog, felt the Rover skid then leap ahead into the void.

Mason felt the adrenaline kicking in, rushing, blotting out the frustration, smashing through his icy Psycho Branch control.

He was slipping all the way over into a pure, murderous rage. He felt himself grinning, and it hurt, but he couldn't stop. The plain, medium face had become a predatory fangs-bared mask.

Nothing had gone right for days. His bandaged hand felt like a well-done hamburger straight from the grill. The side of his face had turned into one large blister about to burst. Bassinetti probably would dock him the forty thousand. And if the General ever got wind of his treachery, he'd garrote him and deep six his remains in a shark tank.

But now, by God, he was going to put paid to that son of a bitch on the horse! Yes, sir, his luck was turning.

He was right about very little, the way things were turning out. But he was right about his luck. The next thing he knew, something unbelievably horrible was happening.

Looking around, Mason realized he was airborne. Somehow he'd lost the Land Rover entirely.

As he flew through the fog he tried to remember what had just happened. It came back to him in quick images, as if illuminated by explosions of gunfire.

It involved a tree stump.

A very wide tree stump about three feet high. It seemed to have darted out in front of him like a particularly ugly, sturdy dwarf. Out of nowhere. Directly in front of him. Mocking him.

The Rover had slammed head on into the stump with a thud that had racketed along the frame, cracked the windscreens, and ripped the steering wheel from his grasp. His spinal column had snapped him back and forth and he'd bitten his tongue. Badly.

The four wheels had kept driving, digging into the slippery grass. The Rover stood abruptly on its front end, catapulting Mason into the darkness, making him a sort of human missile without a guidance system.

He came to earth, his dream of flight in tatters, crunching, hearing lots of things cracking and buckling inside his drenched skin.

The breath was pounded out of him by the sledgehammer impact.

Collarbone? Arm? Neck? Did it really matter?

He shook his head. Groggy. Finally the worst had happened.

He lay on his back gagging, trying to draw a breath. He fought to focus his eyes and ignore the starbursts of pain going off in his head like a third-rate Fourth of July. He looked around, trying to lift himself up on one elbow. He tried to see back into the fog from which he'd come.

Something funny was going on.

First he heard the roar of a Rover engine, then the fog lights came flooding out of the gloom.

"Arnold," he croaked. He gathered his lung power together, screamed: "Arnold . . . look out! It's me! I'm here on the ground . . . Arnold!"

Then the Rover appeared like some demon-possessed piece of junk from a Stephen King novel and bore down on him.

It was gaining speed.

He wasn't sure he could drag himself out of the

way. Arnold had gone crazy! "Arnold!" he screamed, his voice cracking and fading. "You asshole!" But all that emerged was a whisper.

First a horse.

Now a Land Rover.

He tried to move, tried to roll away. . . .

Greco skirted the tree line at a jog, once falling over a root and sprawling among wet oak leaves. He depended on the tree line to lead him in an arc back to the horse barn. Occasionally he saw a fleeting glow from the direction of the house, giving him a geographical center on his right. He heard snatches of engine noise from the Rovers, but it came and went erratically. The rain ran down his face, slithered down his back, soaked his shoes. He was very tired of not being able to see anything, but he knew he needed the cover.

Mainly he was worried about Celia.

Slats.

She was so damn game! He'd never met a woman like her, he was sure of that. Here she was, on totally alien ground, and she was adapting like a marine. He'd had to adapt all his life, particularly in his undercover days. That was all adaptation. But then, he was an ego case, as he'd tried to make her see. Maybe there really was a similarity in her being an actress. And, too, she had this Linda Thurston to fall back on. Maybe she could adapt because she was playing a role, for that matter a role she'd created. He guessed the truth was he couldn't quite figure her out.

Maybe she wasn't figurable.

But he hoped she was all right. He'd hated parting with her, hated entrusting her to the night and the rain and the fog and the horse, but when it came to busting in on the Director about to get murdered, it seemed like he'd had more practice. Whatever, the whole thing was a half-assed improvisation, and the only damn reason he was doing it was for her. Because she had guts, and was the cough-syrup fairy in a tight spot. That's what he'd been thinking as she'd looked down at him from the horse and then yanked the mane, turned, ridden off toward the fog lamps of the Rovers and disappeared. There goes the cough-syrup fairy.

He stifled a wet, raspy sneeze and gave a sigh of relief. He'd reached the horse barn, knowing first by the smell, then by seeing the soaked walls and the ramp. He rested against the side of the barn, then went inside, padding its length between the stalls, glad to be out of the rain for a moment. From the top of the courtyard ramp he saw the faint outlines of the house, heard nothing but the drumming rain on the stones and the heavier dripping from the eaves.

Crossing to the wall of the house that formed one side of the courtyard, he pressed himself under the protection of the eaves and made his way toward the door they'd entered with Mason. He saw a long, sleek Lincoln Mark, which hadn't been there before, then came to the white Rolls Corniche. The Director's Lincoln, Zoe's Rolls, which had carried Charlie . . . probably in the trunk. The players must all be on the board.

The Rolls had a helluva dent in the top of one fender, and he couldn't quite imagine how somebody dinged you from above, but that was Zoe's problem. The least of her problems, he supposed.

The trunk lid was wide open. Rain was blowing into it and collecting on the floor. It was all right on the money, just as it had been outlined in the murder letter, which he seemed to remember from the Pleistocene Age. Yesterday morning he'd met Celia over coffee at Homer's, and everything had been crazy ever since. . . . Well, back to business. He could see the sheet of paper in his mind. Rolls. Trunk. Prowler . . . who was in fact Charlie Cunningham, the poor dumb bastard, minus half an ear, bouncing along in the trunk of the Rolls just so he could do the woman's murder for her. The patsy. The Jerry Lewis of murderers. About to do a very big pratfall.

So where had Charlie gone when he dragged himself out of the trunk?

Greco went along the wall, thought for a moment, went back to the Rolls and slowly closed the trunk lid, hearing it lock with a solid thud.

Now, according to plan, Zoe was writing in the west wing. The Director was settling down with a scotch to get the world in a nutshell from Dan Rather.

But where was Charlie? Maybe he'd hastened the schedule, maybe he'd already shot the Director and was thinking about getting back into the trunk.

He looked at his watch. Six forty-five.

He found the side door, slowly turned the knob, pushed it open.

It was dark in the corridor, with only the one light at the far end. He gently closed the door and stood listening.

He heard water running somewhere. He grinned at the sound. It sounded like someone having a piss.

Quite unexpectedly he sneezed. A loud, violent sneeze that damn near blew his ears off.

Chapter Twenty-seven

✍

Bassinetti unhooked himself from the little device into which he'd stuck his fingertip. It computed his blood pressure and reported it in a tiny red digital readout. His blood pressure was perfect. His heart was also perfect, as another little gadget told him. He was in perfect health. He just couldn't walk. And losing a hundred pounds wouldn't do him any harm. Still, even with the weight and the sedentary fate, he had the constitution of the proverbial ox. Tonight was, he supposed, a kind of test. He intended to come through with all his pennants stiff in a fair wind.

He wheeled over to the drinks table in the study and carefully prepared a double Tanqueray martini with two large green olives for sustenance. He took the first sip, wet his full lips with the gin, savoring it. He looked at his watch. Six forty-five.

The long windows that gave onto the same stone balustrade as the library windows were partly open becuase he hated stuffy rooms. But, like Richard Nixon, he also like fires in fireplaces. With the breeze from the windows behind him, he wheeled across to the logs laid in the grate, lit the kindling with a long match, watched it catch fire. Damn, he was sorry about the rug in the library! It was so unlike Mason, screwing up such a rudimentary task as watching over, baby-sitting, a couple of peripheral individuals for a few hours. Instead they escape, the house is nearly burned down, and Mason himself is scorched in the process.

The fire crackled, flames darting, and his mind was elsewhere when a sound came from outside. But what? He listened again but heard nothing.

Where was Mason now? Where were the Rovers? And where were the woman and Greco?

He rolled across to the windows, swung one of the doors open, and looked out into the shuddering clouds of fog.

No one there.

The Director shook his head. It suddenly occurred to him that he didn't know where anyone was, nor what the devil was going on out there.

He *always* knew what was going on. And the realization that came on him in a twinkling of an eye—that he was suddenly bereft of information— came as an unpleasant shock.

He petulantly swung the chair around, turned on the television with the remote control. As Dan Rather appeared at seven o'clock he heard another noise, a hesitant footfall perhaps, and he slowly turned to the door that led not to the foggy night, but to the inner hall.

A man with a gun was standing in the doorway.

Mason had seen a Psycho Branch man crack once. It had been an unforgettably ugly spectacle, one he'd tried to hide at the very back of his mind behind all the murders and beatings and interrogations, but he could never forget it. All that anger and fear and pressure blowing a guy apart at the seams . . .

When he saw the Rover speeding down on him, when he couldn't make himself heard, when he thought he wasn't going to get the hell out of the way, he began to wonder if he'd had enough, if he wasn't about ready to come apart himself, like poor old Brown had done that time in Montevideo.

But somehow he grabbed a handful of grass and tugged his banged-up body out of the path as the Rover thundered past.

"Arnold!" he bellowed, and tried to cry out again but swallowed the name. He lay on his back, staring up at the fog with a dumb look on his face.

The Rover was empty.

His own goddamn Rover had come after him and tried to kill him. As if in revenge for being run into the stump.

Christalmighty!

Damn near got him too.

It took some doing, stacking up all his broken bones, but he got to his knees, then forced himself to his feet.

He was beginning to sound a little like old Brownie that night when the snakes in the booby trap got him in Montevideo. He wondered if old Brownie had known what was happening to him.

Mason wondered where the Rover had gone. His shotgun was probably still in it. Would it make another run at him?

He stood in the fog, trying to figure out where he was. He'd gotten all turned around.

He couldn't see a goddamned thing.

Thing was, how would you know if you were cracking up if there wasn't someone to see it happen? He wondered where Arnold was.

"Arnold?"

He waited.

"Arnold, you son of a bitch! Where are you?"

Charlie Cunningham was relieving himself in a darkened cubbyhole of a bathroom when he heard somebody sneeze right behind him. It had the effect of a bomb going off in his hip pocket. Reflexively he

levitated about six inches and made rather a mess,
which was hardly his fault.

He stood stock still, afraid even to zip his pants.
Afraid to breathe.

There wasn't supposed to be anyone in the back
hallway. There was supposed to be one Director in
the study, one lethal wife upstairs, and a Cunningham having a whiz.

There was no part for a sneezer in the hallway.

Nobody was moving. Charlie Cunningham wasn't
going to be first.

Finally he heard the faint creak of a floorboard,
then another. Very slow. Moving away.

When he'd gone into the bathroom, Cunningham
had been thankful for the mansion's careful upkeep.
No creaking hinges. He was even more thankful now
as he eased it open. He stuck his head out into the
hallway. He stopped breathing again.

Someone was standing about ten feet away. A little
shorter than Cunningham, much wider, standing
down the hallway and looking toward the end of the
corridor where the light showed dimly.

Cunningham took the gun out of his windbreaker,
holding it like a club. Could he get there and hit the
guy from behind before his footsteps gave him away?

He was calculating his chances when the guy's
shoulders hunched, he grabbed for his face, and
sneezed. His whole body shook and Charlie went for
him.

They say you're never closer to death than when
you sneeze. Charlie figured he would never have a
better shot.

He came down with the gun as hard as he could,
smashing it into the back of the guy's head.

The man grunted as if to say, *Hey, some kinda
sneeze!* He turned a quarter of the way around and
Charlie hit him another glancing blow, which floored
him.

He was dragging the inert body toward the closest door, pulling him by the heels, when he saw the man's face.

Holy Hannah! His mother, who thought he was writing a book about Yogi Berra, always said that. It was the same guy! The eye-patch guy!

The guy on Zoe's terrace, the guy who hadn't been there once they'd packed Friborg away in the trunk of the Rolls. The guy he'd already knocked out once, less than twenty-four hours before.

He couldn't remember the name.

Friend of the damned Blandings woman . . .

For a moment he felt sincerely sorry for the poor unconscious jerk. How many times could a guy get knocked out and still keep waking up again?

He tried the door, and it opened.

He dragged the guy in and laid him out lengthwise on the floor. He didn't want to feel around for a light switch. He could make out high shelves full of what looked like canned goods, jars. A long table in the middle. A pantry or something. He took a straight-backed chair from the table, went into the hall and closed the door. He jammed the chair up under the doorknob, tried to open the door, couldn't.

He took the gun out of his pocket again.

It was time to find the Director.

Chapter Twenty-eight

❧

Celia put all her faith in Roger, mainly because there was no one else to put any faith into at all. Also, because he was so big she couldn't really control him—making faith a necessity. Any anyway, it took all her concentration just to stay aboard.

Once she'd ridden away from Greco, her spirits had begun to flag. She wasn't in the least worried about herself: she had Roger and the fog and two goons in Land Rovers who couldn't see past their front bumpers. But Greco was on his own. He was heading into the enemy camp. And he was unarmed.

At least one person in the mansion would have a gun: Charlie Cunningham was no doubt there by now, earning the pseudonym Mr. Mystery. He was crazy, she was absolutely convinced of that. His performance in her apartment, to say nothing of the condition he was in when he departed, left little doubt of his mental state. If he hadn't been totally nuts before, Ed-the-Mean had certainly pushed him over the edge.

Creating a diversion wasn't as easy as it had sounded when Greco suggested it. First she had to find the guys in the Rovers so she could divert them.

Roger bolted out of the thicket where they'd been hiding and headed toward the open meadow, where she got an occasional glimpse of the yellow fingers of light. She had to get closer, put herself in view somehow, and then lead them away into the fog. But how?

The rain kept getting in her eyes, blinding her, though it didn't make all that much difference since she couldn't see anything anyway.

But when things began to happen, it was all very fast, as if she'd pushed the fast-forward button on her VCR.

One moment she was alone and lost, the next she was suddenly caught in the crisscrossing yellow lights of both Rovers. Roger reared, and she thought she was slipping off, but her fingers held in the mane. Roger wheeled and got the idea that he was getting to stay up late and play games. He galloped away. Celia felt as if the lights were glued to her back, but it couldn't have been more than a few seconds. She thought she heard someone shouting, but the wind was at her ears and Roger was breathing hard and his hooves were whacking at the turf and she gasped with each roller-coaster bump.

She didn't know where Roger was going, but he seemed unconcerned, taking a slow grade swiftly and with ease, the Rovers roaring behind her. She heard a sudden loud cracking sound behind her— not a gunshot, but something bigger and screeching and metallic, as if a Rover had sideswiped a wall— and glancing back she saw that there was only one of them left in the chase. It might have been gaining on her, she wasn't sure. She was just getting into the rhythm of Roger's stride when he began to slow and turn, almost at a walk.

"Roger, come on . . . please, Roger, what are you doing? Don't stop now, come on, Roger. . . ."

Which was when she heard some rocks and gravel slipping away underfoot, felt Roger step quickly. She strained to see what was going on, and saw that Roger was strolling along the edge of a great black abyss. She couldn't tell where it ended, but it seemed free of the fog that floated above it. She tugged at the mane, pulling him farther away from the edge. Her mouth was too dry to speak or swallow. She kept tugging, and slowly he altered his course, moving a few feet away from the loose ground.

Then the Rover appeared again, churning up the hill at full speed, fifteen or twenty yards behind her. Before she was able to register what was happening, the Rover had crested the ridge and there was no time for it to slow down or turn. It flew over the rim of the pit, its lights picking out the fogless emptiness when it was too late to avoid entering it.

It landed a couple of car lengths down the steep side of the ravine, which appeared now to be a wide, deep gravel pit. When the front wheels hit, the driver must have reflexively stood on the brakes. The wheels dug in, there was a squealing of metal on metal, and it turned over headfirst, the lights flashing wildly in every direction at once. It bounced end over end, glass shattering, a tire flying off into space, what she thought was the body of the driver cartwheeling off in another direction, and then the lights were smashed and all was plunged back into darkness and silence but for the taunting whinnying of Roger.

She was quite lost and had to make a choice. One, possibly two Rovers were out of action, and all she could do now was head Roger back in what she guessed was the direction from which she'd come.

Roger, seeming to sense that most of the fun was over, began ambling back down the hill. She kept patting the huge neck, telling him he was a very good, very brave Roger.

Several minutes passed before she saw the yellow lights of the other Rover. It was moving erratically, as if the driver were drunk, swinging in a wide circle, cutting around in back of her without seeming to notice she was there. Then it ground to a halt with its lights behind her, pointing toward what she hoped was the house.

She was thinking about the strange behavior of the Rover and wondering if she was headed the right way. She should have been paying attention to Roger but instead kicked him in the ribs, wanting to get out of the light. When he quickened his pace, she realized too late she was slipping from his wet back.

She landed with a wet noise, half on her tail, half on an ankle that had gotten twisted beneath her.

"Damn," she groaned.

Why wasn't the man in the Rover doing anything? He must be able to see her. She was trapped in the light. But the Rover just sat there, staring at her.

Roger waited a few feet ahead, munching on some grass, standing beside a thick stump jutting up out of the soft meadow.

She stood up, gingerly testing her ankle, which wasn't right at all, and limped after Roger.

The stump was a godsend. Without it there'd have been no way to remount.

She struggled to get atop the stump, which was badly and freshly scarred on one side, and was halfway onto Roger's broad back when—

"Aaarrrrghhhhh!" It was a scream of anger, pain, frustration, hatred.

He'd come from nowhere. His face was distorted, a huge, angry red puffiness on one side, his hand grappling for one of her ankles.

She didn't scream. She couldn't. It was the nightmare of nightmares, a creature rising from the darkness of the underworld to pull her down. . . .

She kicked out, dug her fingers deep into Roger's mane, felt him beginning to pull away from her attacker. She yanked her leg but he wouldn't let go, kept growling and chasing after her as Roger began dancing sideways. The man—it had to be Mason—surely, it had to be! But her mind had cut out, she was running on an atavistic fear she'd never even imagined before, pulling her leg away from the icy

grip, willing herself not to give in. Roger was moving
faster now and her body was being pulled off the
horse, but she wouldn't, couldn't let go of the thick
mane. Slowly the hand began to slide down her wet
ankle. He was being dragged now as Roger circled
away. He couldn't keep his feet as he moved in and
out of the awful yellow light, spinning with Roger,
and he hooked his fingers into her sneaker. She
pulled even harder, using reserves of strength and
nerve never summoned before, and the sneaker
began to give, her foot was sliding out, the heel
almost free . . . and then Mason was hurtling sideways like the end man on a gigantic whip of skaters.
Gravity pulled him away and he was flung backward, hung for a moment in the ghostly illumina-
tion, then slammed over the edge of the stump. He
seemed to bend so far backward that he would break,
but instead there was a howl of pain and he slumped
off the stump and rolled out of sight, only his legs
showing, which twitched slowly, unable to get him
up.

Celia hung on, pulling herself back onto Roger's
reassuring bulk. She tried to say something to him
but the words wouldn't come, and she lay gasping,
hugging his neck, nuzzling her face into the wet
mane.

As soon as she was aware of what was going on,
when she was able to breathe and wet her lips and
sense that Roger must be heading back toward the
house, she looked down at her watch.

Oh, my God! Dan Rather was just beginning!

When Greco came to, he couldn't for several
moments remember where he was. First he thought
he was at home, waking from a bad dream. Then he
thought he might be on Zoe Bassinetti's terrace. No,
he didn't seem to be there either. He lifted his head

and the fireworks began exploding behind his eyes and in his ears, but something told him he'd better not put his poor goddamn head back down and go to sleep. He'd better stay awake, and while he was trying to do that, he remembered where he was. More or less.

He didn't know who'd hit him or what kind of place he'd been stuffed into. He didn't know how long he'd been unconscious either, but when you got sapped you weren't usually out all that long, if you were going to come out of it at all. He remembered that time was short. He forced himself to stand up.

Total darkness, except for all the lights strobing away inside his skull. He felt for a wall, found some shelves, followed the shelves until he came to a door frame, felt for the knob, turned it and pushed, then pushed harder. Nothing. It held tight. Next he felt along the wall next to the shelving. Behind something that felt like a can of Crisco he found the switch and flicked it. The light went on.

It was a can of Crisco. Several cans of Crisco. Enough Crisco to last a lifetime.

He'd been locked into a pantry the size of his own bedroom.

He squinted against the bright bulb overhead and squeezed his temples to stop the Gene Krupa concert. He didn't really expect the squeezing to work—it never had—and sure enough, it didn't.

There was a long table, food sufficient for a supermarket. He'd been sapped in the corridor, where presumably the deliveries of foodstuffs were made. It stood to reason that there had to be another door leading from the pantry to the kitchen. He found it wedged into the far corner of the pantry, between a ceiling-high shelf and a wall fixture that held every known kind of mop.

He tried the door. Naturally it was unlocked. Who locks the pantry door? It didn't even have a lock. He went through the kitchen, moving cautiously so as not to knock over chairs, tables, and dishwashers. As it was, he wobbled a bit and bumped into the doorway on his way out into another hallway, this one carpeted and leading to the foyer with the portraits and the massive staircase, where Mason had relieved him of his gun earlier. He thought to look at his watch for the first time since waking up. Seven o'clock.

The foyer was empty, lit by the chandelier, which sparkled like diamonds strung on ropes. The sliding doors to the library were closed. The smell of smoke hung like fog in the foyer anyway. He stood listening, heard the ticking of a clock from somewhere in the shadows.

Slowly he picked out the murmur of voices. He passed the staircase and struck off down yet another hallway. The murmur became distinguishable as voices.

A light shone from a doorway.

Two men. No, three.

But one of them was Dan Rather.

Greco was trying to think just what he should do. Well, something would come to him.

He moved along the wall, thankful for the thick carpeting.

At the edge of the doorway he stopped to listen.

He heard the clicking of glasses.

Someone said: "Confusion to our enemies . . ."

A toast.

Chapter Twenty-nine

❧

Emilio Bassinetti looked from the hand with the gun into the face of the man he'd been expecting. His wife's lover.

"Ah, Charlie," he said, glancing from his watch to the television image of Dan Rather's serious, movie-star face and very serious blue pinstripe suit, then back to Cunningham. "Right on time. I daresay my lovely wife is even now straining to hear the shot. . . . Come in, my boy, come in."

Cunningham looked around at the elegant study, a room with all the material goods he'd ever wished he could afford. The gun hung limply in his hand. The Director nodded to one of the leather wingbacks and Charlie went to stand beside it, massaging the blood-colored leather with his left hand, getting the feel of it.

"Egad, I hope you don't mind my saying it, Charlie, but you do look a little ragged." The Director was thinking that, in fact, Cunningham and Mason had taken on the appearance of a pair of particularly unattractive bookends. Monuments to their own inefficiency, careworn; surprising in Mason, at least.

"Ragged? You wouldn't believe what I've been through," Cunningham said, his hand nervously checking the bandage on his ear. "Two dead men, did you know that? Did she tell you she killed a guy on the terrace at Sutton Place? Oh, that was beautiful. Guess who got to dispose of the body? She's

crazy . . . it was never supposed to turn out like
this, never—"

The Director raised a hand to interrupt, to stop the
flow of self-pity. "Please, humor me, will you,
Charlie? There are certain bits of information it's
better I don't now. I'm bound to undergo some very
stiff questioning over the next couple days and the
less I actually know the better—"

"So who's gonna be questioning you?"

"We'll get to that in due course. The point is, in my
role as innocent country squire beset by domestic
tragedy in my own home this evening—"

"What domestic tragedy?" Cunningham looked
vaguely concerned—where, the Director observed,
he should already have begun to look wary, were he
as bright as he thought he was.

"Wait and all will be made clear, Charlie. Suffice it
to say it's better if I am quite truthfully unaware of
certain events—"

"Sure, that's all right for you," Cunningham said,
beginning to pace between the leather chairs and the
wall of bookcases, "but there's a dead man in my
apartment—"

"You don't say! Well, we'll go into that in due
course as well—"

"Look, this has all gotten a lot more complicated
than I'd bargained for—"

"In the immortal words of the late Mr. Jolson,"
Bassinetti said, smiling his long, crocodile smile,
"you ain't seen nothin' yet. However, first things
first. My wife has no idea that you and I are now in
cahoots, as they say—is that right? She still thinks
you're down here murdering me?"

"Of course. The egomaniac she is, she'd never
dream a plan of hers would go off the rails—"

"Good, good. Now let me assure you, Charlie, you
can put the body in your apartment entirely out of
your mind. He's caused you all the inconvenience
he's going to. Trust me."

Cunningham looked mollified, stopped pacing, leaned on the chair back as if it were a lectern.

"Here, have a drink, Charlie. You look like a man who might know what to do with a drink. Name your poison." He wheeled himself back over to the drinks table. "How does a double Tanqueray martini sound?"

Cunningham came out from behind the chair, still holding the gun, waiting while Bassinetti made the drink, merely passing the unopened bottle of Cinzano dry vermouth over the cocktail pitcher. A pair of olives plummeted like depth charges into the martini, and Bassinetti held it out to him.

"Here you go, my boy," the Director said. "And Charlie? Your trousers, they're unzipped. There's a good fellow, make yourself presentable." He lifted his own glass, clinked it against Charlie's. "Confusion to our enemies," he said.

Cunningham swallowed deeply and shook his head. He sank down into the leather chair. "Confusion. Well, confusion to everyone. I'm so damn confused sometimes . . . all I know is, I want my money—"

"Absolutely, you shall have it. And soon I have an even more appealing proposal to make to you—just trust me, Charlie. Stay with me while I ramble on." He opened a carved box on the desk. "Cigar?" Charlie shook his head. The Director took one, clipped it and lit it, puffing slowly.

All the frittering of time was getting on Charlie's nerves. "Well, here I am," he said. "I've sent you everything you wanted. All of her notes, everything that documents her plan to kill you, all the notebooks and photocopies of Palisades files, everything she used to research the book. You've got the floppy disks—"

"Tell me, Charlie, what do you think of the book,

now that the two of you have completed it? What do you really think?"

"You know damn well what I think! It's utterly devastating. . . ."

"Yes," the Director mused, nodding his massive, shiny head. He studied the smoke from the cigar. "It's a shame in a way that it can never be published—"

"You'd be destroying yourself, of course—"

"Of course," the Director agreed, kept on nodding, watching the curling smoke. "But then, who am I? In the vast scheme of things? A nobody. Mr. Nobody. A trusted functionary, sufficiently corrupt, suitably paid for his services, just another soldier in the great war. My departure would go largely unnoticed . . . but think of all the others! Well, the mind reels!" He smiled at Charlie, who sank more deeply in his chair and chewed on an olive. "Everyone would go down if the book were published. *Everyone* . . . the White House and its complement of idiots would sink like stones . . . the list of casualties is endless . . . and that's where my power now lies, Charlie— not in what I know, what I carry around in my head. I've known all that from the beginning—kill me and all that would die with me. But *now*! Kill me now," he chuckled, a moist, rolling sound, "and the trouble just begins . . . because of this instrument of destruction, this book Zoe and you have written." He smiled expansively, beatifically. "With this instrument I can destroy them all, and that's what I've now . . ." He looked at his watch. "Yes, right about now, informed them of. The fact that I, too, would be destroyed is immaterial. You might try to think of me now as the Mad Bomber, clad in a vest of dynamite, holding the magic button that can blow us all to smithereens. The fact is, Charlie, to all these mighty people I'm the single most important man in the world. It's a good feeling. Anything happens to me, they all go up in smoke. I'm the safest man in the world, and they know it. If my attorneys open the package in their vaults upon my death, boom! It's over for everyone . . . kablooey!" He smiled at the sound of the word.

Charlie grinned. "Exactly. You've got 'em right where they don't want to be. The end of a job well done. You're safe. You've done a helluva lot to ensure your safety—"

"Oh, I've done far more than that. Don't you see?"

"No, I'm afraid I don't. But that's all right. I'd just like to get my money and get out. Zoe's not gonna like it when you turn out not to be dead, but she's your problem again, I'm out of it. If I'm lucky, I'll never see the bitch again—"

"You'd have to go to Brazil, change your name, live in the jungle . . . and Charlie, chances are she'd still find you and make you wish you'd never been born. That's just the way Zoe is. . . ."

"I'll take my chances," he said, but his face was suddenly shadowed by the doubt that had been just beneath the surface all along. They both knew Zoe too well.

"Will you, at that? I'd say that's not much of a plan, Charlie. Now, consider my position for a moment. I needed the instrument, the book. But how to create it? And I needed to rid myself of a troublesome and—you'll excuse me—unfaithful slut of a wife who was responsible for turning me into a pile of fat who can't walk. How to do it? Then, in a flash, stretched out on my back trying to decide if I wanted to live or not, I knew how to do both. First the book— I made sure my wife, the writer, found out all about Palisades . . . how Palisades is the clearing house for all CIA and Mafia joint ventures, how the CIA and Psycho Branch and the Mafia worked hand in glove, shoulder to shoulder, even sharing command of operations, all to control the drug traffic coming out of Central and South America . . . how Palisades was the banker and money laundry and coordinator for all these group efforts . . . how the CIA and Psycho Branch used the drug money to prop up puppet governments and guerilla movements, without ever having to seek official funding."

The Director passed his cigar over a ferocious-looking cut-glass ashtray, and the gray cylinder of ash dropped off. On the television screen a friendly, rather puckish man was asking if a Tums had ever tickled your nose like an Alka-Seltzer. Dan Rather would be back in a moment. "I let her see these things, I tempted her with files, reports, computer printouts, I left the odd memorandum conveniently—but not too conveniently—here in the study . . . oh, after I had her interest, I made the stuff harder to find. But I knew she'd keep after it because she couldn't resist—she wanted to believe what she was on to. I even confided in her one night, told her the one thing I could never afford was a leak from Palisades, a Pentagon Papers fiasco repeated in the matter of Palisades . . . and I let her vicious nature take its natural course. . . ."

Cunningham had finished his martini and went back to the table, poured the rest of the mixture into his glass. It was diluted by melting ice, but he'd never heard the Director open up like this before. He didn't want to distract him by mixing a new batch. He'd never met anyone quite like Bassinetti. There were bound to be a few Zoe's around, but Bassinetti's were something else again. He came back and sat down again. The gin was doing his ear a world of good. The fire flickered, and a breeze nibbled at the room's warmth.

"Of course," the Director went on, as if he were glad for the chance to talk about his own master plot, "I knew she'd taken you as a lover. The perfect collaborator on her magnum opus. In thrall to her sexually, you'd do whatever she wanted you to do. Now remember, this has been a two-year project of mine. I managed with relative ease to infiltrate your life and hers electronically—yes, I have my own collection of tapes too. Once I knew she'd taken the bait, had done the book and decided to murder me— have a prowler murder me, that is—well, it was all so perfect. Kill me, she inherits, but if I live, there might be some problems with a divorce, sympathy for the cripple being dumped by the beautiful hot number, all that.

"So all that remained was for me to entice you into my camp. One thing I could be sure of, the woman's abrasive nature and chain-mail personality would make you hate her eventually, and I had plenty of time. In that event, you'd think it over and decide to throw your hand in with me. But if you hadn't, I'd have summoned you and given you this chance of a lifetime. Oh, yes, it's been one of those picture-perfect plans. Now, you see, we will be free of my wife, you will be very well off indeed, and I have the leverage to make myself truly wealthy, simply by suggesting that an increase of my remuneration would be a sure way to keep that book from ever being published—"

"Hold on," Cunningham said, swilling gin around his mouth, and waving the gun in front of him. "You're slipping a couple things past me here. In the first place, I wouldn't describe myself as coming off very well indeed, and so far, in the second place, you are still stuck with your wife."

"Cogent points," Bassinetti admitted, "but perhaps we can . . . listen, what am I paying you this evening for your services?" He smiled, smacking his thick lips, stroking his smooth chin, nestled in its setting of fat.

"You know damn well. Twenty-five thousand in cash."

"Ah, you remembered! Well, why don't you take a peek in that Vuitton suitcase over there. Yes, it's not locked. Open it, have a look."

Cunningham snapped the locks, opened the lid, and nearly fainted. "Jesus!"

"Well said, Charlie! How much cash would you estimate you're looking at?"

He shook his head. "I don't know—"

"Have a guess, Mr. Mystery."

"A hundred thousand?"

"Oh, no, more than that. All freshly laundered too. No way to trace it at all. Guess again."

"I don't know, what's the game here?"

"Humor me. Guess."

"Quarter of a million? How do I know?"

"Half a million, Charlie. Cold, very cold, cash. And it's yours. Shows how much I think of you . . . you're quite a chap, y'know. You've been a great help. But there is one more thing—"

"Half a million in tax-free cash." Cunningham sighed, looked up at the Director. "One more thing? Name it."

"Aha, Charlie, I knew you'd see it that way! What a good sport!" The Director chuckled, his vast gut shaking. "All you have to do is kill our abominable Zoe. On the whole it should be a most enjoyable way to earn half a million dollars, what?"

Chapter Thirty

Greco leaned against the wall and wondered if he'd heard what he thought he'd heard.

Palisades overseeing CIA, Psycho Branch, and Mafia drug interests, presumably an enterprise so enormous that neither the Mafia nor the Feds could handle it themselves. It was all so superbly logical, yet immensely daring because of the risk of discovery. Somehow they'd all gotten into bed together, with Palisades fronting the operation, coordinating all their efforts, which had to include dealing with Washington as well as all the individual Latin American countries. It was logical, sure, but the complexity must have been incredible . . . and worth it. And that was what Celia, the cough-syrup fairy, had wandered into. He realized even in that instant that they would probably never know what kind of difficulty she posed for Palisades, because it was all mixed up with the husband/wife mess, the book exposing the whole thing, the attempt by the Director to blackmail everybody. . . .

If he'd heard what he thought he heard, he wanted to burst out with the biggest, longest, loudest laugh of his life. It was priceless! Bassinetti wasn't talking about a few agents free-lancing in the drug business with the Mob: that had been going on for years, it was part of the culture, almost a CIA perk when it came to dicking around in scary southern climes. No, this thing was *policy*, with Palisades as a huge, essentially legitimate front. This was a mainline

organization. This came with approval from the top.
It was the way around begging Congress for money to
work the presidential will south of the border. It took
heavy foreign entanglements out of the advise-and-
consent category. What it did, in fact, was create a
second, secret government within the one you saw
on the TV news every night . . . and the second
government was funded by getting into the drug
business with the Mob.

It was the story of a lifetime. Teddy Birney would
have killed for such a story. And then there was poor
Celia! All she'd wanted to do was keep Zoe from
knocking off her poor crippled husband.

If Greco lived a thousand years, which seemed
increasingly unlikely at the rate his head was being
bashed open and generally maltreated, he doubted if
he'd ever get it figured out.

The General! That had to be General Cates, once
Chairman of the Joint Chiefs, now officially retired
and overseeing most of the intelligence and security
services, a kind of czar, reporting to God only knew
whom. And the manuscript—well, now he knew
what they were talking about.

The thought of trying to explain it all to anyone,
even Celia, left him weak. The problem was, he
really was feeling weak and crummy and light-
headed.

Then the tickling began deep in his nasal passages,
like an army of killer ants setting out, tramp-tramp-
tramping, marching toward his sinuses. He fought
back a sneeze, but they kept coming on like gang-
busters, raping and pillaging and burning. He
grabbed for his handkerchief to clap over his nose
but it was too little, too late.

He sneezed so hard his head smashed forward into
the wall, making a sound that sounded like an
explosion in an echo chamber, racketing on and on.

"God bless you," a voice said.

Greco tried to focus through the tears running from his eye. His head whiplashed again with a second brain-rattling sneeze and a fit of sputtering and coughing. He wiped his nose.

"You must be Mr. Greco," the voice said.

"If you say so," Greco sniffed. He looked down into the black eye of a snub-nosed .38, held in the pink, pulpy fist of a very fat man in a wheelchair. Greco shook the cobwebs out of his head, but could only glimpse spiders. He wished he could do a Bogart impression to get things off on the right foot.

"My name is Emilio Bassinetti. Please, do come in." He wheeled backward, keeping the gun trained on Greco. "You look terrible too. Why is it that everyone I see around here tonight looks as if they'd come directly from a mugging by Hulk Hogan?"

"Do you want an answer, or is that a rhetorical question?"

"Rhetorical, I suppose. Come in, come, come. Have a drink . . . take a load off your feet." The broad beefy face, slightly flushed, wore a grin that made it look very friendly. "To be honest with you, I heard you bumbling around in the hallway some time ago, but I didn't want to interrupt my final seduction of Mr. Cunningham—you are familiar with our Mr. Cunningham?"

"By reputation only."

"Yes. Well, you have been very swift on the uptake, you and Miss Blandings—"

"Mason tells you this stuff, right?"

"I have a variety of sources. In any case, I'm afraid Mr. Cunningham's concentration is rather fragile at the moment—intrigue is not a field in which he naturally shines, of course—and he really needed time to pull himself together. Please forgive this gun, Mr. Greco, it's nothing personal, but I always feel at a disadvantage with my . . . my infirmity."

"You seem to do pretty well," Greco muttered,

edging into the study, feeling cold, tired, and a lot
like the man in the nasal spray commercial who
seems to have drawn his last breath through a
clogged nose.

"Over here by the fire," Bassinetti said. "Goodness,
you're soaking wet. Sounds to me as if the flu's got
you in its grip."

Greco went to warm himself at the fire, felt it
attacking the clammy chill that had worked its way
deep into his bones. "Hey!" He looked around the
room. "Where is Cunningham anyway? I heard the
two of you talking. . . ." His head was hot and his
eyes burning. He had a fever, and his hair was matted
with blood where the gun butt had split his scalp.

"He left through that door over there." Bassinetti
pointed to one of the French doors in the long bank
of windows. "He's gone to pay a call on my wife.
There's an outside staircase to her rooms in the west
wing—"

"Oh, shit! He's gonna kill her!" The conversation
he'd overheard was filtering back through his fever-
ish memory and he tried to get out of the chair but
was moving slowly at the center of a tilted, spinning
room.

"Now, now," the Director said soothingly. "Make it
easy on yourself. Just let nature take its course.
Sooner or later one man or another was bound to kill
the woman. It's her fate, I'm convinced. She's so
immensely killable, but you don't know her like we
do. Ah, your eye patch, your sneezing fit blew it off
to one side. . . ."

Greco straightened the patch. He felt the flu bugs
invading him, calling up reinforcements, out for the
kill. His throat was suddenly raw and tender.

"Well, you got quite an earful, I'm afraid. Sorry to
burden you with it, but let me give you a word of
advice. If I were you, I wouldn't let anyone know you
heard a word. If certain people found out," he

purred, shrugging his massive shoulders, "you wouldn't want to be you. See my point? You're a man who's survived a great deal in your time. You know how the world works. Now, take this drug business. You couldn't stop it if you were willing even to forfeit your life to do so. You can see that. So don't be a silly dead jerk who thought for a minute he could be a hero. This world, this tail end of the century, it's no place for heroes. Their time has passed." He sighed at the way the world had gone downhill. "Now," he brightened, "how about a drink? A brandy?"

"Yeah, sure, a brandy."

"Go ahead. Get it for yourself. Just don't do anything ill-advised."

He went to the drinks table. "A, I'm not a hero, Mr. Bassinetti. And B, I'm too damn tired to make a break for it. And C, what would I do if I did?" He poured brandy into a snifter. "What I need is an antibiotic."

"Indeed you do. These colds can turn nasty. Well, this'll all be over soon enough. Very soon now Mr. Cunningham will have a brief but decisive chat with my wife. Don't be frightened if you hear a shot."

"I'll try to control myself."

"Good man! Then Mr. Cunningham will come down to see me and collect a great deal of money."

Greco wondered where Celia was, but he was so tired and felt so wretched that he doubted he was thinking straight. She was out there in the fog with that gigantic horse. She must be wet as hell. The bad guys would never find her in the fog. The brandy was burning his throat but he drank some more and figured the hell with it, at least he couldn't feel any worse. Dan Rather was long gone. The Director had flicked him out of existence, and the screen was gray as the fog. Somebody was playing violins or cellos on the stereo. "What's that?"

"Beethoven's late quartets. Suits my mood."

They heard a very loud bang.

"What was that?"

"That was Mr. Cunningham killing my wife."

Charlie Cunningham stood at the top of the stairway, feeling the rain plastering his hair to his head and running in thick rivulets down his face. Through the window in the door he saw the white room in which Zoe worked. A creamy white with beige trim. She sat at the desk. She wore a heavy blue sweater, and he knew beneath the desktop were her tight white jeans. He thought about never going to bed with her again. Then he thought about half a million dollars, tax free. He hadn't planned on having to kill her, but the half million was a great persuader. The Director was right, there was no other way to be rid of her. And if the Director got any clever ideas about what to do with Charlie Cunningham, all Charlie had to do was point out that he'd made himself a copy of the manuscript.

He opened the door and came in out of the cold and rain.

Zoe looked up, her sultry face pinched with frustration and impatience.

"Where have you been? It's seven-forty. What have you been doing?" The questions came like machine-gun fire.

Charlie stared at her, couldn't think of what to say. He was still holding the gun in his right hand. The bandage was heavy and wet, rubbing at his torn ear.

"Well? Is he dead?" Her voice had that familiar scraping, tearing edge. Like salt in a wound. "You idiot! Say something! Is it done? Did you kill him? Or did you chicken out?" Slowly her expression of anger turned to one of disgust. "Oh . . . you did, you screwed it up!" She spat the words at him, stood up, glaring. "You poor fool!" Her eyes, so soft and liquid in the heat of passion, flashed like laser weaponry, and he thought about how he could dull them forever, put out her lights for good.

"I didn't kill him," he said tonelessly.

"Idiot!" She came toward him like a fourth-rate Lady Macbeth, checked herself, went back to the desk. "All right, now you must go back down there and do it, Charlie." She took a tiny gun from beside her typewriter. He wondered why she had a gun so close at hand. Then it began to dawn on him. He was supposed to have already killed Bassinetti when, as the prowler, he came to her room. . . .

"Everybody's got a gun," he said. "I've never seen so many guns—"

"Stop babbling, Charlie! Now get out of here. I want you to use that gun. There's still time to go ahead with the plan." She bored twin holes in his skull with those eyes.

He went back to the doorway and the rain. He looked out into the night, felt the rain blowing in on his face.

"Look at the mess you've tracked in here! Charlie, can't you do anything right? Use your head, think! Don't be so hopeless, so stupid, such a loser! Are you listening to me, Charlie? Now use that gun!"

"All right," he said. He drew a mental picture of the Vuitton bag, saw that it was all he'd ever hoped for, and turned back to Zoe. She was so beautiful. He raised the gun.

"Now what do you think you're doing?"

"Using the gun, Zoe."

She realized what was happening at the last second and pulled her own gun up.

They both pulled their triggers at the same instant.

It made a hell of a noise.

Celia heard the crack of the shot, which was carried on the wind blowing rain and fog from the direction of the house, directly into her face. Her ankle was swelling and felt like it had been crushed in a vise. Damn! It was always some damn thing— but the shot roused her from the contemplation of her pain.

Roger's ears perked up.

She saw the lights of the study far away. The fog was either blowing away at last or she'd found a hole in it.

The sound of the shot echoed like a crack of thunder.

There were the glowing lights—

No! They couldn't have failed, not after all this. . . .

No! It just couldn't have come to nothing, not now—

"Come on, Roger!"

She was so cold, so wet, so far over her own precipice of fear and frustration. . . .

Oh, God, what if someone had shot Peter!

And Roger was running again. . . .

Chapter Thirty-one

~

Greco sat silently, feeling as if he'd been waiting since just after the Second World War for something to happen once the sound of the gunshot died away. It wasn't a time for small talk. A woman, however great a bitch she might have been, was lying freshly dead, under the same roof. And the silence bore with it a kind of doom-ridden, oppressive sense of mortality. He was sweating while simultaneously chills shook him. He'd never gotten so sick so fast, but he felt guilty thinking that way, in light of what had just happened in the west wing. He did his best to stifle another sneeze.

Bassinetti sat like a highly contemplative Buddha in his wheelchair, his face void of emotion, the eyes buried in the dark pouches beneath them, the full mouth set firmly, resolved. It was the face of a man who found himself trapped in a wheelchair that he certainly hadn't sought, trapped in a sea of treachery and amorality and money as black as midnight, which he certainly had sought. His face looked as if ideas of right and wrong had been drained from his brain, replaced by craft and cunning and the will to survive, win, in a game without rules. It wasn't a face that gave away much, but Greco sensed in it a kind of surprise that things kept turning out as oddly as they did.

His .38 was trained on the doorway.

He was going to shoot Charlie Cunningham when he came through the door to collect his half million.

Bassinetti had it all figured out. Nerd Charlie kills the wife, his lover. The Director kills the *prowler* who, to his amazement, turns out to be the maddened, newly jilted lover who'd just killed his former mistress. . . .

It was a good story, ironclad. He wouldn't lose if he just stuck to it. And if Peter Greco kept his mouth shut.

But poor Charlie, Greco reflected. Stupid, befogged by sexual desire, dominated by an impossible creature . . . He didn't really deserve to die, did he? The last time Greco had looked it up, stupidity and lubriciousness were not punishable by death.

Without warning the door to the hallway swung slowly open.

From the corner of his eye Greco saw the muzzle of a pistol moving forward like the head of a snake, mouth open.

There really wasn't much time to think of it in a logical sequence. All of Greco's training simply took over. He summoned up in a paroxysm of reflexive action his last ragged bits of energy and hurled himself like a beat-up old warrior from a generation long forgotten to hit the Director from the side as he pulled the trigger.

The gun in the doorway let out a sharp, snotty little bark and Greco felt the bite ripping at the left side of his neck. Hurt like a bitch.

The wheelchair crashed over sideways, and Bassinetti was shouting something crazy that didn't make any sense, just a babble of outrage, which was hardly surprising.

Greco sprawled across the mountainous body, twisted to look up and back at the door to tell Charlie to stop shooting for chrissake—

But it wasn't Charlie in the doorway.

Old Charlie must not have made it out of the west

wing, wasn't going to make it out of this particular nest of vipers . . . because it was Zoe Bassinetti standing there.

She was leaning against the wall, trying to point her gun again and keep shooting. It kept wobbling because she was in pretty bad shape.

One sleeve of her heavy blue sweater was shredded. That arm hung limply. The white hand was red with blood running down the fingers, over the gold and the diamonds.

Her face was blank and pale, showing shock and dismay. She was giving everything she had to raising that gun only far enough to start blazing away at the bodies on the floor.

Greco was caught in the Director's useless legs, and his left hand had gotten wedged in the spokes of the wheel. He kept twisting and turning but only managed to get deeper in debt, getting nowhere, while Zoe just about succeeded in getting both of them in her sights—

And then the wall of windows exploded in a rain of shattered glass!

Roger had taken the balustrade at full tilt, unworried about the windows since it was still foggy and blurry and he'd never been here before.

Celia had dug her heels into his flanks, and the bank of windows had been no match for him. He hardly even noticed them.

The panes imploded, spraying glass across the Director's study. Roger stopped just short of the drinks table. He looked around as if to say, Hey, you *know* this isn't the barn, right, lady?

Celia tried to see what she'd interrupted, but all she saw was one hell of a mess.

Greco and a fat man seemed to be wrestling on the floor at Roger's feet. They were covered in a snowfall of glass.

Zoe Bassinetti was dripping blood, holding a gun, staring in open-mouthed amazement at a world gone quite mad. She took a few steps toward the men entangled on the floor. She was weaving, wiped her face with one hand and smeared it with blood like war paint. She started to say something, looking up at Celia . . . the gun pointed down at Greco's head . . .

Celia kicked out at her hand, caught the wrist with the point of her remaining sneaker and watched the little pistol spin away toward the corner of the room—

"Zoe!" It was a scream in the night, a shriek, disembodied.

"Zoe!"

Zoe turned sluggishly, suddenly disarmed, back toward the doorway.

Celia looked too.

Charlie Cunningham stood in the doorway. The front of his windbreaker was soaked with blood. He looked like he was trying to laugh.

Instead he began shooting.

Zoe jumped off the floor with the impact of the slugs smashing into her beautiful, bloodied body.

She hit Roger's hindquarters and left a sticky smear on his flank as she slid to the floor.

Charlie made it halfway into the study before he lay down almost gently, a crooked little smile on his face, and died.

It was quite still.

Greco slowly got to his knees, kicked free of the spinning wheel of Bassinetti's chair. He reached up and took Celia's hand, pulled himself upright.

"Peter, oh, Peter . . . are you okay?"

"Gotta helluva cold, Slats . . ."

She felt him squeezing her hand.

The Director was wheezing and snorting.

Roger tried to ignore the whole scene.

Celia looked down into Greco's face, his weak smile, his runny nose. His neck was bloody.

She had no idea what was going on. And Linda Thurston wouldn't have either.

AFTER

The tiny, dusty dressing room was crowded to bursting: with flowers, telegrams, popping bottles of champagne, and smiling, shouting, babbling well-wishers and fellow actors and friends. Celia sat on a stool, her back to the mirror and the makeup table, and tried to hear what they were all saying to her.

The lights had gone down on the opening night of *Misconceptions* five minutes before, when she and Debbie Macadam had taken their final curtain call as co-stars, Celia's part having been beefed up in the rewrites. Debbie had insisted that she would take no solo curtain calls just because people has seen her in movies, so they'd come off hand in hand, relieved and happy and bursting with hope, leaving the tight little off-Broadway stage and finding Billy Blumenthal, the director, waiting to kiss and hug them both at the door to the dressing room. The two guys in the cast were there, too, and then everybody started arriving and the chaos began.

The crowd out front was still milling around in the ninety-degree June night, which had been spent without aid of air-conditioning. Morris Levy came in, mopping his face with a red bandanna, a happy author who'd diligently done his work through the past three weeks. He gave Celia a heartfelt hug and whispered a thank-you for her performance; then Joel Goldman, her agent, was whispering in her ear, telling her he had a feeling about this show. "It's got it all, kid," he said. "You're gonna be doing it for a long time. And you'll have time to play with Linda Thurston!" He grinned broadly, kissed her cheek again, and somebody handed her a Styrofoam cup of warm, cheap champagne that bubbled nobly and tasted like heaven.

She was almost afraid to admit it, but Joel was right, it did have that feeling. It had all been out there on the postage-stamp-size stage: all the scary lighting cues had worked to perfection, the rewrites had worked, the gasps and laughs and tense silences had all been right on the money.

Greco came in after the first wave of first nighters had departed. He stood in the doorway, looking around shyly, self-consciously. Celia had never seen him in a suit before, and he looked unsure of himself, didn't seem to realize what an imposing figure he was in the dark blue summer suit, his scarred face deeply tanned and the eye patch you couldn't ignore. A kind of energy seemed to pulsate from him. She felt it even where she sat.

Celia caught his glance, held it, and watched as he smiled slowly, still hanging back from the crowd that encircled her. She excused herself and stood up. Even in her garish, ghoulish back-from-the-dead costume, covered in stage gore, she looked up at him and was unable to stop smiling.

There were some events of which she still knew nothing, would never know. But her mind was crowded with a tumult of images she knew she'd never forget.

Greco with a bullet wound in his neck and pneumonia in both lungs, and Celia taking a bouquet of tulips to his hospital room and kissing him to wake him up. . . .

The flurry of people from Washington, from mysterious agencies that were never quite identified, who'd come to New York to speak to her, telling her she had to forget what had happened because the security of the republic was at issue and she didn't want to let her country down, did she?

And the prominent account in the *Times* of the

tragic death of mystery novelist Miles Warriner at the hands of a terrified burglar, interrupted while writing at a New Jersey country estate.

And Admiral Malfaison and General Cates locking the only copy—other than that damn Bassinetti's—of the Palisades manuscript in a vault so far beneath the Pentagon it was closer to Beijing than Washington.

And the funeral in Queens of an Italian restaurateur and hit man, Vincenzo Giraldo.

And the tiny obituary of Mr. Mystery, dead after a West Village street mugging.

And the note in *Publishers Weekly* about Jesse Lefferts, newest senior editor at Pegasus House.

And the blur of rehearsals, going to visit Peter as he recovered and got out of the hospital, began coming to her place with Chinese for dinners with her and Hilary, and began tentatively to get his pool stroke back.

"Peter, thanks for the beautiful roses—"

"Listen, Slats, you were wonderful, scared the hell out of me—"

"And you're a pretty hard guy to scare."

"Medium hard," he said.

She felt herself starting to cry, but he put his arms around her and kissed her.

"Oh, Peter, you'll get this bloody gunk all over you."

"You've seen me bloody before . . . and anyway, who cares? You look . . . just . . . just—"

She laughed and threw her arms around his neck.

"I've got bad news for you, Greco. This is how I always look in the morning."

He laughed. "I'm tough, I can take it."

Debbie Macadam had joined them. "So, you must be the man in the Hathaway shirt ad we've been hearing so much about . . . the one-eyed wonder!"

Greco laughed. "That's me."

Billy Blumenthal was clapping his hands in the doorway. A champagne cork popped in the quiet.

"Okay, kids, give me just a minute here. I've got an announcement you might be interested in. As you know, we have a movie studio backing us through this first stage of production. Frankly, based on what I saw out there tonight, they'll be sticking with us—"

A cheer went up but he waved them quiet again.

"I'm very pleased to tell you now about something that's been in the works for the past week or so. We have a definite second commitment—are you ready for this? Another half-million dollars!" He was drowned out by shouts of excitement. Celia felt a shiver of excitement and felt Greco squeeze her shoulders. "And . . . and," Blumenthal went on, "we're going to take this little mother all the way to Broadway!" Pandemonium, hugs and kisses all around, champagne spilling and foaming.

"The Martin Beck Theatre," Billy said. "We open late in August after two months in this little Chelsea sauna"—laughter, moans—"and we're the first show of the new season!"

From among the excited cries Debbie Macadam's voice could be heard. "Who is it, Billy? Who's our angel?"

"Ah, my darling, you have but to ask. I'd like you to meet our new back—a true lover of the theatre . . . an angel beyond our wildest dreams . . . a wonderful guy you're all gonna love . . . here he is!"

Billy stepped out of the doorway and everyone peered forward, applauding, as a very fat man, blushing pink, perspiring profusely, rode his wheelchair into view.

Celia felt her breath catch as the others crowded around him. Linda Thurston couldn't have worked it out better. She put her mouth to Greco's ear.

"You are a scoundrel, you darling man—"

"And a bit of a blackmailer . . . but listen, he told me he loved the show."

"You talked with him tonight?"

"Hell, we sat together. I figured he had this half million sitting around gathering dust. . . ." He shrugged.

"I love you, scoundrel!"

"I've earned it, right?"

"I guess you have at that. . . ."

Peter Greco winked his big brown eye.

ABOUT THE AUTHOR

DANA CLARINS is a pseudonym for a bestselling novelist who lives and works in New York City. Bantam also published the author's previous two novels, *Woman in the Window* and *Guilty Parties*.

BANTAM
SHOP-AT-HOME
C·A·T·A·L·O·G

Special Offer
Buy a Bantam Book
for only 50¢.

Now you can have Bantam's catalog filled with hundreds of titles plus take advantage of our unique and exciting bonus book offer. A special offer which gives you the opportunity to purchase a Bantam book for only 50¢. Here's how!

By ordering any five books at the regular price per order, you can also choose any other single book listed (up to a $4.95 value) for just 50¢. Some restrictions do apply, but for further details why not send for Bantam's catalog of titles today!

Just send us your name and address and we will send you a catalog!

☐ 25789-7 **JUST ANOTHER DAY IN PARADISE,**
Maxwell $2.95

Fiddler has more money than he knows what to do with, he's tried about everything he'd ever thought of trying and there's not much left that interests him. So, when his ex-wife's twin brother disappears, when the feds begin to investigate the high-tech computer company the twin owns, and when Fiddler finds himself holding an envelope of Russian-cut diamonds, he decides to get involved. Is his ex-wife's twin selling high-tech information to the Russians?

☐ 25809-5 **THE UNORTHODOX MURDER OF**
RABBI WAHL, Telushkin $2.95

Rabbi Daniel Winter, the young host of the radio talk show "Religion and You," invites three guests to discuss "Feminism and Religion." He certainly expects that the three women, including Rabbi Myra Wahl, are likely to generate some sparks . . . What he doesn't expect is murder.

☐ 25717-X **THE BACK-DOOR MAN,** Kantner $2.95

Ben Perkins doesn't look for trouble, but he isn't the kind of guy who looks the other way when something comes along to spark his interest. In this case, it's a wealthy widow who's a victim of embezzlement and the gold American Express card she gives him for expenses. Ben thinks it should be fun; the other people after the missing money are out to change his mind.

☐ 26061-8 **"B" IS FOR BURGLAR,** Grafton $3.50

"Kinsey is a refreshing heroine."—*Washington Post Book World*

"Kinsey Millhone . . . is a stand-out specimen of the new female operatives." —*Philadelphia Inquirer*

[Millhone is] "a tough cookie with a soft center, a gregarious loner." —*Newsweek*

What appears to be a routine missing persons case for private detective Kinsey Millhone turns into a dark tangle of arson, theft and murder.

Look for them at your bookstore or use the coupon below: